"Hey, are you okay?"

She forced a grin. "Yeah, I… It all just hit me. We could have died. Brady could have killed us… What if he comes back here?"

"Then I'll be ready for him. I won't let him hurt you, Chelsea. I promise." Jake reached for her cheek and dried a tear with his thumb. A warm tingle spun through her. His blue eyes held hers, lit with a hard-edged but reassuring determination. A sense of security flowed through her. After the way he'd come through for her already this afternoon, she had no trouble believing Jake could protect her from the escaped convict, should he return.

She studied Jake's face, admiring the way the fire's glow highlighted the rugged cut of his cheekbones and square jaw. Good Lord, but he was handsome.

"Who are you, Jake Connelly? And what put you at the right place at the right time to stumble into my nightmare?"

Black Ops Rescues: Putting lives—and hearts —on the line

D1510501

Dear Reader,

It's Jake's turn! In *Cowboy's Texas Rescue,* black ops pilot Jake Connelly takes on a Texas-size blizzard and an escaped convict in order to rescue girl-next-door Chelsea Harris. Chelsea's worst nightmare, being kidnapped at gunpoint by an escaped murderer, turns to fairy tale when ultra-handsome Jake swoops in to save the day. As they survive a massive winter storm together and pursue an escaped felon, Chelsea and Jake learn lessons about unconditional love, sacrifice and redemption.

Cowboy's Texas Rescue is the last book in my Black Ops Rescues series, and I've had so much fun creating these sexy and dangerous guys that I'm sad to see the series end. Action and adventure scenes are my favorite to write, and the Black Ops Rescues series gave me many opportunities to indulge that love. I hope you've enjoyed getting to know Alec, Daniel and Jake and seeing them find true love. These guys will always be near and dear to my heart. What's coming up? Three Louisiana brothers. Three babies in jeopardy. Three emotional stories of lost love, edgy danger and the courage to give love a second chance. Watch for the Mansfield brothers coming soon!

Happy reading,

Beth Cornelison

COWBOY'S TEXAS RESCUE

BY
BETH CORNELISON

MILLS & BOON

All the characters in this book have no existence outside the imagination of the author, and have no relation whatsoever to anyone bearing the same name or names. They are not even distantly inspired by any individual known or unknown to the author, and all the incidents are pure invention.

All Rights Reserved including the right of reproduction in whole or in part in any form. This edition is published by arrangement with Harlequin Enterprises II B.V./S.à.r.l. The text of this publication or any part thereof may not be reproduced or transmitted in any form or by any means, electronic or mechanical, including photocopying, recording, storage in an information retrieval system, or otherwise, without the written permission of the publisher.

This book is sold subject to the condition that it shall not, by way of trade or otherwise, be lent, resold, hired out or otherwise circulated without the prior consent of the publisher in any form of binding or cover other than that in which it is published and without a similar condition including this condition being imposed on the subsequent purchaser.

® and ™ are trademarks owned and used by the trademark owner and/or its licensee. Trademarks marked with ® are registered with the United Kingdom Patent Office and/or the Office for Harmonisation in the Internal Market and in other countries.

First published in Great Britain 2013
by Mills & Boon, an imprint of Harlequin (UK) Limited,
Eton House, 18-24 Paradise Road, Richmond, Surrey TW9 1SR

© Beth Cornelison 2013

ISBN: 978 0 263 90359 1
ebook ISBN: 978 1 472 00719 3

46-0513

Harlequin (UK) policy is to use papers that are natural, renewable and recyclable products and made from wood grown in sustainable forests. The logging and manufacturing processes conform to the legal environmental regulations of the country of origin.

Printed and bound in Spain
by Blackprint CPI, Barcelona

Beth Cornelison started writing stories as a child when she penned a tale about the adventures of her cat, Ajax. A Georgia native, she received her bachelor's degree in public relations from the University of Georgia. After working in public relations for a little more than a year, she moved with her husband to Louisiana, where she decided to pursue her love of writing fiction.

Since that first time, Beth has written many more stories of adventure and romantic suspense and has won numerous honors for her work, including a coveted Golden Heart Award in romantic suspense from Romance Writers of America. She is active on the board of directors for the North Louisiana Storytellers and Authors of Romance (NOLA STARS) and loves reading, traveling, *Peanuts'* Snoopy and spending down-time with her family.

She writes from her home in Louisiana, where she lives with her husband, one son and two cats who think they are people. Beth loves to hear from her readers. You can write to her at PO Box 5418, Bossier City, LA 71171, USA, or visit her website, www.bethcornelison.com.

For Paul, who loves me just the way I am.

Thanks to Rita® winner and author extraodinaire Darynda Jones for lending her name to Chelsea's neighbor and for sharing her dog Dooley for the story. Thanks, Darynda, for supporting the NOLA STARs!

Thanks to Jodi Israel, who won the chance to be a secondary character through the Brenda Novak Diabetes Auction for the Cure in May 2012!

Thanks also to Aida Alberto for allowing me to feature her cat Nela in the story.

Thank you to Carmen Parks, who won the chance to have her dog Sadie featured through the PAWS of Northeast Louisiana online auction.

Prologue

Jake Connelly crept down the corridor of the under-ground bunker, his senses on full alert and his Colt M4A1 assault rifle at the ready. When his black ops team reached the reinforced steel door at the end of the dim passageway, they moved silently into position—or as silently as they could while wearing CBRN suits. The military issue, head-to-toe protective clothing, designed to protect a soldier from chemical, biological, radiological or nuclear contamination, was cumbersome but critical for this op.

His team leader signaled for the men up front to work their magic and get them past the relatively low-tech security on the door. Or low-tech for a U.S. black ops team. Not so low-tech for a developing nation, even if that nation's government had the means to kidnap a nuclear scientist and consign him to work in this hidden bunker developing a dirty bomb.

With the door breached, the team leader led the charge into the underground lab, barking in Farsi, "Everyone down! On the floor!"

"Now!" Jake shouted when the lab workers hesitated. "Hands on your head!"

One of the protective suit–clad workers tried to run, and one of Jake's teammates stepped from the corridor to block the man's escape. Jake tackled the fleeing worker, landing with a knee-jolting crash on the floor.

The team leader aimed his assault rifle at another man's head. "On the floor!"

Jake quickly frisked the worker beneath him for weapons and, finding none, jerked the man to his feet. He bound the man's hands behind him and led the lab tech into the corridor with a rifle muzzle between the man's shoulder blades.

"Clear the room! Let's get 'em to the helo." The team leader whipped out a riot cuff and bound the wrists of the lab worker he had pinned to the floor. "All right, guys, set the fireworks."

"Move!" Jake shouted in Farsi when his captive resisted. Grabbing the man's arm, he ran, hauling the combative lab tech behind him. The rest of the team was on Jake's heels as he sprinted back down the tunnel they'd just cleared of guards and out into the predawn darkness.

Their driver was waiting in an armored SUV, and the team piled into the vehicle, shoving their captives in first, then crowding onto the bench seats, even as their driver hit the gas. They tore away from the nondescript brick building that hid the entrance to the underground bunker, leaving the last two team members to follow in a second vehicle once the C4 and detonators were set.

Their SUV sped through the night-darkened desert

the short distance to the helicopter that would get them all out of Dodge. Jake's copilot, Bruster, had the helo's turbines whirring, the rotor blade spinning. The bird was ready to take off.

The doors of the SUV popped open as their driver skidded to a stop, and the team disgorged from the vehicle, shoving the captive laboratory workers toward the helicopter.

"All yours, cowboy!" the team leader called to Jake as Jake handed off his prisoner and climbed in the pilot's seat. "I want us in the air the second the rest of the team gets here."

"Roger that," Jake replied, tugging off the hood and breathing mask of his CBRN suit and checking the helo's controls. When everything was set, he peered through the windshield, searching the night for his teammates' vehicle. Under his breath he muttered, "C'mon, c'mon, c'mon. Hurry, guys."

"Connelly," Bruster shouted over the noise of the turbine, "HQ radioed earlier for you. You had an emergency call from the States. You're supposed to report in as soon as we get back to base."

A chill nipped the back of Jake's neck as he remembered a different emergency call his family received years before. He frowned as he fastened his seat belt. "What kind of emergency?"

Bruster shrugged one shoulder. "Don't know. Just delivering the message."

Jake jerked a nod and scanned the terrain again for their teammates, but his thoughts dwelled on the worrisome message. An emergency call from the States? That didn't bode well.

"There they are!" the team leader shouted, yanking Jake back to the danger at hand. "Let's go!"

Jake's teammates appeared like specters crossing the barren landscape, and Jake had the helo in the air even before the other agents finished clambering aboard.

"Twelve seconds!" the explosives specialist barked, and the team assumed brace positions while Jake and Bruster goosed the helo to move faster, climb higher, get out of range. *Now.*

Jake swung the bird in a wide arc, gaining as much altitude and latitude as quickly as he could.

"Five seconds," his teammate called.

Jake took over the countdown in his head.

Four. Three. Two.

He gripped the cyclic tighter. Braced.

One.

Below them, a flash of explosives rocked the tiny building above the bunker. A fraction of a second later, the shock wave hit the helicopter, and Jake steadied the bird as it shuddered and pitched.

Bruster whooped. "How's that for a kick in the ass?"

"Nice flying, cowboy," the team leader shouted from behind Jake. "Now let's go home."

"Roger that, chief."

Two hours later, once the nuclear scientist had been secured at the black ops team's Mideast base and the other lab workers had been detained for debriefing, Jake marched into the communications center. He'd changed out of the CBRN suit into jeans, a T-shirt and his trademark cowboy hat. Scanning the room, he found the officer in charge. "I was told I had an emergency call from the States. What's up?"

The chief of communications nodded and directed Jake toward a phone near the center of the room. "Your sister called. She's standing by at the Dallas office to talk to you. Let me patch you through."

Jake's heart drummed an anxious rhythm as his call was connected via satellite to a secure line in the States. Moments later, he heard his older sister come on the line, her voice rife with emotion. "Thank God they reached you, Jake. I wasn't sure they'd find you in time."

The mission group's bus was attacked by a militant gang, a long-ago voice echoed in his memory.

Jake squeezed the phone receiver and furrowed his brow. "What's wrong, Michelle? They told me there was an emergency."

"There is. It's Dad."

Jake's stomach dropped to his toes, and he held his breath. Not even the shock wave from the bunker explosion had shaken him this hard. "Tell me."

"He's had a massive heart attack, Jake. He's in intensive care at Northwest Texas Hospital in Amarillo and…" She sighed heavily.

Jake swallowed hard. "Will he make it?"

"It's touch and go. The doctors think…" Michelle paused, clearly struggling to speak. "Jake, you need to come home."

Chapter 1

A brutal winter storm was looming.

As she crossed the grocery store parking lot, Chelsea Harris cast a worried gaze to the dark clouds rolling in from New Mexico and quickened her step. She still had to stop for gasoline, or her mother's boat of a car wouldn't make it all the way back to their rural West Texas ranch house. The gas-guzzling 1985 Cadillac Fleetwood had been her father's wedding gift to her mother. Despite the worn seats—held together by the always-ready duct tape kept in the glove box—the rusting body and the seemingly monthly repair bills, her mother treasured the car and refused to give it up. Chelsea was babysitting the car, along with her parents' house, while her folks took a well-deserved and overdue three-week cruise to Hawaii.

An icy wind buffeted her as she keyed open the driver's door. *Hawaii would be nice right about now.*

Shivering, Chelsea brushed her long, wind-blown hair from her face and huddled deeper into her pullover sweater. This morning she'd raced out of her parents' ranch house without a coat, because the temperature had been a balmy sixty-five degrees. But since she'd left for work at the blood center, the temperature had plunged as a cold front moved through town. *Thank you, fickle West Texas weather.*

Dropping a grocery sack and her purse on the seat beside her, Chelsea cranked the Caddy's engine, coaxing the car with a muttered, "Come on, Ethyl. I know you hate the cold, but we gotta get home before the storm hits."

She breathed a sigh of relief when the engine finally caught, and she backed out of her parking space and headed to the gas station down the block. Her own apartment was only a few blocks from the blood center where she worked as a phlebotomist, so she usually rode her bike to work. But her parents' home, the ranch house she'd grown up in, was twenty-two miles from town, necessitating pressing Ethyl into service. The cost of gasoline to and from town was eating her paycheck for lunch. But how could she refuse her parents' ranch-sitting request after all they'd done for her through the years?

Chelsea pulled up to the gas pump, cut the engine and gritted her teeth, dreading stepping out into the wintery wind again. *The sooner you fill up, the sooner you'll be home in a hot bath with a glass of wine.* The promise of unwinding sounded heavenly, so Chelsea shouldered open the car door and stepped out into the cold.

As she turned toward the gas pump, she almost collided with a disheveled man in orange coveralls who appeared from nowhere. "Oh! I'm sorry. I didn't see—"

"Get in the car!" he growled, jamming something hard in her belly.

She glanced down at the object poking her, and a chill that had nothing to do with the weather raced through her.

A gun. The man had a gun!

Chelsea's throat dried. Her heart rate spiked. "I d-don't have any money. I—"

He crowded her, forcing her to step backward, and he opened the driver's door on the Caddy. "Get in!"

She jolted when he barked the command at her. He shoved the gun harder into her ribs, and panic flooded Chelsea's brain. Sheer survival instinct kicked in. With her heart pounding a frantic cadence, she slid back onto the driver's seat.

The gunman climbed in the backseat, moving the muzzle of his weapon to the base of her skull, and grated, "Drive."

"But—"

"Drive!" His shouted order brooked no resistance.

Hands shaking, Chelsea cranked the engine again and pulled away from the pump. "Wh-where are we going?"

"Just drive! And don't try anything stupid. I've already killed two cops today to make my getaway. I'll shoot you without blinking if you give me trouble."

He leaned over the front seat and snatched her mother's GPS from its mount on the dashboard. After he'd pushed a few buttons, the disembodied voice of the GPS intoned. "Go home?"

He tapped the screen, and the GPS voice said, "Continue west on Highway 244 for one point six miles, then turn left."

Chelsea's stomach pitched. The last thing she wanted was for this cretin to know where her parents lived. She bit her lower lip and met the guy's dark glare in the rearview mirror. Okay, maybe the last thing she wanted was to be raped and tortured to death. But having him know where she was staying ranked near the top.

"You live with anyone?" he asked.

"Wh-what?" Dividing her attention between the road and monitoring the man in her backseat, Chelsea fought the panic swelling in her chest. She needed to keep her head if she was going to survive, but the constant pressure of his gun against her skull made it difficult to think calmly.

"It's an easy question. Do you live with anyone? Will there be anyone else at your house when we get there?"

"It's my parents' house."

He jabbed her again with the gun. "And are Mommy and Daddy home?"

She considered lying for a moment, but the gun poking the base of her skull gave her pause. She wasn't a good liar, and if he guessed she was bluffing… "N-no. I'm house-sitting while they're out of town."

A leering grin twisted his mouth. "Perfect."

The lettering stenciled on the breast pocket of his jumpsuit caught her attention. *Texas Department of Criminal Justice—Inmate*. Her pulse spiked, and she sputtered, "Y-you're a prison inmate?"

He leered at her via the rearview mirror. "Not anymore."

Her mouth dried remembering his warning that he'd already killed two cops today. No doubt the gun he wielded had been stolen from one of the cops.

"Wh-who are you? What do you want from me?"

"For now, all I want is a ride out of town, maybe a place to hole up for a little while, until I can plan my next move."

She noticed he didn't give her his name. Not that she really expected him to.

"Then you don't h-have any place in mind you're heading? No one on the outside is helping you?"

"You're helping me now, aren't ya?" Another leer.

Chelsea swallowed hard. Dear God, she *was* aiding and abetting a criminal. But under duress. They wouldn't convict her for helping a prisoner escape under duress, would they? Her heart stutter-stepped. Lord, she hoped not.

As she approached the turn for the highway to her parents' house, she considered driving straight. The road to her parents' ranch was long and nearly deserted. She had a much greater chance of finding help if she stayed on this road. She accelerated as they neared the turnoff, then cringed when her mother's GPS reminded her to turn left.

"Turn, damn it!" he yelled as they reached the intersection.

Gulping oxygen, she cut the wheel hard, and Ethyl's tires squealed as they whipped a sharp turn at the last second.

The man shot her a dark look and jabbed harder with the gun. "You weren't gonna turn, were ya?" He smacked the back of her head with the butt of his gun, and pain ricocheted through her head.

Narrowing a lethal glare on her, he growled, "I warned you not to pull anything! Drive me to your house, or I will shoot you and drive myself! Got it, girlie?"

Chelsea drew a shuddering breath and nodded. *Just do as he says, and you might stay alive,* the voice of fear and caution whispered to her.

Tears filled her eyes as a sense of futility and helplessness rushed over her the farther she got from town. She didn't want to die. But she didn't want to go down without at least attempting to save herself either.

As her initial shock and panic settled into an even level of terror, Chelsea mentally raced through her options. Could she crash the car into something and make a run for it?

She glanced around the isolated stretch of ranchland and saw nothing but miles of flat, empty earth. No trees, no roadside buildings, not even a highway sign substantial enough to make Ethyl undrivable. And if she did crash her mother's Caddy out here, where would she run? Her captor would shoot her before she took three steps.

Despair wrenched her chest, and she blinked back the tears that gathered in her eyes. Could she somehow get the gun away from him? He didn't look all that well muscled, but he was taller and was most likely stronger than she was.

She cut her eyes to her purse, where her cell phone was nestled in a front pocket. If she could distract him, could she dial 9-1-1 before he stopped her?

She met his gaze in the mirror again, and his eyes narrowed with suspicion before darting to her purse.

"Don't even think about it, girlie." He grabbed her purse and dragged it into the backseat with him. "You got a gun in here or something?"

"N-no."

He started rifling through her purse, and Chelsea's skin crawled, seeing him touch her personal things. She squeezed the steering wheel, searching for another plan of escape when Ethyl's engine coughed.

The man's head came up. "What was that?"

"I don't—"

The motor sputtered again, and a sinking realization settled over her, as dark as the clouds rolling in from the west.

Ethyl choked again as the man leaned over the front seat to scan the dashboard lights and gauges. "What the hell are you doing?"

"Nothing. But we—"

The engine sputtered loudly and cut off. Icy dread shimmied through Chelsea.

Her captor ground the muzzle into her nape and grated, "Don't screw around with me, sister. I'll blow your damn head off!"

Chelsea whimpered fearfully and cleared her throat as she coasted to the side of the road and stopped the car. "It's not me! I swear. W-we're out of gas!"

"A winter storm warning has been issued for the Texas panhandle and parts of New Mexico and Oklahoma, with accumulations of two feet or more of snow and ice possible tonight along with high winds and temperatures dropping into the mid-twenties," the radio announcer droned from the speakers of Jake Connelly's F-150.

"No kidding." Jake leaned forward to peer through his windshield at the line of dark clouds gathered on the horizon. The readout on his truck's thermometer said the temperature outside had dropped ten degrees just in the past thirty minutes. The cold front was closing in fast. He checked his truck's clock and mentally calculated his arrival time at his dad's house near Amarillo. He might just make it before the storm hit, if he hurried.

"In other news, an inmate escaped this afternoon from a Texas work detail, killing two police officers in the process."

Jake turned the radio volume down and drummed his fingers on the steering wheel as he sent another considering glance to the clouds and hedged. Maybe he should go straight to the hospital and ride out the storm there. Michelle had said time was of the essence.

"Authorities are still searching for Edward Brady, convicted six years ago for armed robbery and two counts of second-degree murder. The public is warned that Brady is armed with a handgun belonging to one of the fallen officers and should be considered extremely dangerous. Brady is described as having—"

Jake snapped off the radio. Even the suggestion that he might not get home in time to see his dad made Jake's chest tighten. Regret and concern sat heavily on his lungs. His dad had been so proud of him for being chosen for the elite black ops team, but the demands of the job kept him away from his family for months at a time. He'd missed last Christmas and hadn't made time to visit his father in more than a year. When Jake had apologized to his dad during their two-days-late Christmas call, his father had dismissed Jake's absence, saying, "The work you're doing is important. You're making a difference. I understand."

But Jake had heard an undertone of disappointment in his dad's voice in that call that knifed his heart now.

Time is of the essence.

Jake nudged the gas pedal, bumping up his speed. He'd never forgive himself if he didn't make it home before his dad died.

* * *

Chelsea cringed as the escaped inmate cursed a blue streak, railing in her face. Spittle flew from his mouth as he blasted her with invectives and blamed her for their predicament.

"That's why I'd stopped at the gas station where you hijacked me," she said, frustration and defensive anger battling her fear.

The man's dark eyes narrowed, and he ran a hand over his thinning brown hair. "Are you saying this is my fault?"

Chelsea bit the inside of her cheek. Don't get him angry. Or rather *angrier*. Her stomach flip-flopped.

"M-maybe someone will stop and help us," she offered, trying to infuse her tone with a note of optimism that would calm her captor. But a glance down the isolated road told her everyone with sense was already hunkered down at home, bracing for the storm.

The inmate's eyebrows beetled, and he shifted restlessly on the seat. "No. No, we can't have that. Can't risk someone calling the cops." He looked down at the orange coveralls he wore, as if realizing his attire screamed his status as an escaped felon. Raising a speculative glance to Chelsea, he waved the gun at her. "Give me your clothes."

She blinked. "What?"

Her captor started peeling off his prison garb, revealing a second weapon he'd tucked in his underwear. Another gun, although this one had a funny shape and was painted with yellow stripes on the wide muzzle. Maybe a stun gun?

He caught her curious stare and grated, "Strip! Now! I want your clothes."

"But it's freezing!"

He gave her a sneer. "That's your problem, girlie, not mine."

A shudder rolled through Chelsea, and she fought down the wave of nausea that churned in her gut. Her brain scrambled for something, *anything,* that would distract him. Anything that would give her the upper hand and a chance to call for help.

"Come on. Hurry up! Gimme your clothes, damn it!" He waved the gun under her nose. "Don't test me, girlie. I swear I will shoot you and take the clothes off your corpse if you don't get 'em off *now!*"

Hands shaking, Chelsea grasped the hem of her sweater and tugged it off over her head. Tears filled her eyes as the chilly air nipped her skin.

He snatched the pink pullover from her, then bent to shove the orange coveralls and second gun under the front seat. And Chelsea seized what might be her only chance.

Lunging for her purse, she grappled for her cell phone and thumbed the call button. *9-1—*

"Bitch!" Her kidnapper yanked the phone from her, jabbed the power button and threw the phone on the floor of the backseat. "That's it," he growled. "Get out."

Fear rippled through her. Heart thundering, gut roiling, Chelsea blinked back tears. "N-no. Please! I won't try it again. I just—"

"Damn right you won't try it again." He climbed out of the car, opened the driver's door and poked her with the gun. "Get the hell out of the car!"

Shivering with cold and terror, Chelsea scanned the horizon again, praying for help. No one. Nothing. She struggled for a breath as dread squeezed her lungs. Was this it? Was this how she'd die?

The encroaching storm clouds blotted out the sun

and made the afternoon seem more like evening. Despair darkened her hope.

The convict yanked her out of the car by the arm. "I said get out!"

Chelsea screamed as loud as she could. Maybe someone, somewhere, would hear and—

A stunning blow found her cheek.

"Shut up! Give me those jeans now, or I'll do it myself." The man's dark eyes narrowed on her.

Hands shaking, she stripped off her jeans, while humiliation and tears stung her cheeks. Icy wind whipped around her, and she shivered. "You have what you want. Please, just let me go."

"And let you sing to the cops where you saw me and which way I was headed?" He scoffed. "No chance." He reached out and stroked her face, sending a ripple of revulsion to her core. "But because you've been so helpful, I'll let you live. For now."

Chelsea released a breath of relief...too soon.

After snatching the key from the ignition, the gunman grabbed her arm and dragged her toward the back of the Caddy. He keyed open the trunk and turned to her. "Get in."

Chelsea eyed the trunk, and her knees wobbled. "Please, just...just let me g—"

"Get in!" he roared, pointing the gun at her.

"But you said—"

The convict grabbed her, his arms pinning hers to her sides, and shoved her toward the open trunk.

"No! Please!" She fought him, fought hard, clawing, biting, struggling. But in the end, all she got for her efforts were another smack on the head from the butt of the gun and scraped legs when he forced her into the trunk.

Chelsea gasped in terror as he slammed the trunk closed and she was swallowed by darkness. She wrapped her arms around her stomach and fought to remain calm. She could get out of here. She had to. *Just think. Stay calm and think….*

As long as she didn't give him a reason to shoot her, she still had a chance to figure out how to escape. Tears stinging her eyes, she sent up a prayer…and started searching for a way out of Ethyl's trunk.

Edward Brady stomped back to the driver's seat of the old Cadillac, chafing his cold arms and grumbling. Of all the women and all the cars that stopped at the gas station that afternoon, he had to pick the troublemaker who was driving on fumes. He hiked up the jeans that sagged on his hips, then dropped onto the front seat and scowled. Stupid girl's pants didn't even fit.

Squeezing the steering wheel, he glared through the windshield and fumed over the bad turn of luck. He was a sitting duck, stranded here on the highway, and the dark clouds rolling in warned his luck was about to get much bleaker. He needed a new plan.

He slapped the steering wheel and bit out a blistering curse. He'd spent months plotting this day, planning his escape, and thanks to stupid rotten luck and the bitch with the too-big jeans, his dream of freedom was all going in the toilet. If he were caught now, he'd be put on trial for killing those cops. In Texas, that meant the death penalty.

Brady shuddered. He refused to get caught now. He'd come too far, had too much at risk. He needed transportation, a hideout that was off the cops' radar, weapons, food…and he needed it fast. When that storm hit, if he didn't have shelter, he could die of exposure. And wouldn't that be sorry freakin' irony?

In the trunk, the woman started banging on the lid and shouting for help.

Brady gritted his teeth. Maybe he should kill her and be done with it. "Shut up!" he yelled. "I'm trying to think out here!"

Movement in the rearview mirror caught his attention. A truck was approaching. Half of him wanted the truck to stop. He could shoot the driver and take the truck.

But if the truck's driver heard the woman's shouts for help, he'd be screwed.

Brady slumped down in the seat. *Just drive on by, pal. Just drive on by.*

But the truck slowed as it passed.

The banging from the trunk got louder. "Help! Someone help! Please."

Turning the ignition key one notch to access the battery power, Brady opened the window, switched on the radio and turned it up full blast.

Jake narrowed his gaze on the ancient Cadillac sitting on the shoulder of the isolated highway. As he drove past the parked car, he spotted a man in the driver's seat, slumped low, his expression dour. Car trouble? If so, the poor schmuck could be waiting hours for a wrecker out here. Big trouble, what with the winter storm approaching.

Jake's conscience kicked him. Be the Change You Wish To See had been his mother's mantra, paraphrasing Gandhi, as he grew up. She'd lived by those words. *And died by them.*

No matter how pressed for time he was, trying to

reach the hospital before the snow hit, he had to at least offer the guy help. Pulling to the shoulder in front of the Caddy, Jake jammed his black Stetson on his head and cut his engine. The screech of electric guitars and chest-vibrating thump of bass wafted to him, growing exponentially louder when he opened his truck door to climb out. The dude in the Caddy had a heavy metal rock party for one blaring through open windows.

Before exiting the truck cab, Jake recalled the report of the escaped prisoner, took his SIG-Sauer 226 from the glove box and stuck the pistol in his jeans at the small of his back.

He scowled as he walked toward the Cadillac. Open windows when the temperature hovered in the low thirties? Maybe the guy was high on something. "Hey." He shouted to be heard over the blaring music as he approached. He flashed a friendly smile and tugged the brim of his cowboy hat. "You need any help?"

The man, wearing a rather effeminate pink pullover sweater, shot Jake a wary look but didn't answer, didn't bother to turn his radio down. The bass continued thudding, and high-pitched voices screamed unintelligible lyrics.

"Can you turn the music down?" Jake asked, stopping a few steps from the driver's door and stooping to peer through the window at the man behind the steering wheel. His feminine attire, his odd behavior and his unresponsiveness all rang warning bells in Jake's head.

The man shook his head and leveled a flat stare.

"Are you having car trouble? Do you need help?" Jake asked, yelling to be heard over the ruckus.

"I'm fine." The man shifted slightly and jerked his head toward the looming clouds. "You best move on before that storm hits."

Jake lifted an eyebrow. "I could say the same for you."

"Mind your own business," the guy snarled.

Jake gritted his back teeth and swallowed his retort. If the surly jerk didn't want his help…screw him.

He'd turned to leave when the pounding he'd assumed was the bass from the speakers sounded from the rear of the Caddy. From the trunk. He stopped and listened, turned back toward the driver.

Was that scream part of the music or…

His senses ramping into high alert, Jake edged toward the rear of the vehicle, reaching behind him for his pistol. The guy could be a drug smuggler. A human-smuggling coyote. Or about a half-dozen other options that sprang to mind. Jake divided his gaze between the man and the interior of the car as he did a fast check for weapons, for hiding passengers, for contraband as he crept backward to check the trunk. "Buddy, why don't you step out of the car and—"

Jake's adrenaline spiked.

An orange jumpsuit had been stuffed halfway under the backseat.

The escaped prisoner lunged from the car, whipping a gun out from under the pink pullover.

Instantly Jake raised his own weapon and squeezed off a shot. Spinning, he dived behind the protective cover of the Caddy's rear bumper. The inmate— Edward Brady, the radio had called him—returned fire. Brady's rounds deflated a back tire and pinged off the heavy steel fender.

Hearing the scuffle of feet, Jake peered around the back of the Cadillac. Brady was running toward Jake's truck.

"Oh, hell no, you're not takin' my truck," he growled.

Jake leveled his pistol, aiming for the guy's leg rather than a kill shot. He'd leave the cretin alive for the local authorities to deal with. He fired once, and the inmate fell to the ground, clutching his left leg. Staying behind the protection of the Caddy, Jake crept to the passenger door, reached inside to turn off the blaring music, then eased forward to the front fender. "Toss your gun toward me *now,* or I'll shoot your other leg!"

Brady returned a scathing epithet and fired twice toward the Caddy.

Jake scowled his irritation but kept his focus on subduing Brady. He narrowed his eyes on the weapon Brady had. It looked like a .40 Smith & Wesson M&P. Pretty typical police sidearm. Sixteen rounds in a standard magazine. Call it eighteen rounds, in case he was wrong about the model of pistol, and it was a 9 mm instead. Jake made a few calculations—two shots to kill the police officers in his getaway, four shots fired at him just now. Brady could have as many as a dozen rounds left. Brady needed to surrender the gun or spend those remaining rounds.

"Toss me the gun!" Jake repeated.

Brady answered with two more shots toward the Cadillac. Jake fired near Brady once to encourage returned shots. The escaped inmate didn't disappoint. Five more shots.

By lifting his hat into Brady's view, Jake drew three more rounds. Jake monitored the injured convict from behind the Cadillac, waiting for more shots.

Instead the gunman struggled to his feet and headed toward Jake's truck again.

Muttering a curse under his breath, Jake darted after Brady, overtaking him easily and knocking him to the pavement. With a punch to the jaw, Jake disoriented Brady enough to wrest the police sidearm from the escapee, which he quickly stashed at the small of his back. Then twisting the man's arms up behind his back, Jake dragged Brady to his feet and shoved him back toward the Caddy. "Had to do it the hard way, didn't you?"

Brady glared at him and bit out another curse that would make a sailor blush.

In the glove compartment, Jake found a roll of duct tape—probably the same one the owner of the car had used liberally on the vinyl seats—and he helped himself to a strip for Brady's filthy mouth. Next Jake bound the inmate's ankles and wrists, leaving Brady's arms in front of him so that he could self-administer pressure to his bleeding leg. After dumping the inmate on the backseat, Jake ripped a larger hole in the jeans around the man's gunshot wound and gave the injury a cursory inspection. The gash was deep but was still a flesh wound. No broken bones or major blood vessels damaged. The thug would live to be a burden to society.

Jake yanked off the man's sock and pressed it against the wound. "Hold still while I tape that up to stanch the bleeding."

Brady glared at him the entire time as he pulled the duct tape around the man's leg, creating a makeshift bandage. Nothing fancy, but good enough to stop the bleeding until the authorities arrived. "Keep pressure on that to slow the bleeding."

With his prisoner subdued, Jake took the Cadillac's keys from the ignition and moved toward the trunk to investigate the thumping noises he's heard earlier. Leveling his weapon with one hand, he keyed open the trunk and cautiously raised the lid.

Chapter 2

Tremors racked Chelsea, a combination of the cold, her fear and the surging adrenaline in her veins. She curled in a tight ball, trying to stay warm and keep her panic at bay. She'd never been claustrophobic, but being locked in the Cadillac's trunk was making her rethink that position.

Fumbling blindly, she'd tried to open the trunk from the inside to no avail, and her attempts to punch out a taillight and flag a passing car had been equally futile. Ethyl was a tank, and no amount of awkward kicking or beating on the walls of the trunk had made any difference.

And then she'd heard a car approach. Slow. Stop. But as soon as she'd cried for help, her captor had cranked the radio loud enough that the car shook.

The exchange of gunfire had been terrifying and deafening. Whoever had stopped to offer his help had been armed—not such a big surprise. This was Texas after all. But not knowing who'd won the battle, if the escaped convict had killed again, had her strung tight. Tears stung her eyes knowing help was so close…and still so far.

A rattle came from the trunk lock, and she tensed. *Oh, please, God, let it be someone to rescue her and not that maniac killer!*

The lid lifted, and daylight poured into the pitch-dark of the trunk. She shuddered as a stiff icy wind swept into the well of the trunk, blasting her bare skin.

"Ah, hell," a deep voice muttered.

Her pulse scampered, and she squinted to make out the face of the man standing over her.

The gun in his hand registered first, then his size—tall, broad-shouldered, and his fleece-lined ranch coat made him appear impressively muscle-bound. Plenty big enough to overpower her if he was working with the convict.

A black cowboy hat and backlighting from the sky obscured his face in shadow, adding to her apprehension.

"Are you hurt?" he asked, stashing the gun out of sight and undoing the buttons of his coat.

"N-no." When he reached for her, she shrank back warily. Her dishabille caused nervous skitters to dance along her nerves, left her feeling vulnerable. Awkward. Cold as hell.

And where was the convict? She cast an anxious glance around them, down the side of the car, searching. Was he dead? Waiting to pounce when she climbed out of the trunk?

She jolted when her rescuer grasped her elbow.

"Hey, I'm not gonna hurt you." The cowboy leaned

farther into the trunk. "Let me help you out of there, and you can have my coat."

His coat... She almost whimpered in gratitude, anticipating the warmth. Heat from his fingers burrowed to her core as he steadied her and helped her rise to her knees. When she caught her first good glimpse of his square jaw and stubble-dusted cheeks, her stomach swooped. *Oh, Texas!* He was a freaking *Adonis.* Greek god–gorgeous with golden blond hair, cowboy boots and ranch-honed muscles. He lifted her out of the trunk, and when he set her down and her knees buckled with muscle cramps, cold and fatigue, she knew she couldn't dismiss old-fashioned swooning for at least some of her legs' weakness. He draped the coat around her shoulders, and the sexy combined scents of pine, leather and man surrounded her. She had to be dreaming....

Relief surged through her. *Rescue!*

"You can sit in my truck and get warm while I deal with Brady and call the cops." He stepped past her and reached up to close the trunk lid. Keeping a kind blue-eyed gaze on her, he slammed the trunk lid closed.

She nodded her understanding. "Th-thank you."

A movement in the backseat of the car drew her attention. The convict glared at her through the shattered rear window, and a chill raced through her. As she held the inmate's malevolent leer, he raised his tape-bound hands. Clutching the stun gun.

He aimed.

Terror shot through her, and she screamed, "Look out!"

Too late.

She heard the hiss and crackle of the electric current. She watched helplessly as the cowboy stiffened, his face contorting in pain. His body jerked and writhed as the convict continued to feed a disabling electric current through the twin probes piercing her rescuer's neck.

"Stop! You'll kill him!" Tears of horror, fear and sympathy puddled in her eyes. She rushed toward the cowboy, desperate to do something to help. But...if she touched him, would she receive the debilitating shock, too?

Overwhelmed by the current coursing through him, the cowboy's legs crumpled. As he slumped to the ground, his head hit the back fender, then thumped hard on the pavement.

Chelsea gasped and staggered toward the cowboy's prone form. He lay eerily still.

Oh, God. Ohgodohgodohgod. Please don't let him be dead!

When the crackling noise stopped, Chelsea plucked the prongs from the cowboy's neck and felt for a pulse. She released a shaky sigh when she palpated a steady throb.

Hearing scuffles from the car, she rose warily to peer into the backseat. The convict pulled the tape from his mouth, wincing and growling obscenities, then set to work gnawing at the tape on his hands with his teeth.

Fresh prickles of fear spun through Chelsea. The inmate would be free soon, and she had no doubt he'd be set on vengeance. She needed a way to protect herself. Think!

She glanced around. The cowboy's truck sat about one hundred feet down the road. If she made a dash for it, could she get there before the inmate shot her? Unlikely. And what about the cowboy? She couldn't steal his truck and abandon him. Taking a deep breath, she tried to calm her adrenaline-charged brain enough to make quick, logical decisions. With another glance over the trunk, through the shot-out window, she watched the inmate rip tape from his wrists, then bend down, presumably to work on freeing his feet.

Her gaze darted to the broken glass. *Gunfire*...

The cowboy had been holding a gun when he opened the trunk!

Dropping to her knees beside the cowboy, she shook him. "Where's your gun? I need your gun!"

Still no response. Either the stun gun or the hit he took to his head had knocked him out.

She heard Ethyl's back door squeak open. The inmate was coming....

With frantic hands, Chelsea patted down the cowboy. Chest, waist, hips...dear God, the man was solid muscle. Finding nothing, she grabbed an arm and tugged, struggling to turn him over. Groped behind him...

"Nice try, girlie."

Gasping, Chelsea jerked her gaze up.

The convict hovered over her, a gloating expression twisting his face.

Icy fear slithered down her spine. Finally, her fingers closed around the butt of a gun, and she yanked it from the cowboy's belt. Swinging the weapon toward her kidnapper, Chelsea gritted her teeth. "Stop where you are!" She worked up enough spit in her dry mouth to swallow. "Don't come any closer, or I'll shoot."

The convict hesitated, eyeing the gun. He had a wad of white cloth taped to a bleeding wound on his leg. "You won't do it. You could never live with yourself knowing you'd killed another human being."

Her pulse kicked. Was he right? Could she pull the trigger if she had to? "If you force my hand, I will kill you to save my life—" she nodded toward the unconscious cowboy "—and his."

The convict's expression hardened. "Get back in the trunk, girlie, or I'll fry you like I did John Wayne."

The frigid wind and her fear brought the sting of tears to her eyes again. She blinked hard, fighting to keep the inmate in focus, her attention glued on him. *Shoot him. Just shoot him. It'd be justifiable homicide.*

Her hands shook, and her stomach roiled. "Just... t-take his truck and leave us here."

The inmate's eyes narrowed, and his brow furrowed as he studied the gun in her hands. "Good idea. But... you'll still be in the trunk. Just in case you had any ideas about goin' to the cops."

He took a step forward, and Chelsea tensed, her finger curling around the trigger. "I said stay back! Don't touch me."

"Go ahead," the convict taunted, "shoot me. I dare you."

He took another step toward her, and Chelsea squeezed the trigger.

Click.

Her insides clenched at the telltale sound.

With a low rumbling laugh, the inmate closed in on her. "Well, well. Maybe you would shoot. Too bad you're out of bullets."

Brady knocked the emptied gun out of the brunette's hands and nudged the cowboy with his toe. The guy was out cold. Good. He gave the guy a hard kick in the ribs. "Sorry son of a bitch."

"Don't!" The brunette moved between him and the cowboy. "Leave him alone! Haven't you hurt him enough?"

"He shot me!" Brady growled back, pointing to his bleeding leg. "I should put a bullet in his head and be done with him."

"No!" She draped herself over the cowboy's body like some modern Pocahontas saving John Smith, and Brady scoffed. The girl had guts, standing up for the cowboy, trying to protect him, but Brady had other plans for the jerk.

"Get out of the way, or I'll kill the both of you!" He shoved her with his foot, and pain radiated up his leg.

"With what? The gun's empty." She raised her chin, visibly shivering in the cold. Or fear. He liked the idea that he scared her.

He leaned toward her, getting in her face. "With my bare hands if I have to. But I hear if you get juiced long enough with one of these babies—" he waved the stun gun "—you'll go into cardiac arrest." He leered at her. "Care to try it and see?"

She gasped and pulled away but stayed planted between him and the unconscious cowboy. Firming her jaw, she rallied for another show of chops. "A car could come by anytime. Do you really want to be seen standing here with me nearly naked, you holding that gun thing and him slumped on the ground? We're bound to cause a passerby to take a second look."

Brady frowned. She had a point. He had to do something with them and get moving. Before the cowboy woke up. Before a cop spotted him. Before his leg bled out.

Before this sucky day took another piss on him.

He needed to cover his tracks and find a hideout. Fast.

He opened the Caddy's trunk and faced the girl.

"Get up!" he ordered the brunette. "Get his arm. Help me put him in the trunk."

Limping forward and keeping most of his weight on his good leg, he shoved a hand under the cowboy's armpit and waited for the girl to comply. When she hesitated, he snarled, "Look, girlie. I'm in pain, and I'm in a hurry. I have exactly no patience left." He aimed the stun gun at her. "Get him up."

With wide eyes locked on the stun gun, she grabbed the cowboy's other arm, and they heaved him up, dragged him to the trunk and draped him over the back of the open well. When he lifted the cowboy's legs and swung them into the trunk, Brady's injured leg throbbed, and he dumped the cowboy in the Caddy with an unceremonious shove.

The brunette sent him a disgruntled look. "You bully. Your mother must be so proud of you."

Brady bristled, then lobbed a glancing blow to her chin. The brunette gasped and clutched her face.

"My mother could care less," Brady grated.

"*Couldn't* care less," she muttered, picking up the cowboy's hat and carefully putting it in the trunk beside the unconscious man. "Learn English, jerk."

Brady's temper spiked. He grabbed a fistful of her hair and yanked her head toward the trunk. "Get in! Now. Or I'll give hero boy another jolt."

"No! Don't hurt him!" Whimpering in pain as he towed her forward, the brunette climbed in the trunk and tucked herself into a ball beside the cowboy. He released her hair and was about to slam the trunk closed when he saw the woman's expression change, and she gave a soft gasp.

He followed the direction of her gaze…and saw the second gun tucked at the cowboy's back.

Her hands lunged for the weapon. Fumbled.

"Don't!" he warned. He raised the stun gun, shoved it against her shoulder and squeezed the trigger.

The brunette screamed. Jerked stiff. Dropped the pistol.

"I'll take that." Brady took the pistol as well as the cop's empty service weapon and shoved them in the waist of the girl's oversized jeans. "You're not the first chick to screw me over, and because I am, as you said, a bully…" He leered at the brunette, who gaped at him with tear-puddled eyes and an expression of horror. He wished he could put Angi, his backstabbing ex, in a trunk to freeze, but this girl could pay for Angi's sins. "I think I'll let you die slowly. Suffering." He wrenched the ranch coat off the girl and shoved his own frozen arms in its warmth. "Thanks. I'll take this, too. Call it payback for the bullet in my leg."

He closed the trunk, retrieved the ignition key and locked them inside. Slapping the trunk lid, he shouted, "Have fun, girlie. You should freeze to death by morning, if you don't suffocate first!"

With that he limped to the backseat of the Caddy, collected his prison jumpsuit, the girl's purse and cell phone, then glanced about for any other evidence he'd been there. He couldn't do anything about the broken rear windshield or bullet holes in the Caddy, but he could take the cowboy's truck and get the hell out of there before a witness showed up.

Hobbling to the pickup, Brady tossed the armload in the back of the truck and sent a disgusted look toward the darkening sky. The wind had started gusting, and the first wet snowflakes swirled from the sky.

Time to find shelter.

* * *

Jake woke by degrees, fighting the black abyss that sucked at him. He cracked his eyes open slowly, taking in information from all of his senses. He lay on his side, a hard, cold, lumpy surface beneath him. His head throbbed. Darkness surrounded him. He could smell motor oil, mildew and…something sweeter. Flowers? Peaches?

All was quiet, except for the whoosh of gusting wind…until a quiet sniff and muffled sob reached him through the blackness. He wasn't alone.

A soft body nestled against him, shivering, shifting. He tried to move, to sit up, but he immediately hit his head on an unyielding barrier above him. Lightning bolts streaked through his skull, and with a groan, he sank back to the cold surface below him.

A soft gasp filtered through the dark.

"You're awake?" a female voice whispered.

Jake raised a hand to his pounding temple. "Yeah. I… Where are we?"

"He put us in the t-trunk." The woman sniffled again, then added, "I'm sorry. I tried to stop him, to shoot him, but your gun was out of bullets."

A flurry of memories scrolled through his brain. Gunfight with an escaped con. A nearly naked young woman in the trunk—a brunette with big green eyes and freckles on her pale cheeks. Pain screaming through his body. "Taser," he groaned. "Hell."

"A-are you all right?" she asked, and her teeth chattered.

"I'll live. You?"

"J-just scared. And c-cold."

He felt the tremor that rolled through her and reach blindly for her in the darkness. Her arms, torso and legs were bare except for her bra and panties. That matched his memory of her lack of clothes when he'd opened the trunk earlier, but…

"What happened to the coat I gave you?" But he knew the answer.

"The convict took it," she confirmed. "H-he stole your t-truck."

Jake gritted his teeth, fury and frustration coursing through him. Reaching behind him he felt for his pistol and the police sidearm he'd lifted from the convict. Both were gone. "Hell."

Drawing a slow breath, he focused on the situation at hand and the more immediate need to get them out of the trunk and warmed up. Based on his companion's shivering and state of undress, she was well on her way to hypothermia. "What's your name, ma'am?"

"Ch-Chelsea Harris." Her voice cracked with emotion and from the cold.

Compunction and compassion twisted inside him. He was cold, but she had to be miserable. And if he'd been more thorough ensuring the area around his prisoner was secure, they wouldn't be in this mess. *Hell and damnation.*

"Hi, Chelsea," he said in a calm, reassuring tone. "I'm Jake Connelly, and I'm going to get us out of here. I need you to trust me. Okay?"

She hesitated, her skepticism obvious in the silence, then she whispered, "Okay."

"First things first. I'm going to chafe some warmth into your arms and legs. Your shivering means you're dangerously low on body heat. I'm not groping you. Got it?"

"Y-yeah."

Jake wrapped his hands around her arm, which was

frighteningly cool to his touch, and vigorously rubbed her skin. "Did he hurt you?"

"Not as b-bad as he hurt you."

"Meaning he *did* hurt you." Jake pressed his mouth in a tight line of disgust and fury.

"He h-hit me once. Gave me a z-zap from the stun g-gun. Grabbed my hair. S-stuff like that." She said it as if getting jolted by a stun gun was nothing, but he heard the telltale warble of fear in her voice.

He muttered an invective under his breath.

"Hey, w-we're alive," she said, putting steel in her voice. "That's all I c-care about."

"True that." In his head, he began working through the possibilities for getting them out of the trunk. "Does your bra have an underwire?"

"Wh-what?"

He chuckled under his breath. "That sounded skeevy, didn't it? Sorry. I need something I can use it to pick the lock and get us out of here."

"Oh. Uh…yeah. It d-does, but how—"

"Permission to manhandle your bra?"

Chapter 3

Brady pressed a hand to his throbbing leg. The duct tape bandage the cowboy had fashioned over his wound had worked for a while, but fresh blood was seeping from under the tape. As his adrenaline receded, his pain grew, along with his impatience.

Gusts of wind battered the pickup and made it difficult to control the truck. He swerved as if he were drunk and battled to stay in his lane. The last thing he needed was to let erratic driving draw the attention of a passing cop.

Squinting through the windshield, he spotted a farmhouse ahead and tried to remember how far the GPS voice had said they were from the brunette's house. Damn it, he should've brought the GPS with him, but he'd gotten in a hurry.

Get a grip, man! You've come too far, risked too much to screw up now! Brady squeezed the steering wheel. He refused to go back to prison. Confinement was sucking the life from him. He'd eat a bullet before he let them cage him up again.

He pulled into the driveway of the farmhouse and surveyed the scene. An old pickup was parked out front, and a small stable sat a hundred yards or so behind the house. A black-and-white dog noticed his arrival and started barking from behind the fence of its pen. He glowered at the dog, knowing the ruckus was likely to attract unwanted attention.

Sure enough, he'd just cut the engine, intending to take a look around, when an old man stepped out of the stable and sent a curious look his way. Brady cursed under his breath and pulled the cowboy's gun onto his lap. He rolled down the truck window and waited as the old man ambled closer.

"Can I help you?" the white-haired man asked.

Brady sent him a friendly smile and curled a finger around the trigger of the pistol. "I'm afraid I'm lost. I'm looking for a friend's house." Brady called an image to mind of the brunette's key chain, dangling from the Caddy's ignition. The miniature Texas license plate clipped to the ring read *Chelsea*. "Chelsea said her parents were on vacation, and she was house-sitting for them. I'm supposed to meet her for dinner, but I think I missed a turn."

The man's face brightened. "You must mean the Harrises. I heard they were taking a cruise or some such." The old man walked a few steps closer. "Their place is the next driveway on the left. About four miles, I think." He grinned. "Nice girl, that Chelsea. How did you meet her?"

Brady shoved down his rising impatience. "Mutual friend." He jerked a nod. "Thanks for the directions."

He moved his hand from the gun to the ignition key, then hesitated. The old man could identify him if the police did a house-by-house search. He glanced back at the old codger, who wore a bright orange hunter's cap, and his brain started clicking.

Wrapping his hand around the cowboy's pistol again, he called to the man, "You're a hunter?"

The old man flashed a crooked grin. "Yep. Have been since I was six, and my daddy took me deer hunting near Tyler."

Brady smiled. A hunter would have rifles, shotguns, maybe even a bow. Weapons he might need.

"Good to know." He popped the driver's door open and slid out, keeping the pistol hidden from the man's view.

The old guy frowned. "Whatcha doing? Shouldn't you be gettin' to the Harrises' before this storm hits?"

"I'll be heading out soon enough. Anyone inside? A wife? Kids?"

"Who wants to know?" The man's gaze dropped to the bloodstains on Brady's leg, and he narrowed a suspicious look toward him. "Who are you? What happened to you?"

Brady swung the gun up. "I'll ask the questions. Who's inside?"

The man tensed when he saw the pistol, then gave Brady a defiant glare. "What do you want, boy? You think you can frighten me with that thing? I saw combat in World War II. Spent weeks under fire in a trench in France. I've already survived hell on earth." The man straightened and squared his shoulders. "You're nothing but a punk. I'm not scared of you."

Brady sneered at him. "Maybe you should be, gramps."

* * *

Permission to manhandle her bra? A strangled sound rose in Chelsea's throat. Humiliation and modesty warred with her common sense and will to survive. The cowboy's request made sense. His idea was inspired, logical.

But she couldn't help the prickle of self-consciousness. Bad enough that her nearly naked size 14 body was pressed intimately against his male perfection. *Awkward.* Stripping in front of the convict and being discovered by Jake wearing only her skivvies had been mortifying enough, especially knowing the extra weight she'd gained in the past year gave her love handles and unsightly cellulite on her thighs.

Maybe if you hadn't let your appearance go— Todd's voice echoed in her head and lanced her heart.

"Chelsea?" Jake said, still waiting for her answer.

She swallowed hard, and mustering her practicality like a shield, she shoved down the twinges of embarrassment. "All right. Should I take it off?"

"Let me see what I can do with it on. I'd hate for you to lose even the tiny scrap of protection from the cold it's giving you. Hold still, okay?"

She tried not to move, but when his warm fingers slid under her bra and nudged the side of her breast, a current of sensation, a hyperawareness of the über-sexy cowboy's touch charged through her. And she flinched. She bit the inside of her cheek to stifle a moan of pleasure.

Oh, Chelsea...so inappropriate under the circumstances.

Their lives had been threatened, they were trapped in a car trunk, and she was literally freezing to death. But, oh, heavens, the brush of his fingers on her bare skin, the press of his hard chest spooned next to her back, the juxtaposition of his groin against her tush...

How could she not react to him?

He tugged on the fabric at the end of the underwire, flexing and twisting the material until the wire poked through. He pulled the wire, but it held fast.

Chelsea's breath hitched in her chest as he slid his hand around to the other side of her demi-cup and repeated the process.

"I usually don't p-put out like this on a first date," she said with a nervous chuckle. "You owe me d-dinner and a movie when we g-get out of here, pal."

He gave a short laugh, his breath fanning the back of her neck and sending a thrill to her core. "You got it, darlin'," he said with a lazy Texas drawl.

She heard the pop of a seam, then felt the tug, as the underwire slid free, and the vibration at her back as he gave a low growl of satisfaction. Maybe it was wrong for such simple things to turn her on, given the gravity of their situation, but tell that to her crackling nerve endings. The cowboy had her every skin cell charged and her heart racing.

"Got it," he said. "I don't suppose there's a flashlight in here, is there?"

"N-not that I could find. Wh-what about a cell ph-phone?"

He jerked. "You have a cell phone?"

"I— No. I w-was hoping you did."

His muscles relaxed again, radiating his disappointment. "No. I left mine in my truck, charging. If Brady stole my truck, then he has my phone, too."

Chelsea's pulse tripped. "Brady? You knew that guy?"

"Naw. I heard the news reports about his escape. I

only realized who he was after I saw the orange jumpsuit stuffed under the seat. By then Brady had pulled his gun and...well, you heard the shootout."

"Yeah." She shivered again, remembering the echoing shots, imagining the carnage that could have happened just feet from her, fearing a bullet would pierce the trunk and hit her.

"Okay, I'll go by feel. Hang on, now. I've got to work around you." His body canted closer to hers, his arms shifting and reaching past her for the trunk lock.

She tried to give him room to work, but her legs had grown stiff and cramped, and her arms were almost numb from the cold. While before she'd been certain she would die, either by the convict's hand or from exposure, Jake's presence, his level-headed thinking, gave her a morsel of hope, which she clung to with both hands.

"H-have you ever picked a lock before?"

He grunted. "More than once."

"Oh? Is b-breaking and entering a hobby of y-yours?"

He didn't answer right away. "Let's just say picking locks comes in handy at times in my line of work."

She frowned. "A-and what line of w-work would that be?"

The rattle of metal answered her, but Jake said nothing.

A draft blew through the confines of the trunk as the wind outside gusted harder, and Chelsea couldn't stop the shudder that rolled through her. Thanks to the darkness that surrounded them, she couldn't tell if Jake was making any progress on jimmying the lock or not. But for the first time since the escaped con had grabbed her and shoved the gun in her ribs, Chelsea believed she might actually survive this ordeal. Thanks to Jake.

What he did for a living didn't matter in the scheme of things if he could get them out of the car.

While Jake worked on the lock, Chelsea tried to steer her thoughts away from the biting cold long enough to strategize. Before now, she'd been so focused on not getting shot, then on staying warm and getting out of the trunk, that she hadn't thought beyond those threats. With the real possibility of escaping the trunk at hand, she needed to make a plan. She was determined to stay positive, think clearly and not give up. She could get out of this pickle if she didn't panic.

Step one: How would she get home if Ethyl was out of gas? While waiting for Jake to wake up, she'd heard a few cars pass by, but increasingly fewer people were out on the road as the storm closed in. She was in her bra and panties. Her parents' house was still at least six miles away.

The weight of despondency sat on her chest, and she doggedly shook off the negativity.

"Come on," Jake grumbled under his breath as he worked.

"C-can I help?" she asked, her teeth chattering.

"No." He moved his hands back to her arms and rubbed her skin briskly again. "The lock is sticking, probably because of rust, maybe ice, but I'll get it open."

Seconds later she heard a click, and Jake released a sigh.

"Well?" She held her breath.

"I think the locking pin moved, but the underwire broke off." He banged on the lid, but nothing happened.

Chelsea battled the disappointment that tried to swell in her chest. *Stay positive.*

"Watch out," Jake said, pushing her legs aside with his hand. "Give me some room."

She scooted as far back from the lock as she could. "What—"

She heard a thud, then another, and the trunk hook bent slightly so that a crack of light and chilly air seeped in. In the weak light that filtered inside, she could see Jake bring his knees to his chest, then kick out with an abbreviated thrust. The heel of his boot hit the lock once, twice...and suddenly the lid sprang open. Chelsea gasped as a blast of icy wind swept over her and relief flooded her veins.

"Hallelujah," she whispered.

Jake rolled his head to face her, grinning. "And amen."

He smacked a kiss on her forehead, then grabbed the car frame to pull himself out of the trunk in one swift motion. As he jumped to the pavement, he clutched a hand to his temple, and she remembered the blow to the head he'd taken as he collapsed from the stun gun.

"Are you okay?"

He raised a startled look to her. "Me? You're the one turning into a human popsicle."

"I saw you grab your head. You hit it pretty hard when you fell."

He waved away her concern with a flick of his hand. "I'll be fine. Right now we have to get something for you to wear."

She climbed out of the car and tested her cramped legs' ability to hold her upright. Weak, but she stayed vertical. Spotting his cowboy hat in the trunk, she reached for it, then turned to hand it to him.

He took the hat but jammed it on her head instead of his. "You need this more than I do."

Admittedly, without the trunk's protection from the wind or Jake's body heat cuddled near her, her cold factor had risen exponentially. Along with her awkward, self-conscious factor. Being nearly naked with a stranger in a dark trunk paled to being nearly naked with a hunky cowboy outside in the light of day.

Jake raked his gaze over her, and he frowned.

Her cheeks stinging with humiliation, she wrapped her arms around her middle, both fighting off the cold and hoping to hide her love handles from his scrutiny.

He marched past her and opened Ethyl's back door. She thought about the horrid orange jumpsuit the escapee had been wearing, and her stomach roiled. Even as cold as she was, the idea of wearing the creepy killer's prison castoffs disgusted her. But when he backed out of the car shaking his head, she knitted her brow. "The orange jumpsuit?"

Jake shrugged and headed toward her with his hands upturned. "He must have taken it with him. It was evidence of his trail after all. So…unless you have an emergency blanket or some spare clothes stored in there…"

Chelsea heaved a shivering sigh. "No."

Already large snowflakes danced around her head and dusted the ground.

Her shoulders slumped. "Now what? The car is out of gas."

Jake stopped in front of her and started unbuttoning his shirt. "For starters, you take my clothes."

She jerked her chin up and met his gaze. "B-but then you'll freeze. I can't—"

"So be it." He stripped off his long-sleeved chambray shirt and dumped it in her hands. "A gentleman doesn't let a lady go without."

Tears of gratitude prickled her eyes. Being a good Samaritan, stopping to help the stranded driver, could have cost Jake his life, and he was still making sacrifices on her behalf.

"Th-thank you." Her voice cracked as she wrapped the shirt around her and jammed her arms in the sleeves. The fabric still held his body heat and traces of his woodsy scent. A quiver spun through her that had nothing to do with the chilly weather.

When she glanced up from buttoning his shirt, he'd kicked off his boot and shoved his jeans to his feet. Her breath backed up in her lungs. The sight of his broad bare chest, tautly muscled legs and clingy boxer briefs rooted her to her spot. *Oh, Texas, the man was sexy!*

"Here." He extended the jeans to her, rousing her from her gawking stupor, and a new level of awkward reality slapped her. No way would his jeans fit her size 14 butt. If she tried to zip his jeans and couldn't, she might as well rent a lighted sign with arrows that blinked *Chubby*.

"I, um… Keep those. You n-need to wear s-something."

He shook his head. "I wouldn't feel right wearing them if you were—"

"Jake." She grabbed his arm. "I… God, this is embarrassing." She squared her shoulders and raised her chin. "They won't fit me." She exhaled harshly, creating a white cloud that slowly dissipated, along with her pride. "I'm too fat for them."

Jake scowled, his gaze wandering over her as he shook the jeans out to put them back on. "If you say so."

Chelsea turned away, biting the inside of her cheek and choking down the burn of humiliation that climbed her throat. Even Todd's cruel bluntness when he'd dumped her hadn't stung this much. She knew she shouldn't be so sensitive, shouldn't care what Jake thought of her appearance. She'd probably never see him again after today. But her waist size was a sore spot for her. And not just because Todd had used her weight gain as an excuse to break up with her.

The extra pounds reminded her of a dark time in her life, long months spent at the side of a hospital bed, weeks of eating fast food and junk snacks from a vending machine so that she could stretch extra minutes from the day. She'd turned to comfort food when she thought she might lose her mother. The added pounds represented grief and a loss of control in her life that she was still struggling to reclaim.

"For the record—" Jake's voice drew her from her gloomy thoughts "—you're not fat."

She cringed mentally at his attempt to comfort her. She didn't want his pity or his false flattery. "Todd thought so," she mumbled under her breath.

"You're *not.*"

"Whatever."

She heard the rasp of his zipper as he re-dressed, the thump as he stomped his foot back in his boots. She stared down at her own feet. At least Brady—or whatever the convict's name was—had let her keep her tennis shoes. They had miles to walk before they'd reach shelter and a phone.

"And along those same general lines, when you tell your friends about today, be kind." She lifted a puzzled look to Jake, and he sent her a wry grin. "Remember that it was *cold* out here."

When his meaning became clear, she darted a glance at his groin, then back to his face. And laughed. "Seriously? *That* was c-cold mode, and you're worried what I'll tell my f-friends?"

He arched an eyebrow. "Just sayin'."

An icy wind buffeted her, burrowing to her bone and stealing the return quip from her tongue. Chelsea hunched her shoulders and blew into her hands. "My parents' house is about s-six miles that way." She aimed a finger down the road, her teeth chattering. "That's where I'm staying while they're on vacation."

"Is that where you were headed when the car ran out of gas?"

She nodded.

Jake folded his arms around her, blocking the brunt of the wind with his body. He lifted her hand and rubbed her frozen fingers between his palms. "Is it safe to assume Brady headed there when he left here? Did he know where your parents lived?"

She ducked her head to look in Ethyl's front window. "Well, the GPS is s-still in the car, so it's hard to s-say. I was driving, and the GPS only g-gives one step of direction at a t-time. He knew the general d-direction we were headed but maybe n-not a specific address."

The idea of an escaped criminal breaking into her parents' house, eating their food, sitting on their sofa to watch their new flat-screen TV made her skin crawl.

"Is your parents' place the closest house?" Jake asked, twisting at the waist to scan the empty horizon.

"N-no. Henry Noble's house is about t-two miles from here. Then Darynda Jones and her kids live about a mile d-down Haverty Road. Her husband is deployed in Afghanistan until July."

"Okay. We'll head to the Nobles' because it's the closest. From there we can call the cops to check out your house before you go home." He took her hand

and started down the road, casting a wary eye to the sky. "Let's hurry. These flakes keep getting bigger and coming down faster."

Jake stopped walking after Chelsea stumbled for the third time in as many minutes. Facing her, he blinked as giant snowflakes battered his face, driven by a biting wind. "Am I going too fast?"

"S-sorry. I j-just… M-my legs are so c-cold, they're numb. I can't feel them, m-much less walk straight."

Frowning his worry over her worsening condition, Jake glanced down the road, gauging how much farther they had to walk to reach her neighbor's house. Two inches of snow had already accumulated, and the wind blew harder by the minute, dropping the temperature with each gust. His head throbbed where he'd hit it, but he couldn't do anything about his aching skull, so he shoved thoughts of it aside to concentrate on Chelsea. "Climb on my back. I'll carry you."

She stared at him blankly, her slowing mental faculties another sign of hypothermia.

"Chelsea, do you understand what I said? Can you hold on to me if I put you on my back?"

If needed, he could carry her fireman-style over his shoulder. Checking for some sign of coherence, he looked straight into her eyes—gorgeous, green bedroom eyes, he noted again, feeling a kick in his pulse. And, hot damn, but her generous bottom lip begged to be nibbled like a fresh strawberry.

Chelsea frowned. "I—I'm too heavy."

That again? "Nonsense. I've carried men bigger than you, under worse circumstances." He thought about how his comment sounded, then added, "Not that you're big… I just mean—" Another lightning bolt of pain shot through his head. He gritted his teeth. "Hell, just get on my back and hold on. Okay?"

Crouching in front of her, he pulled her arms around his neck. When her hold on him tightened, he slid his arms under her legs and stood. If he weren't so concerned about how red and cold her skin felt, he'd really enjoy having her breasts pressed against him and her legs wrapped around his waist....

His knees still hurt from tackling the worker in the radiation lab the day before, and as he stood, a grunt of pain slipped out.

Chelsea sighed and wiggled weakly. "See. I t-told you I'm too heavy."

"Relax." Jake tightened his grip and trudged on down the road. "That grunt was not about you. It was about the abuse my knee took on the job recently."

"Wh-what do you do?" she asked.

Conversation was good. If he could keep her alert and talking, he could monitor the extent of her hypothermia.

"I do security work." His standard vague response.

"Like a m-mall cop?"

He chuckled. "No. Overseas contract work." More nonspecific generalities. Even his family didn't know the full extent of his top secret black ops work.

"O-oh." She fell silent for a moment. "I'm a vampire."

Jake scowled. "A vampire?"

Was this his first sign she was losing touch with reality, disoriented, hallucinating? Not good.

She gave a small laugh. "Y-yeah. I take people's b-blood."

"To drink?" He'd heard of weirder things.

A scoff. "No! For s-surgeries and s-stuff. I'm a phlebotomist at the b-blood center."

A grin of relief tugged Jake's lips. "Gotcha. For a minute there, I thought you were losing it."

She chuckled weakly, then sighed. "Y-you smell good."

"Uh…thanks." He thought he smelled like airports and twenty hours on a stuffy plane, but…whatever. *Keep her talking.*

He asked her basic, easy questions, general get-to-know-you fare. Was she dating anyone?

Where did she go to college? What were her hobbies?

No. Local community college. Reading and quilting. Barrel racing.

Barrel racing? Jake quirked an eyebrow. *Interesting.* Did she like sports?

Football and some baseball. Rodeo.

Between the blowing, blinding snow and the extra weight on his back, Jake made slow progress down the highway. He tried to keep his mind on the mundane conversation and not on the bitter temperatures and frigid wind. He'd endured worse conditions in the line of duty, so he could handle a snowstorm with no shirt or coat. No matter how cold he was, Chelsea had to be colder. He admired the fact that she wasn't complaining, that she kept a sense of humor even though she had to be miserable. Having her body pressed against his back provided him a little added warmth, and he hoped his body heat was helping her against the freezing temperatures.

He cast a narrowed glance around him to figure out how far they'd come. Visibility had quickly diminished once the storm descended.

"How long have you worked at the blood center?"

"Three years. No, almost f-four." She sounded drowsy, her speech beginning to slur.

"Chelsea, stay with me. Talk to me. How much farther is it to the Nobles'? Am I going the right way?"

Her finger wiggled. "Down that d-driveway."

Jake squinted through the blowing snow and spotted two reflectors poking through the snow, marking the end of a driveway. Target sighted. Jake ducked his head against the wind and picked up his pace.

As he plowed through the storm, he thought briefly of his father, lying in the hospital in Amarillo, fighting for his life. Jake's heart sank. Given the weather, Chelsea's condition and his stolen truck, he doubted he'd make it in time to tell his father goodbye. As much as he hated missing his last chance to see his father, his job with the black ops team had taught him plenty about sacrificing for the greater good, about priorities. And his first priority now was saving Chelsea, getting her to safe shelter and warming her up.

His second priority was finding Brady. He wasn't sure when the escaped convict had landed on his radar, but sometime between stopping to help a stranded motorist and finding a woman locked in a car trunk, he'd made Brady his business, his priority. According to the radio, Edward Brady had already killed two policemen. The guy was dangerous, desperate.

But Jake had made a vow years ago when evil men like Brady had taken his mother's life. He would not turn his back and let evil win again. Jake was determined to put an end to the convict's reign of terror, no matter what it took. Because stopping dangerous men was what he did, and Brady had made it personal when he crossed Jake.

* * *

"Wait here." Jake set Chelsea down behind an old truck parked in the neighbor's front yard. "I'm going to scout things out, make sure Brady isn't inside ready to ambush us. If there's trouble, stay hidden. Got it?"

Chelsea gave a jerky nod and slid to the snowy ground, huddled in a shivering ball. She needed heat—and fast—but Jake wasn't about to go charging into a situation blind. Not while there was an escaped convict in the area. He might not see his stolen truck or any tracks in the snow on the property, but that didn't mean Brady wasn't around.

Crouching low, Jake hurried across the lawn to the front window, where he peered inside. Despite the increasing gloom and encroaching evening darkness, no lights were on in the house, making it harder to see the home's interior. The possibility existed that the homeowner was not there, though the truck parked out front suggested otherwise.

Moving to the next window, Jake peeked inside again, still finding nothing to suggest Henry Noble was home. When he rounded the corner to the back of the house, he discovered a dog pen with a small doghouse in a back corner of the yard. He didn't see a dog in the pen, but there were paw prints in the snow inside the caged area. Because there were no footprints leading to the dog pen, Jake decided the dog must be huddled inside his doghouse. Another indicator no one was home at the Noble residence. Why would anyone with good sense leave their pet out in such horrible weather?

An uneasy feeling stirred in Jake's gut. Where was Henry Noble? Had the bad weather stranded him in town? The roads and visibility were bad, but not impassable at this point.

He continued around the outside of the home, checking through windows, scanning the yard for clues of occupancy. As he crept through the backyard, the dog, a medium-sized black-and-white heeler or Australian cattle dog, saw him and charged out of his doghouse barking and pacing inside his pen. Jake waited and watched from behind a woodpile to see if the dog's barking brought anyone to the back door, if even to look out at the yard for the source of the dog's agitation.

Nothing. No one.

Not even from the horse stable, one hundred or so yards behind the house. The wind had blown the main door to the stable open, and it banged noisily on the stable wall with each gust of frigid wind. If Henry Noble owned horses, the stable should have been shuttered and secured to protect the animals from the storm. Most ranchers were far more concerned with their animals' welfare. That Henry Noble seemed not to be didn't sit well with Jake.

Frowning his puzzlement, Jake completed a full circuit of the house, then approached the front door cautiously and knocked. Pressing an ear to the door, he listening for sounds of someone moving around inside but heard nothing except the dog out back and the howl of the wind in the eaves. Turning the knob, he tested the door and found it unlocked. His pulse kicked uneasily. Where the hell was Noble and why hadn't he locked his home when he left?

"Hello?" he called into the dark house as he crept into the foyer, wishing he had his gun for self-defense. He made a quick sweep of each room, knowing he needed to get Chelsea inside…like an hour ago.

Empty. No Noble, but more important, no Brady.

He hurried back outside to the old truck where Chelsea huddled, shaking with near-convulsive tremors.

"Okay, sweetheart, let's get you inside." He scooped her in his arms, and she looped a limp arm around his neck. He carried her across the yard and into the house, where he laid her on the living room couch.

She turned her head slowly, teeth chattering, and frowned as she studied the dark room. "Wh-where's M-Mr. Noble?"

"That," Jake said, taking a throw from a nearby recliner and wrapping it around her, "is a good question. Short answer—not here. Any ideas where he could be?"

Chelsea furrowed her brow and clutched the decorative blanket around her. "N-no." She sank back in the cushions of the sofa and closed her eyes. "H-he's retired. M-Mom said that s-since his wife died last s-summer, he never g-goes anywhere. H-he's like a hermit."

"He lives alone?" Jake found another blanket, one of the recent marketing gimmicks, that had sleeves, piled in the seat of the recliner and pulled it around his shoulders like a robe. Moving to the sofa, he pulled Chelsea onto his lap and included her in the circle of the sleeved wrap. She snuggled in as if to nap, and he jostled her. "Hey, I know you're tired, but you need to stay awake. I'm going to get you something warm to drink and some clothes to put on in a second."

His gaze landed on the fireplace where three small logs were stacked, and he decided lighting a fire was a good next step. "Hey, do you see any matches or a lighter around here? I'm going start a fire."

He reached under the shade of a lamp beside the couch and twisted the switch. Nothing happened.

He tried again. *Nada.*

Frowning, he glanced to the DVD player across the room, to a digital clock beside the recliner and to the cordless phone charging station on the end table beside the sofa. The display screen on each device was dark. He huffed his frustration. "I think the power is out. That's why it's so dark in here. And unless he has a corded landline or cell phone lying around somewhere, we have no phone either. The cordless is useless without a working base."

He chafed Chelsea's icy legs and rubbed her fingers, praying she didn't have frostbite. Even though she'd been significantly underdressed for the conditions, her saving grace might be that the temperature had been near freezing and not subzero.

"S-Sadie," Chelsea croaked.

"What?"

"H-his dog. I h-hear her."

Jake nodded. "She's in her pen out back. I'll bring her in when I get some more wood for the fire."

Chelsea shook her head, scowling. "No. N-now. It's freezing out th-there!"

Jake arched an eyebrow and flashed her a lopsided grin. "All right, I'll get her. Do you know if she bites?"

"Sadie's a s-sweetheart." She shuddered again, but he noticed a healthier color was already returning to her cheeks. She licked her pinkening lips, and his libido kicked hard. Her lush mouth tempted him to forget he was raised to be a gentleman and steal a taste. Now might not be the right time, but later…

Squelching the spike of arousal that spun through him, Jake shifted her off his lap and gave her the sleeved blanket as he pushed off the couch. "I'll be right back."

Before venturing outside, Jake checked the front

closet and found a heavy camouflage hunting jacket, which he commandeered, along with a fleece sweater, which he took for Chelsea. He tossed her the sweater as he passed the sofa on the way to the back door. "Put this on, and I'll check the bedrooms for more clothes when I get back with the dog."

"Aye-aye, C-Captain," she returned, the corner of her mouth twitching in a teasing grin. Her good humor and alertness boded well for her recovery, and Jake drew a deep breath of relief as he headed outside.

Sadie paced and barked at the gate of her pen as he crossed the yard.

"Hi, Sadie," he said in a soothing, friendly tone. "Good girl. Where's your person? I bet you're cold, huh?" He let the dog smell his hand through the fence, and Sadie wagged her tail as she wiggled excitedly waiting for him to open the gate. "Let's go inside. Okay, girl? Good dog." Judging Sadie not to be a bite threat, he opened the gate.

Sadie charged out…and tore across the yard toward the stables, barking.

A tingle raced down Jake's spine. Had the dog seen something he missed?

"Sadie! Here, girl. Sadie!" Blowing into his cold hands, he headed at a trot across the lawn toward the stable. "Sadie?"

The dog appeared in the door of the stable for a moment, as if to say, *Are you coming?*

Jake jogged to the stable, approaching the open door cautiously. "Hello? Mr. Noble, are you there?"

No answer. Hearing only the agitated nickering of horses, the whip of wind and Sadie's dog tags tinkling as she paced, Jake moved into the shadowed stable.

His gaze assessed every dark corner and egress as he crept inside. "Hello?"

Sadie appeared from one of the horse stalls and gave an uneasy whine.

Apprehension pooled in Jake's gut. He eased around the half wall of the stall and peered inside.

An elderly man lay on his back, staring sightlessly at the rafters. A bullet hole marred his forehead.

Chapter 4

Brady poked another log into the fireplace, then rose to his feet, groaning when his injured leg throbbed in protest. Rubbing his thigh where the bullet had left a deep gash, he clenched his back teeth and cursed under his breath. He hoped the damn cowboy was freezing his ass off, gasping for his last breath.

As he rubbed his hands together, warming himself in front of the fire, he studied the pictures on the mantel. Most were of the brunette he'd carjacked. Baby pictures. Prom pictures. Rodeo pictures. High school graduation. He had to admit, the girl had been a looker. Pretty face, hot body.

Brady grunted. So what if she'd packed on a few pounds recently? He'd do her. In fact, maybe he'd been wrong not to bring her with him. Six years in the pen was a long time to go without any tail. He shrugged and turned to hobble into the kitchen.

The power had gone out five minutes after he'd broken in the brunette's house. At first he'd panicked, thinking it meant the cops had found him and were executing some kind of takedown. But one look out the window at the howling wind and whipping snow had eased his mind. Blackouts during winter storms were pretty common. Ice or tree limbs on the power lines. Wind-fallen power poles.

Brady opened the refrigerator and helped himself to a beer and leftover lasagna. He had no way to heat the lasagna without electricity, but even cold, the leftovers were a hell of a lot better-tasting than the glop he'd eaten in prison. Forking up huge bites straight from the container, Brady headed into the bathroom next. Surely the brunette chick had some kind of pain reliever in her medicine cabinet.

Setting the lasagna aside, he opened the mirrored cabinet over the sink and had to hold the bottles close to the fading sunlight from the window to read each label. The first two were for nausea, prescribed to someone named Marian Harris. The brunette was Chelsea, so maybe Marian was her mother? Whatever. He tossed the bottle aside and went on to the next.

Bingo. Marian also had oxycodone for pain. *Thank you, Marian.* He popped two and washed them down, cupping water from the faucet into his hand. Any extra pills he didn't use, he could sell for gas money or food. Maybe trade for sex. With a gloating smile, Brady pocketed the bottle, reclaimed the dish of lasagna, and headed back to the living room. Things were starting to look up for him.

Turning from the dead old man, Jake shuddered and heaved a dejected sigh. Brady had definitely been here.

Tensing, Jake swept another keen glance around the stable, listening. He moved from stall to stall, searching, looking for clues that Brady might still be in the area. But other than Sadie and three restless horses, no one was around.

Because there were no footprints or tire tracks in the thin layer of snow surrounding the stable, Jake concluded that Brady had been there and left before the snow started in earnest. Had probably arrived at Mr. Noble's within minutes of locking Jake and Chelsea in the trunk. Which gave him at least an hour head start to have been here and left again.

Gritting his teeth, Jake returned to the first stall. Kneeling by the body, he felt for a pulse, even though the man's wound left little doubt he was dead. The old man's murder shook loose old memories and left a gnawing anger inside him. He'd seen his share of dead bodies on the job, but being back in Texas, heading to his father's hospital bed meant his mom was not far from his mind. Another senseless tragedy. His chest tightened with the grief he'd carried for the past twelve years.

A sense of urgency pounded through Jake. A killer was on the loose, and Jake's lack of transportation, communication or weapon put him at a distinct disadvantage. He refused to cede the upper hand to a scum like Brady, but he couldn't abandon Chelsea until he knew she was out of danger.

Sadie sniffed at her master's hand, and Jake scratched the dog's ear. "Sorry, girl. Let's close this place up and get back to the house."

After putting blankets on all of the horses and securing the stable doors, Jake led Sadie by the collar back to the house. Sadie gave a hard shake as she trotted inside, flinging droplets of melting snow. Jake headed back to the living room, dreading breaking the news to Chelsea that her neighbor was dead. Murdered. "Chelsea?"

The sofa was empty. The living room was dark and silent.

His gut tightened, and his hand reached instinctively for his gun. Which Brady had stolen. Silently, Jake mouthed a curse word and moved deeper into the house. Sadie followed him, giving him a curious look and a tentative tail wag.

Before he reached the hallway to the bedrooms, a thump from the opposite end of the house drew his attention. Sadie heard the noise, too, and hurried off toward the kitchen, tags jingling. Jake followed, and as he eased toward the kitchen, he noticed the gun cabinet in a recessed corner of the living room. The case doors stood open, and every rack had been emptied.

He clenched his back teeth. Wherever he was, Brady was now well armed.

Another scuffling noise from the kitchen drew his attention, and he continued in that direction, picking up a fishing trophy from a bookshelf to use as a weapon if needed. He peered around the corner into the dim kitchen. Saw no one. Sadie paused to sniff around her food bowl.

A squeak of hinges pulled his gaze to a utility closet at the other side of the room. Then Chelsea's voice. "Oh, thank God."

Sadie raised her head and perked her ears.

"Chelsea?" Jake crossed to the closet.

"In h-here." She pushed the utility room door open and shuffled out, into a weak beam of light from the kitchen window. "Gas water heater." She shot him a wide grin, and Jake's breath backed up in his lungs.

Her bedroom eyes sparkled, and her smile transformed her face. Sure he'd noticed her sexy mouth before, but he hadn't *really* appreciated how attractive she was. Okay, her near-nudity *had* been distracting, and because of their dire situation, he'd tried to keep his mind on the business of saving her life. But gentleman or not, he'd have to have been dead not to notice her womanly curves and smooth skin.

A flash of heat swept through him, reminding him it had been months since he'd been with a woman. *Down, boy. Wrong time and place.*

Chelsea pulled the throw tighter around her shoulders as she stooped to give Sadie's head a pat. "I c-can have a hot b-bath!"

Jake set the trophy on the kitchen counter and cleared his head. "No. I mean…later. A hot bath now could cause heart arrhythmia." Her grin faltered, and he felt as if he'd kicked a puppy. "But hot water is good news. We can fix something warm to drink and wrap you up with a hot water bottle."

His body tightened, and heat crawled through him. *That wasn't all he wanted to wrap around her.…*

She shuffled to a kitchen chair, the dog at her heels. "The b-bad news is the kitchen phone is c-cordless, too. We have n-no way to call the c-cops, unless we find a cell phone."

Jake grimaced. He considered for a moment keeping his recent discoveries to himself but decided Chelsea needed the truth. "Actually, there's worse news."

She met his gaze, her mesmerizing green eyes wide with alarm. "Did you find Brady? Is he here?"

"No, not that I can tell. But…he was." Jake dragged a hand over his mouth and sighed. "The gun case is open and empty."

Chelsea puckered her brow. "That doesn't necessarily mean—"

"I found Mr. Noble in the stable."

She sat taller, stiffening her back as if bracing for a blow. "And?"

"He's dead. Gunshot wound to the head."

Chelsea gasped and slumped back in the chair, shaking. "Oh, my God…"

"I'm sorry. We're you close to him?"

"I— No, not really. I mean, he's been our neighbor for as long as I can remember, but…it's just—" Her gaze drifted down to Sadie, and she stroked the dog's head. "Sad. Scary."

"My best guess is Brady came upon the house shortly after he left us locked up, searched the house and took whatever he thought he might need. He ran into Mr. Noble and shot him rather than leave a witness. Don't know yet if he shot him in the house and dragged him to the stable or killed him there. Hell, Noble could have confronted him with a weapon, for all I know. But however it went down, Brady armed himself from Noble's gun cabinet and was gone before the hardest snow started."

She frowned. "Not that I'm sorry Brady left, but…if Mr. Noble was dead, why not hide out here?"

"He could have thought someone else would show up here. Mrs. Noble, for instance. He had no way of knowing she was dead."

Chelsea nodded.

"Maybe he thought Noble had called the cops and wanted to clear out before they showed up. Or…he could have some other specific destination in mind, someplace he felt more confident he'd be safe to lie low for a while."

Her face fell, and she groaned. "My parents' house. He knows they're out of town, that I was house-sitting."

Jake raised his chin and met her gaze, hope flaring in him. "No, that's good. If we have an idea where he's staying, we can send the authorities to pick him up—"

"How?" She flipped up one palm and tipped her head. "No phone, remember?"

Jake slammed a hand down on the table and barked a curse word. Pressing his mouth in a taut line, he drew a deep breath, trying to calm the roiling disquiet and futility inside him. He needed to be hunting Brady. His training, his instincts all demanded action, yet here he sat.

He paced to the kitchen window and stared out at the snow that blew harder and heavier by the minute. He could barely see past the front lawn, and daylight was rapidly fading. An accumulation of close to four inches had already collected on the old truck parked—

Jake straightened, his pulse kicking into overdrive. "Keys." He swept a look around the kitchen, searching for a pegboard or key hook. "Chelsea, you see any keys around here that look like they might go to the truck out front?"

She glanced around, shaking her head. "No. Maybe by the front door?"

He jogged toward the entry hall, calling, "Be right back!"

On an old phone desk by the door, Jake spotted a wooden bowl with a variety of keys, bolts, pens and peppermint candies. He rifled through the assortment until he found a key with the Ford logo. "Bingo."

Bracing against the stiff, icy wind and stinging snow, Jake crossed the yard to the old pickup and climbed in the cab. He put the key in the ignition and turned it.

The truck's engine whined and sputtered, but refused to catch. "Come on!"

He tried again and again with the same results. Each subsequent attempt produced a weaker-sounding engine noise as the cold battery gave up the ghost.

Finally Jake dropped his hand from the key and squeezed the steering wheel in frustration. He itched to set out on foot, hunting down the escaped killer. But heading out in a raging storm, unarmed, blinded by whipping snow and dark of night was not a smart move. Leaving Chelsea unprotected and still recovering from hypothermia rankled, as well.

Idleness didn't sit well with Jake. Waiting, no matter how advisable, felt too much like the reckless disregard and selfishness that he'd indulged in the summer he was sixteen. Since that painful summer, he'd been a man of action. But as he stared out at the blizzard and darkening night sky, he forced himself to swallow the bitter pill of defeat. Temporary defeat, he amended.

He might be stranded for the night, hands tied by his limited resources, but at first light tomorrow, he *would* find a way to catch up to Brady.

Chapter 5

From the kitchen, Chelsea heard the lifeless whine of the truck engine, and her spirits sank. She'd harbored a faint hope that she would be back at her parents' house, in her own clothes and snuggled in her own bed by nightfall. That fantasy sputtered out, even as she heard Jake try again to start Mr. Noble's old Ford.

She glanced down at Sadie, who sat beside her, getting her ears rubbed. "Well, Sadie girl, do you think Mr. Noble kept any of his wife's clothes?"

Sadie wagged her tail, acknowledging Chelsea. The dog was an orphan now, she realized. Someone would have to care for Sadie until a new home could be found for her. Chelsea's apartment management didn't allow pets, but she could keep Sadie at her parents' for a while. Chelsea leaned over and hugged the dog's neck. "Don't worry, Sadie. I'll find you a good home."

Mustering her strength, Chelsea pushed away from

the table and headed slowly toward the living room, clutching the blanket around her shoulders and pausing to lean on furniture as needed for rest. She'd made it as far as the end of the hallway when Jake bustled back in from the front yard, bringing with him a blast of cold air.

"No luck?" she said, as much to alert him that she'd left the kitchen as for confirmation of what she suspected.

He strode into the living room, blowing into his hands, and shook his head. "I'll start that fire now. We're gonna need it."

She hitched a thumb over her shoulder. "I was gonna look for something to wear. Maybe some of Mrs. Noble's things or some of his pajamas. Anything that will fit at this point. I'll bring you a shirt. Okay?"

He nodded. "Can you do it alone or do you want help?"

"I'll call if I need you." Sadie followed her down the hall to the first bedroom, which looked as if it had been Mrs. Noble's sewing room. Chelsea checked the closet and found extra linens, pillows and blankets, all of which would be handy for camping out in front of the fireplace tonight, but no clothes.

As she turned to leave the room, a movement in the corner caught her eye. Her pulse tripped, and she yelped. She swung toward the shadowed recess of the room, nearly tripping over Sadie as she backpedaled toward the door. "Who's there?"

A black-and-gray tabby with a white chest stretched lazily and sauntered over to rub against Chelsea's leg. Chelsea exhaled and fought to calm her racing heartbeat. "Geez, cat, you scared the crap outta me."

Jake appeared at the door. "Chelsea?"

"I'm okay. I think I just lost ten years of my life expectancy thanks to kitty here, but…" She stooped to lift the cat in her arms. The cat's collar had a tag that read Nela. "Meet Nela."

"Hello, Nela." Jake gave the tabby's head a little scratch. "Fire's going. I'm going to fix us something to eat, something warm to drink."

She nodded and set Nela back on the floor. "There are extra blankets and pillows in that closet if you want to grab some. I'm guessing we'll be m-making our beds in front of the fire, unless we get power back soon."

"Roger that. We need to close all the doors to these back rooms. It'll help keep the heat from the fire more in the living room."

She nodded, her teeth chattering. "R-right."

While he raided the sewing room closet for bedding, Chelsea moved on to the next room, the master bedroom, and found his and hers closets. Mrs. Noble's closet looked untouched, and her heart broke for Mr. Noble, who'd clearly been reluctant to get rid of anything following his wife's death. She flipped through the matronly dresses and blouses until she found a pair of khaki pants and a long-sleeved cotton blouse she thought would fit. The pants had an elastic waistband, not the most flattering fashion statement for someone her age, but she wasn't going to quibble. She added a soft pullover sweater and the fleece cardigan Jake had given her earlier, layering on warmth. Still she shivered. The cold sank to her bones, and she wondered if she'd ever feel warm again.

After she'd donned the clothes she'd picked out, she took a heavy flannel shirt from Mr. Noble's closet for Jake to wear while his shirt dried out. Wrapping the throw around her shoulders again, she returned to the living room with Jake's snow-soaked shirt. After spreading the shirt on the hearth to dry, she huddled close to the fire now crackling in the grate. Nela walked up to investigate the fire, tail twitching, and gave a lazy stretch. Sadie lay down in front of the hearth, resting her chin on her paws and giving Chelsea a sad look.

Mr. Noble had been killed. The tremor that raced through Chelsea now had nothing to do with the cold. She'd been plenty scared in the past few hours, facing the escaped convict, getting locked in her trunk, braving the cold, but she'd held the full extent of her terror at arm's length. She'd forcefully shoved down the fear that served no purpose other than to distract her and get in her way. But now…

She felt the tears sting her sinuses and adrenaline kick-start her pulse. She saw Brady's evil glare, the pistol aimed at her. She heard the concussion of gunfire and remembered the pain that twisted Jake's face as the stun gun's electric current coursed through him. Her elderly neighbor was dead, and the murderer was still on the loose, probably within miles of here. Maybe hiding out in her parents' home…

"Here."

She jolted when Jake spoke, and she swiped at the tears dampening her cheeks.

"More good news. The stove uses gas, too." He held a steaming mug out to her, which she took with shaking hands. "I'm heating a can of soup, but start with this coffee. It's instant, but it's not too bad if you add enough sugar."

He settled on the floor beside her and glanced her direction. "Hey, are you okay?"

She forced a grin. "Yeah, I… It all just hit me. We could have died. Brady could have killed us like he killed Mr. Noble. He still could. What if he comes back here?"

"Then I'll be ready for him. I won't let him hurt you, Chelsea. I promise." Jake reached for her cheek and dried a tear with his thumb. A warm tingle spun through her, and her pulse gave a giddy kick. His blue eyes held hers, lit with a hard-edged but reassuring determination. A sense of security flowed through her. After the way he'd come through for her already this afternoon, saving her from Brady and from Ethyl's trunk, she had no trouble believing Jake could protect her from the escaped convict should he return.

She studied Jake's face, admiring the way the fire's glow highlighted the rugged cut of his cheekbones and square jaw. Good Lord, but he was handsome.

"Who are you, Jake Connelly? And what put you at the right place at the right time to stumble into my nightmare?"

He arched a golden eyebrow. "If you're asking how I happened to be on that stretch of highway tonight, then the answer is I was driving through to Amarillo." His expression darkened, and his forehead creased as he frowned. "My dad had a heart attack, and I flew in, hoping to see him before…" He hesitated. Sighed. "They don't think he'll pull through."

Chelsea's heart twisted. "And now you're stuck here with me instead of seeing your dad. Oh, Jake, I'm so sorry."

He patted her knee. "Not your fault. You didn't ask for this any more than I did."

"No, but…" A selfish sense of comfort tripped through her. As terrible as it was to admit, she was glad Jake was with her. Besides the fact that he'd rescued her from the locked trunk, she couldn't imagine going through this terrifying scenario alone. She thought about what he'd said for a moment, then tipped her head in query. "You flew in?"

"Yeah."

"From where?"

He shot her an odd look. "I...can't tell you."

"You can't? Why?"

"Because I can't. It's the nature of the job I do. I can't disclose my location, even to my family."

Chelsea's eyes widened. "Are you, like...a spy or something? CIA?"

"Not CIA. Not a spy."

"Security. You said you worked in security. Overseas." She searched her foggy memory for any other details he'd given.

"I can't talk about what I do beyond that. Sorry."

"Are you a SEAL? Like the guys who killed bin Laden?"

He twitched a grin. "Those guys get all the high-profile jobs and glory. But no, I'm not a SEAL."

"But you're some other kind of special forces. Am I right?"

He gave her a mysterious smile. "How's your coffee? I guessed on the amount of sugar."

She grunted. "I see. You could tell me, but then you'd have to kill me. Is that how it works?"

"Nothing personal. I'm just not allowed to discuss my job."

"Okay. Next question... Why not fly directly to Amarillo?"

"Because I hitched a ride with the Air Force to Dyess Air Force Base in Abilene."

"So you're in the Air Force?"

He gave her a patient grin. "I didn't say that. Dyess is where I stored my truck when I left the country."

She narrowed a speculative look on him. "But the Air Force doesn't let just anyone fly with them."

He wrapped his fingers around her wrist and squeezed. "Chelsea, let's just say some higher power knew you were in need of someone with my particular skill set and put me on that road so I could help you."

"Is that what you believe?"

"I don't know." He sipped from his mug, then set it aside. "Maybe. I believe life is 10 percent what happens to you and 90 percent how you play the cards you're dealt."

She nodded her agreement. "You're right about that."

"I also know that I've been in worse situations before and come out alive. A snowstorm with no power is a cakewalk by comparison."

"Uh…have you forgotten the armed-and-deadly escaped felon?"

He scowled. "Oh, I haven't. I have every intention of capturing Brady and turning him in."

Chelsea blinked at him, and her gut pitched. "Wait… Capturing him? You plan to go after Brady?"

"Damn straight."

"But, Jake—"

"Hey…" He caught her shoulders and met her gaze with a hard, level look. "Keeping you safe is my top priority. But I can't ignore the fact that Brady is out there, that he's already killed three people we know of. I have a duty to find him and bring him in."

"But…he's dangerous!"

A muscle jumped in Jake's jaw, and any trace of humor or comforting warmth fled his eyes. "So am I."

Chapter 6

After they drank their coffee and ate some hot soup, Jake arranged a pallet on the floor in front of the fire using sofa cushions and blankets. Chelsea settled in on the makeshift bed, still feeling weak and shivery despite the hot food and clothes. All she had to do was look out the window at the driving snow or think of poor murdered Mr. Noble and a deep-seated chill would shimmy through her.

Before long Sadie crowded onto the pallet with her, and she rubbed the Australian cattle dog's ears. Nela also joined the party near the fire, perching on the hearth and blinking sleepy eyes at the strangers in her house. Jake returned from taking their soup bowls to the kitchen and had a package of Oreos. He popped a whole cookie in his mouth and chewed, offering her a chance to take one, as well. After the embarrassment of having been seen in her underwear and hearing Jake grunt when he lifted her onto his back, she waved away the Oreos. No time like the present to start the diet again. He could make all the polite excuses about knee injuries from his job that he wanted, but the truth was carrying her had been no picnic for him. Chelsea was determined to lose those extra pounds before bathing suit season.

"You sure?" Jake put another cookie in his mouth and hummed happily. "Man, I can't remember the last time I had Oreos. I'd forgotten how good they are."

"I'm sure." She watched Jake eat another cookie, and she wrapped her arms around her middle when her stomach growled.

He tugged a lopsided grin and arched one eyebrow. "I can see what else is in the pantry if you want."

"No, I..." Chelsea turned to stare into the fireplace. "It feels weird to be eating Mr. Noble's food, being in his house. I mean, I understand the circumstances make it necessary, and he's...he's dead and all, but..."

"But he was your neighbor, and it feels like an invasion of privacy," Jake finished for her.

"Exactly."

He squeezed her shoulder, his fingers rubbing the tense muscles near her neck. Despite their dangerous predicament, the deep massaging of his hands turned her to goo. Chelsea bit the inside of her cheek to muffle the groan of pleasure that rose in her throat.

"If he were alive, what do you think Mr. Noble would have done when we showed up on his doorstep, given the situation with the storm and Brady being in the area?" Jake asked.

She gave Jake a quick glance, considering his question. "He'd have...invited us in, offered us something hot to drink and insisted we'd be safer if we stayed with him rather than trying to get to my parents' house." A pang twisted in her chest remembering previous visits with the widower. "He always loved having company stop by, especially after his wife passed."

Jake nodded slowly. "And I bet he'd want someone looking after his horses, Sadie and Nela, too. Which we are." Jake paused, setting aside the cookie package and dusting crumbs from his fingers. "This is only temporary, Chelsea. As soon as the weather clears, I'm moving you somewhere safer, and we'll send the authorities out here to handle the scene in the stable."

The crime scene. She shuddered. Everything about the situation rankled. She was hunkered down in the home of a murdered neighbor with a mythically handsome man who may or may not be a CIA spy or elite forces soldier, while a colossal winter storm raged outside. She gave her head a shake as if she could clear the fog of surrealism. And today had started so normally....

Chelsea curled her fingers in the warm folds of Sadie's fur and cut a worried glance to Jake. "I've been thinking about the other neighbors in the area, especially Darynda Jones. She's alone at her place with young kids. What if Brady was going house to house scavenging weapons and money and..." She swallowed hard, not wanting to contemplate the tragic possibilities. "What if he killed Darynda and her children, too? Or Mrs. Posey, who lives a couple miles past my parents' house. Who knows what—"

"Hey—" Jake caught her hand in his, his blue eyes a smoky shade in the darkening room "—let's not borrow trouble. Taking out one old man and stealing his guns is one thing, but I doubt Brady would risk being seen by more people than necessary. Just the same, when the storm eases and we can get out, we'll check

on the neighbors or send the cops to make sure everyone's safe."

Meanwhile, she had, in Jake, the best protection a
girl could ask. She should be counting her blessings
rather than dwelling on all the things that had or could
go wrong. "Okay."

He moved the Oreo package aside and scooted closer
to her. His shoulder bumped hers as he leaned back
against the base of the sofa, stretching his long legs out
in front of him, and a heady tingle swept through her.

"The snow's really piling up out there. I used to
love weather like this when I was a kid." He grinned
at her, his change of topic clearly designed to distract
her. What diverted her thoughts instead were the sexy
crinkles beside his eyes when he smiled and the tiny
chip missing from the corner of a bottom incisor. Otherwise his teeth, his smile, like the rest of him, was
perfect. And she was alone with him all night.... *Oh,
my!* Another flash of prickly heat shimmied through
her and coiled in her belly.

"School would be canceled," Jake said, drawing
her out of her musings, "and we'd roast hot dogs and
marshmallows over the fire, even if the power was
still on." He sighed and drew his eyebrows together.
"Of course, my dad would be worried about his herd.
He'd disappear for hours with his ranch hands, checking on the cattle and hauling stored hay into the fields
for them to eat."

She tipped her head sideways as she looked at him.
"You didn't go with him?"

"Once I got older, sure. I remember the first winter
storm I helped him with. I was thirteen, I think. Man,
I remember coming home cold to the bone and so exhausted I could barely stay awake through supper."

He lifted one cheek in a grin. "Best kind of tired in the world. My dad used to say, you sleep well at night when your pillow is an honest day's work."

"I'm sorry about your dad. That you're stuck here, instead of with him."

He angled a sad smile toward her. "Yeah. Thanks."

He fell silent, staring into the fire, and Chelsea fidgeted with the edge of the throw, weaving it around her fingers. "My mom spent several months in the hospital about year ago, fighting breast cancer that had metastasized to her lung. It's scary to think about losing a parent, you know. I mean, you take them for granted and roll your eyes when they try to micromanage your life, but then something like that happens and you think, wait a minute! My mom can't die! I need her!" A familiar worry knotted her gut and fluttered in her chest. She took a slow breath to calm herself, reminding herself aloud, "She's a lot better now. The Hawaii trip is to celebrate her being in remission."

"That's good." He flashed another lopsided grin, but it seemed tinged with sadness.

"Yeah. Her doctors are hopeful, but I still get a little panicky when she has a bad day or acts tired. Now I'm the one nagging her about eating healthy and getting enough sleep."

She was rambling, she realized, chattering nervously because the fire, the dark room and quiet house felt too intimate.

He'd seen her in her underwear, for cripes' sake! Carried her on his back...

And now they were alone together. All night. Her pulse stumbled.

She rearranged the throw around her shoulders and shifted her weight from one numb butt cheek to the other. Sadie yawned, then propped her chin on Chelsea's leg.

Glancing at Jake's profile, she asked, "When was the last time you saw your dad?"

"Hmm." He scowled and scratched his chin. "Thanksgiving."

"So…at least you saw him recently." She infused her tone with a note of optimism, trying to lift his spirits. "That's good."

He glanced at her, his expression guilty. "Not this past Thanksgiving. The one before that. Like fourteen months ago."

"Oh." She blinked at him and fumbled. "That's—"

"Not so good."

"Well," she hedged, "but you were working, right? Doing important, top secret security stuff. Protecting lives…"

He cut her off with a side glance. "I could have made time between missions, but there was always another assignment calling, more bad guys to chase around the world."

"So…why didn't you stay with ranching? What made you get into the spy game?"

He quirked one eyebrow. "I'm not a spy."

"So you say. But maybe you are, and you're just telling me you're not to try to throw me off track." She gave him a teasing grin. "And you didn't answer the question. Why did you give up ranching with your dad?"

His expression grew pensive as he stared into the flames. "I'd made a promise I had to keep."

"What kind of promise? To whom?"

He didn't answer right away, and she feared she'd crossed a boundary. Finally he sighed and said, "To my mom. She used to tell me and my sister to be the change we wanted to see in the world."

"Gandhi."

His eyebrow lifted. "Yeah, very good."

She shrugged. "I think I heard it on *Jeopardy* last week."

He flashed a grin before turning back to the fire and growing pensive again. "Ranching was fine for my dad, but I wanted to make a difference in the world, do something to counter the evil that's all too prevalent in our world. I'd started college working on an ag science major, but I decided pretty quickly I wanted to do something that mattered in the big picture."

"I'd say you've done that, Spy Guy." After a moment, Chelsea asked, "What did your dad say about your leaving the family business?"

"He was a little irked at first, probably because I dropped out of school without talking to him first. I think, mostly, he was disappointed I didn't want to follow in his footsteps."

She put a hand on his arm and squeezed. "How can he not be proud of what you're doing for your country? You risk your life to protect others...."

He nodded. "Oh, sure. He's happy for me now, but I left home during a rough time for my family. Later when I joined the Air Force, he told me he respected my decision." His cheek twitched in a quick lopsided grin.

She wrinkled her nose in query. "I thought you said you weren't in the Air Force."

He turned up one palm. "I'm not anymore. I left for my current position. The military experience and working knowledge of planes and helicopters serves me well on the job."

Chelsea arched one eyebrow. "The top secret, can't-tell-me-what-it-is job."

His mouth curled up in a wry grin. "Yeah, that's the one."

"What about your mom? How does she feel about your top secret spy gig?"

His eyebrows whipped together in a deep crease, and his eyes darkened. "I don't know. She died when I was sixteen."

"Oh." Her heart wrenched in sympathy. "I'm sorry."

He acknowledged her condolence with a quick nod but didn't pursue the topic. Chelsea mentally kicked herself. She'd been yammering about how scary it would be to lose her mother and Jake *had* lost his. She felt like a heel. *How does that foot taste, Harris?*

"Probably the hardest thing about my job for my dad is that we can't talk very often," Jake said, yanking her out of her self-recriminations. "I can't tell him where I am, what I'm doing, when I'll see the family again..."

"Are you and your dad close?"

"We were. Before I left home and took this job." He paused a beat. "Or maybe it started when Mom died. A lot changed that summer." He snapped his mouth closed and clenched his teeth.

She didn't miss the melancholy that drifted over his face.

"But he knows you care, that you'd be there if—" She caught his darkening expression and huffed her frustration with herself. "Crap. I'm not helping, am I?"

He moved his hand to her knee and flashed a lopsided grin. "None of this is your fault. And if I have to be snowbound, at least I have pleasant company to help pass the time."

She twisted her mouth in a wry moue. "Pleasant

company who promises to find lighter topics for discussion from here on out."

He winked at her, then turned back to the fire. When he winced and raised his hand to the bump on his head, she remembered how hard he'd hit his head when he fell after being shocked by the stun gun.

Concern twisted inside her. "You okay?"

"Hmm? Oh, yeah. Just have a headache." He gave her a dismissive shrug.

"I bet you do. You hit your head pretty hard and were out cold for a scary long time. You probably have a concussion."

He hummed his agreement. "Wouldn't be my first."

"Mr. Noble probably has some OTC painkillers in his bathroom. Want me to get you some?" She let the blanket drop from around her shoulders and started to push up off the floor.

He caught her arm. "I'll go."

She shrugged away from his grip and rose shakily to her feet. "No, let me. You've been taking care of me the last several hours. It's my turn to do something for you."

"Suit yourself." He climbed to his feet anyway. "I'll go out and get us more firewood before it's completely buried under the snow."

As he headed to the door, she noticed that he wavered a bit. "Jake, are you dizzy?"

He waved her off. "I'll be fine."

Chelsea pressed her mouth in a line of disapproval. Her dad was stubborn about seeing a doctor or admitting he felt bad. As if accepting help or acknowledging he hurt was a show of weakness. Men!

Chelsea headed down the hall toward the bathroom, which because of its lack of windows was pitch-dark.

Retracing her steps, she searched every drawer in the living room and kitchen until she found a flashlight. Switching it on, she returned to the bathroom and opened Mr. Noble's medicine cabinet. And blinked. The man could supply a pharmacy. She checked each bottle, shining the flashlight on one label at a time. High-blood-pressure medicine. Asthma medicine in Mrs. Noble's name. A popular antidepressant. Poor Mr. Noble had missed his wife so much....

Pushing the prescription bottles aside she found a bottle of ibuprofen in the back of the bottom shelf and took it down for Jake. Heck, she'd probably take one, too. As her muscles thawed out, they'd started to ache.

She reached the living room just as Jake came through the back door with an armload of split firewood. He stumbled, lurching sideways, and his shoulder bumped the doorframe. Two of the logs in the stack tumbled to the floor, startling Nela, who scurried away from the fireplace with her fur bristled.

Jake grumbled a curse under his breath, then hesitated when he noticed Chelsea watching him. "Okay, so I'm a little dizzy. Yes, I probably have a concussion, but I'm fine."

He retrieved the logs he'd dropped and walked slowly to the fireplace. Without looking at her, he began poking more wood in the fire and blowing on the embers to stoke the flames.

Chelsea set the bottle of ibuprofen on the end table and, studying Jake with a worried gaze, she cuddled back inside the throw. Mentally she reviewed what she knew about concussions. Did she need to keep him awake tonight or was that an old wives' tale? What other symptoms should she be watching for?

And what would she do, stranded as they were, if Jake's concussion became a real medical emergency?

Chapter 7

Darkness settled over the house as night encroached, and the residual heat in Mr. Noble's living room dissipated as the outside temperature dropped and snow piled up. The wind picked up, driving the snow harder and stirring drafts from the chimney that made the fire in the grate dance and writhe. A powerful gust blasted the house, rattling the windows and howling in the eaves.

Chelsea suppressed a shiver and shifted uncomfortably. "Man, that wind sounds spooky."

"Reminds me a little of the sandstorms in the desert. When the terrain is flat, with no buildings or trees or other landscape to block the wind, it can gust forty or more miles an hour, kicking up sand and debris until there's nothing but a suffocating cloud of grit blowing around you. You can't breathe without choking on the dust."

Chelsea narrowed a speculative look on him. "Why do I think you're not talking about the dust storms in California?"

He lifted an eyebrow. "Because I'm not."

She shook her head in awe. "You've traveled all over the world, haven't you?"

He shrugged one shoulder and poked at the fire. "I wouldn't say *all over* the world, but...I've worked a lot of foreign locations. It's the nature of my job."

She propped her elbows on her bent knees and her chin on her hands. "Where have you been?"

Jake leaned back against the sofa and stretched his arm along the cushions. "I did some work in Colombia recently. Iraq and Afghanistan, as you probably guessed. A couple other places in the Middle East I can't tell you about." He gave her a wry grin. "Indonesia. Mexico." He rubbed his chin. "Jamaica."

Chelsea sat straighter. "Jamaica? What kind of security job did you do there?"

His grin spread. "Bikini inspector. That's where my class went for our senior trip in high school."

She snorted and rolled her eyes.

Jake chuckled. "You didn't specify work travel." He nudged her foot with his. "So where have you traveled?"

She groaned and propped her chin on her hands again. "Nowhere," she grumbled. "Well, Dallas. San Antonio. Oh, and we went skiing in Steamboat Springs one year."

"What do you mean, nowhere? I hear Steamboat Springs is great."

"Compared to West Bumbleshmuck, Texas, maybe. Compared to Jamaica or Colombia? Not so much."

He screwed his face in a skeptical frown. "You

would *not* have liked the parts of Colombia I visited. Definitely not on the tourist maps."

"Maybe so, but at least you're not in a rut. Your life is exciting, interesting. Challenging."

"But also dangerous. Often tedious. Frequently dirty, smelly and bug-infested."

"But important." She met his gaze with an honest enthusiasm. "What you do saves lives. Am I right? You make the world safer for the rest of us boring people back home."

Another shrug. "Well, yeah, I suppose. And *boring* is your word, not mine."

"And you love your job." She flashed him a lopsided grin. "Admit it. Even with the dirt and smell, you love what you do. It's an adrenaline rush. A reason to get up in the morning. It's a roller-coaster ride, the Peace Corps and a Jason Bourne movie all rolled into one!"

He sputtered a laugh. "Um, wow. I don't know if it's all of that." He cocked his head and sent her a crooked smile. "I think you've mistaken me for some kind of saint-superhero hybrid."

She opened and closed her mouth, then turned her gaze back to the fire. "Well, you saved my life. That makes you something of a saint in my eyes."

He grunted and ran a hand through his hair. "I'm no saint, Chelsea. I'm glad I happened along when I did and could get you out of harm's way, but—" another dismissive shrug "—I was just doing what I've been trained to do."

In other words, he'd have done the same for anyone. *So don't go forming any attachments or lopsided bonds with him.*

Chelsea felt a small pang of disappointment, but schooled her face to hide any reaction. Jake might be kind, thoughtful and handsome as the devil, but the little touches, the sweet smiles of encouragement, the friendly banter had nothing to do with her and everything to do with Jake's character. As if an über-gorgeous warrior hero would fall for a plain-Jane country girl. *Dream on.*

Chelsea dragged her gaze away from his magnetic blue eyes and tried to calm her racing heart. Crushing on the hunky soldier who saved your life was to be expected, right? She just had to keep her feelings—and his lack thereof—in perspective.

"In my view, you're a hero, too," he said.

She scoffed a laugh. "What?"

He turned up a hand as if the answer should be obvious. "What you do helps save lives."

Chelsea shook her head. "Don't pander to me."

His eyebrows shot up. "Said the pot to the kettle, Miss You're-a-Saint-to-Me." He aimed a finger at her. "Don't sell yourself short, Chelsea. What you do is important, too. I hope to God if my dad needs blood while he's in the hospital that there'll be some available... maybe even some you drew from a donor."

She flashed him a small grin, appreciative of his kindness. "Let's hope so."

She'd always viewed her job as contributing something to society, worthwhile. But hardly heroic. She was a cog in the wheel that helped keep all the moving pieces working. Phlebotomy paid the bills, and for that she was grateful. But compared to the work Jake did, she was small potatoes. Still, his kindness, trying to buoy her spirits and crediting her for helping save lives, touched her.

Not only was Jake drop-dead gorgeous, but he was

also a gentleman and good-hearted. A warrior with a heart of gold. She had to be dreaming....

Brady peered out the window at the snow piling up and chuckled smugly. The timing of this storm couldn't have worked better for him if he'd planned it. The cops would be kept busy helping stranded motorists, handling medical emergencies, dealing with panicky citizens who'd lost power. Roads were impassable thanks to the mounting snow. And the only two people who could tell the police which direction he'd fled would soon be frozen to death, if they weren't already.

Brady shivered at the thought. A nasty, miserable way to die, for sure, but the damn nosy cowboy deserved as much for shooting him.

He rubbed his aching leg, then hobbled back to the couch where he'd piled extra blankets for the night. He'd cleaned his gunshot wound with alcohol, which had burned like hell but was better than risking infection, then shredded a bedsheet to make himself a bandage. The wound would heal in time, and he'd be no worse for wear. He was lucky on that count, but having a gimpy leg slowed him down. Until he was across the border in Mexico, he needed all the speed and stealth possible.

Brady leaned his head back, savoring the soft cushions, and let his eyes slide closed. Yep, this snowstorm was sure a lucky break for him. He had a safe hideout and time to regroup before making his final run to freedom.

"Do you want me to get you another blanket?" Jake asked later that evening. "The temperature in here is dropping fast now that it's dark outside."

After eating some dinner, they'd raided Mr. Noble's bathroom cabinet for toiletries and found new tooth-brushes, unopened deodorant and clean washcloths. She felt better having freshened up and now was snuggled under a coat and two blankets.

Chelsea shook her head and sent him a grateful smile. "I'm okay. I can even feel my toes again. Look." She lifted the quilt from her feet and wiggled her toes. "Movement and everything. I can even make the Vulcan salute with my feet." She parted her middle toes while keeping the others closed. "Live long and prosper!"

"Such talent," he said, flashing a wry grin.

She laugh. "I know, right? My mother's so proud."

When he chuckled, his eyes lit, and the warm glow in his handsome face stole her breath. She even found his chipped bottom tooth sexy. She wanted to pinch herself to see if she was dreaming. Then again, if she was hallucinating in some hypothermia-induced dream state, she didn't want to wake up. She was stranded with a gorgeous cowboy/supersoldier who was doting on her every need. Homicidal escaped felon, murdered neighbor and massive blizzard aside, she was loving the current situation.

Enjoy it while it lasts. Men like Jake didn't give her the time of day under normal circumstances. Soon enough the storm would clear, Jake would make good his promise to capture Brady, and her cowboy rescuer would ride off into the sunset without looking back. No doubt, to him she was just another damsel in distress, another rescue mission, another notch on his sniper rifle.

An inconvenience on his way to see his dying father.

Jake put another log on the fire and stirred the coals

with the poker. "So your parents picked a pretty good time to take a cruise. Hawaii beats a snowstorm any day in my book."

"Yeah," she answered distractedly, her thoughts churning. Chelsea chewed her bottom lip, her heart heavy when she thought of what Jake might be missing. When her mother had been hospitalized last year, battling cancer, Chelsea had told her she loved her every day as she left the hospital for work, fearing her mother would take a sudden turn for the worse and she'd miss the chance to say goodbye.

Jake finished stoking the fire and sat back on the floor, leaning against the sofa, his long legs stretched out in front of him. He pulled a blanket around his shoulders and stared into the now-crackling blaze.

Sadie got up from the spot where she'd been sleeping and curled up next to Jake's legs, propping her chin on his knee with a whine.

Jake rubbed the Australian cattle dog's ears. "Good girl, Sadie." As he stroked the dog's head, his expression grew pensive. "Did I tell you that when I opened Sadie's cage, she ran straight for the stable where Mr. Noble was? She knew something had happened to him and was determined that I follow her."

Chelsea pressed a hand to the ache that swelled in her heart. "That's so sweet. And…heartbreaking." She sighed. "I promised her earlier that I'd take care of her until I found her a new home. All of his animals will need new homes."

Jake glanced at her. "Do you know if he had family? It'd be their say what happens to the animals."

"I think they had grown children. In Oklahoma, maybe? My parents will know how to reach them, I bet."

Jake's hand stroked down Sadie's back, ruffling her fur. "Dogs can be pretty amazing."

Chelsea cocked her head. "I agree, but…exactly how do you mean?"

He didn't answer right away, and his expression said his thoughts were miles away.

"I was on assignment with a small team of guys in Afghanistan a couple of years back," he said at last, his eyes trained on the fire in the grate. "Our mission was to find this guy believed to be the head of a local terror cell. We stayed in this little town for weeks getting to know the locals, learning what we could." He paused and scratched Sadie behind the ear. "Well, there was this dog, a stray that kinda adopted us—which is to say we felt sorry for him and fed him scraps from our dinner, gave him water, patted him…"

"And made a friend for life," she finished for him with a smile. "If he was like most dogs."

Jake sent her a quick smile, then stared at Sadie again. "He was. Stuck to us like glue, our friend to the end…"

A cold apprehension skittered down her back. "Wait. This dog isn't going to die at the end of this tale, is he? 'Cause I don't think I can handle another heartbreaking—"

He flashed her another grin. "No, he lives."

Chelsea exhaled in relief and wiggled her fingers at him. "All right, then you may continue."

"So this dog, we called him Rex, hung with us most every night to get fed and patted and to huddle near our fire, but he disappeared every day to do who-knows-what dog stuff, right? Which was fine with us, because we had our own work to do, and the dog could potentially have been in the way."

"The dog belonged to the terrorist," Chelsea guessed.

Jake drew his eyebrows together and sent her a bemused look.

Her eyes widened as she played her hunch forward. "The dog was a spy!" She waved a finger at Jake as her scenario unfolded in her head. "It was wired for sound, and the terrorist found you through the dog's surveillance equipment. A chip in his collar!"

Jake rubbed his chin and gave her a level look. "No."

"Oh."

"Do you want to hear this?"

She gave him a sheepish grin. "Sorry. Continue… please."

"One day we got word from a local that the guy we were after had just gotten back from a trip. He was going to be at a certain home for a party that evening, so we prepared to raid the home and take the guy prisoner." He paused and cast her a side glance as if expecting her to interrupt again.

She waved a hand. "And?"

"And we showed up at the house, and as we were told, the guy was there. We made our move, but the guy wasn't going to go quietly. He grabbed a woman, held a gun to her, classic standoff situation. He shot at us, we were pinned down, he was cornered in an alley behind the house…you get the picture."

She did, and another chill ran through her, imagining Jake in such a dangerous position. Her chest tightened realizing how casually he told the story, as if he were describing a trip to the grocery store or a baseball game. Life-or-death situations were his job, his normal.

She thought of how terrorized she'd been when Brady pulled the gun on her. She'd cooperated with him out of blind fear and the instinct to stay alive. But Jake...

"We didn't want to hurt the woman, of course, but we knew if it came to it, we'd have to. He was too valuable of a target, and civilian casualties..." He frowned. "Well, they happen sometimes."

Chelsea swallowed, not liking the direction the story was going. Her fingers curled into the blanket around her shoulders, her attention fixed on Jake.

"And?" she reluctantly prompted, drawing out the word.

"From out of nowhere, Rex came charging onto the scene. Apparently he'd followed us and saw the guy shooting at us, read the situation and...took action."

Chelsea felt herself leaning forward in anticipation. "How?"

"Rex ran right up to the guy and bit down on the terrorist's leg, growling for all he was worth. Caught the guy completely off guard, and put quite the hurtin' on him." Jake lifted a corner of his mouth and ruffled Sadie's fur as if congratulating her for Rex's accomplishment. "Ole Rex served as enough of a distraction that the woman was able to wiggle loose of the guy's grip. We dropped him with a leg shot, and Rex kept him busy until we moved in and subdued the terrorist for transport to our base of operation."

"Rex was protecting you," she said, feeling her heart melt.

"Yeah." When Jake turned toward her, she'd have sworn his eyes were damp. Knowing her hard-core soldier had a soft spot for his one-time pet only endeared him to her more. He cleared his throat and added, "Ole Rex had seen what guns did, knew we were in danger and took it upon himself to help us out."

"So...what happened to Rex?" She wrinkled her nose and bit her lip, dreading the answer.

"We took him back to our base, and last I heard, they were training him to work with the military police." Jake patted her leg, and the warmth of his touch sent a sweet frisson spiraling through her. "He was being well cared for and loving the attention of his trainers."

She settled back, savoring the glow Jake's story stirred. "You're right. Rex was amazing. Courageous and loyal and protective..."

A comfortable silence fell between them, punctuated by the pinging of icy snow as it hit the windows, driven by the raging wind. Her fingers and toes tingled as they thawed out, and the energy her body had spent keeping her warm and surviving the hypothermia left her exhausted.

Stretching out on the floor and propping her head on her folded arms, Chelsea tried to sleep, but the howling wind and pinging snow were an ever-present reminder of the day's tumultuous events. She turned toward Jake and studied his chiseled profile. She'd always imagined someone with such a perfect straight nose, kissable lips and square jaw would be making movies about special ops soldiers, not actually *doing* such dangerous and demanding work.

He shot at us, we were pinned down....

Jake's eyes were closed in slumber, but even with him asleep, she felt infinitely safer than if she'd been enduring this nightmare alone.

Heck, who was she kidding? If not for Jake, she wouldn't be enduring anything. She'd be dead—frozen to death in the trunk of her mother's Cadillac. Her parents would have returned from Hawaii to learn their only daughter had perished at the hands of an escaped criminal. Her heart squeezed thinking of her parents' grief, and another ripple of fear spread through her. Brady was still out there....

She scrunched sideways, scooting a few inches closer to Jake. Then a couple inches closer. And another couple inches—

Jake's arm snaked out from his blanket and wrapped around her waist. She swallowed a startled gasp as he pulled her backward until they were spooned together, bodies touching from shoulders to feet.

"This work better for you?" he asked, his warm breath fanning her ear.

"Um, yeah." Chelsea felt the flush of embarrassment sting her cheeks and was grateful the darkness hid her telltale blush. As his body heat penetrated her clothes, she drew a mental picture of his male physique and taut angles pressed intimately against her. Her entire body thrummed with a sexual awareness. Dear Lord, he smelled good...like pine and fresh air and manly musk. Having his arm around her, holding her close, with her head pillowed by his muscular arm was an experience straight out of her dreams.

She squirmed a bit trying to find the most comfortable position for her arms and hips, and he gave a little moan.

"Chelsea, I'm trying to be a gentleman, but all your wiggling up against me is tempting me to—"

The crash of shattering glass rang through the dark house.

Chelsea gasped and shot to a seated position, apprehension nipping her spine. "What was that?"

Jake pushed up onto his elbow. "Sounded like a window breaking."

The tinkle of more glass being knocked to the floor followed, and Chelsea's gut knotted. "It's Brady! He's back!"

Chapter 8

"Wait here." Jake rose to his feet, his hand itching for his stolen pistol. Damn Brady for leaving him unarmed. Instead, he took the fire poker from its stand. "I'll go take a look."

Chelsea's eyes widened, and her apprehension touched something primal inside him, something that fired his protective instincts on a personal level he didn't stop to analyze.

"Stay here? Alone?" She scoffed. "Not a chance." Scurrying to her feet, she crowded close to him. "Until Brady is caught, I'm sticking close to you."

"Chelsea—" Jake looked into her frightened green eyes and snapped his mouth closed. She was right. If anything happened, he wanted her close, where he could protect her. "Okay, but stay behind me and stay quiet."

She gave a nod and handed him the flashlight. Together they inched toward the back of the house. An icy draft wafted into the hall, confirming Jake's theory that a window had been broken. The howling of the wind grew louder. Jake opened each door and swept the flashlight beam into each room as they moved deeper into the house. Nothing in the sewing room. Nothing in the bathroom. All still in the guest room. Which left the master bedroom.

Chelsea grabbed the back of his sleeve, her grip tightening as he peered cautiously around the door-frame into the last room. A dim shadow moved on the opposite wall. Jake tensed, adjusted his grip on the fire poker.

A scratching noise filtered out of the bedroom, and Jake aimed the flashlight beam toward the eerie sound. The window in the wall to his far left had been shattered, and the skeleton-like branches of a tree limb dangled through the jagged glass. Each gust of icy wind made the creaking branch sway and scrape the wall. But had Brady broken the window with the branch, or had the wind?

Jake searched the room carefully with the flashlight beam, illuminating every corner and potential hiding place.

"Well?" Chelsea asked, her question the merest of whispers.

Satisfied that no threat lurked in the dark bedroom, Jake allowed the coil of tension inside him to ease, and he faced her. In the weak glow that seeped down the hall from the fireplace, Chelsea was little more than a shadowy figure in the dark hall, but her fear was palpable. Jake cupped her chin in his hand and stroked her cheek with his thumb. "The wind sent a broken tree limb through the window."

"Not Brady?"

"Not Brady."

She released a sigh of relief and sagged weakly against him. He hugged her close for a moment, allowing her time to calm her jangled nerves.

After only a few seconds, she levered away from him, her tone surprisingly steady. "We need to find something to cover that window or the temperature in here is going to plummet."

"Roger that." Her pragmatism surprised him, though maybe it shouldn't have. She was understandably shaken by the day's events, yet she'd not complained once. Her concern for her neighbors' welfare and quick assumption of responsibility for Mr. Noble's pets and home demonstrated a selflessness and reliability he admired. "Any ideas?"

"Don't suppose you noticed any handy-dandy sheets of plywood in the yard when you cased the place earlier, did you?" she asked with a note of wry humor.

Jake grinned, even though he knew she couldn't see it. "Sorry, no. Maybe we can scout out some heavy plastic or cardboard, though."

"Oh!" she said, brightening with an idea. "A pattern cutting board! I think I saw one in the sewing room earlier before the cat scared a year off my life."

"A what?"

She grabbed his hand and towed him toward the sewing room. "Light, please?"

He handed her the flashlight, and she quickly located the large folded sheet of thick cardboard, printed with a measuring grid. "A pattern cutting board. You use it to protect your table when you lay out a pattern, pin it to the fabric and cut the pieces of a garment that will be sewn together."

"Ah, got it." He pulled the pattern board out from behind the desk where it was propped. "Yeah, this should work, at least temporarily. We'll need to reinforce it with something waterproof, though, or it'll fall apart when it gets wet from the snow."

She bit her bottom lip and scrunched her nose. "The shower curtain?"

He squeezed her shoulder. "Good thinking. Let's get them up. It's already getting cold in here."

With a bit more hunting through the house they found a few small nails to tack the cutting board and shower curtain in place over the broken window, and some packaging tape to seal the edges.

Chelsea scrutinized their handiwork when they were done and frowned. "Not the best long-term fix, but good enough for now I guess."

"That's what matters." He hitched his head toward the bedroom door. "Let get back to that fire. It's got to be twenty degrees colder in this room now."

"Fine by me."

He followed her out to the hall, closing the bedroom door behind them. When they reached the living room, she piled back inside the blankets of the makeshift bed, while Jake stirred the coals in the fireplace and added another log.

"Now," he said, settling on the floor beside her, "where were we?"

She tipped her head. "Pardon?"

"Before the window broke?" He laid down and curled his body around hers, pulling her close. "I think you were here, like this." He wrapped his arm around her waist, and his warm breath fanned her neck. "Hmm… That feels about right."

Chelsea's blood whirred past her ears, and tingling heat coalesced low in her belly.

But soon Jake's quiet snores joined the night sounds, leaving her hanging.

All your wiggling up against me is tempting me to—

To what? If the branch hadn't broken the window, what would Jake have done?

A metallic clang woke Jake the next morning, and before he could blink his surroundings into focus, he sensed something was different. Something was... missing.

Chelsea.

He jackknifed to a seated position, then groaned when his head rebelled with a sharp bolt of pain. Yeah, he probably had a concussion. He battled down the swell of nausea that followed the lightning ache in his head, then glanced about him, assessing. Chelsea was definitely gone.

"Chels?" he called, his voice craggy with sleep as he tossed aside the blankets and rolled to his knees. Another clang and a loud scraping noise drew his attention to the back window. Someone was outside.

His pulse kicked up as he moved to his feet to investigate. As he had yesterday, more than once, he instinctively reached for a weapon he no longer had on him, then gritted his teeth in frustration. He felt naked without his gun, especially because he had Chelsea to protect and a known killer on the loose.

Edging toward the window, he fingered the drape open a crack to peek out. And goggled at the sight that greeted him. Chelsea was in the yard with a shovel, scooping two-foot-deep snow and hefting it onto an ever-growing pile. "What in the world?"

He jammed his cowboy hat on his head, pulled on the coat he'd borrowed yesterday from the front closet and headed outside.

She looked up and stretched her back when he opened the door, and Sadie, who'd been sniffing the ground near her feet, pranced over to greet him with a "Ruff!"

"Oh, good morning. Did I wake you?"

"What are you doing?" he asked.

She spread her hands as if the answer was obvious. "Shoveling."

"Uh-huh." He rubbed his chin, which was bristly with two days' beard, and screwed up his face. "Okay... why?"

"Um...for Sadie."

"Sadie?"

Chelsea nodded. "She was pawing at the door when I woke up and all but crossing her legs, poor girl. But when I opened the door to let her out, the snow was past her armpits." She paused and wrinkled her nose. "I guess you'd call them armpits. Do dogs have armpits? *Legpits* doesn't sound right." She waved a hand. "You know what I mean. Anyway, I had to clear a potty patch for her."

"A potty patch?" Rubbing a hand on his stubble-roughened chin, he glanced down at Sadie, who wagged her tail and blinked dark eyes at him. He'd had dogs when he lived on his parents' ranch, so he was familiar with the special concessions and arrangements one sometimes made for a pet's needs. Good thing for Sadie, Chelsea was, as well.

She bent to heft another scoop of snow for Sadie, and Jake stepped over to her, putting a hand on the shovel handle. "I'll do that."

"No need. I think Sadie's done, and this is a big enough patch to accommodate her until the snow melts some."

When she stretched her back again, he frowned at her. "You should have had me do the shoveling."

She tipped her head and gave him a charmingly puzzled look. "Why?"

"You had hypothermia yesterday."

She twisted her lips in an amused grin. "Yeah, *yesterday.* I'm fine now." She glanced down at her shoes. "Although my feet are wet and cold now. I didn't have boots when I trudged out to the toolshed for the shovel."

His scowl deepened. "Again…should have had me do it."

"You were asleep, and after yesterday, carrying me for miles, saving my life, you deserved to sleep. Not to mention you have a concussion."

"But I'm—"

"The man?" she asked, cutting him off and giving him a slitty-eyed warning look. "Don't tell me you were about to play the Y-chromosome card. I know you're like…some super-spy-guy soldier and all…and I know I was little help yesterday because of the hypothermia and all…but we're in this together. I can pull my weight." She clapped a hand to her chest. "I can shovel snow for a dog that's gotta pee."

Jake couldn't help the smile that tugged at his cheeks. Not only did Chelsea look cute as hell with her nose red from the cold, her green eyes ablaze and her lips set in a pout of stubborn determination, but her thoughtfulness, her hard work, her moxie also tangled inside him and stirred an odd warmth in the center of his chest.

He raised his hands. "Uncle. Heaven forbid I play the Y-chromosome card." He took the shovel from her and propped it against the side of the house. "However, if you don't want to go another round with hypothermia, you'd better get those wet shoes off and warm up by the fire."

She started for the door with an eager nod. "Actually, I'm thinking it's time for that hot bath I put off yesterday."

Tapping his hat back from his face, Jake surveyed the snowy landscape, blanketed in more than two feet of the white stuff with large flakes still fluttering from the clouds. "Might as well. Not sure we're going anywhere for a while. At least nowhere we can't walk, but even walking will be tricky in snow this deep. Roads will be closed, power's still out…"

Which sucked. Because the more time passed, the more likely Brady might get away. And the more likely Jake wouldn't make it to Amarillo before his father… Jake sighed. He couldn't finish that thought.

Chelsea stomped her feet, knocking off clinging snow from her shoes and pant legs before going back in the house. He started to follow her, then thought of Mr. Noble's three horses. He should check on them, make sure they had hay, see if the water pipes to their troughs had frozen, muck their stalls. He may have been gone from Texas for several years now, but the lessons he'd learned growing up on the family ranch were ingrained. A cowboy took care of his horse.

Tugging his hat down against the still-blowing flakes, he trudged to the stable through the snow, slow-going considering its depth, and kicked enough of the snow piles away from the stable door to push it open enough to squeeze inside.

The three horses, one a dapple gray and two bays, nickered and tossed their manes when he clucked his tongue and whistled softly. "Hey, guys. How are you holding out?"

As expected, the water in the horses' trough had a top layer of ice, which Jake broke and threw in a corner of the stable. Below the ice was an ample supply of water for the horses to drink, but Jake checked the water spigot and managed to get a slow trickle to flow out. He left it dripping into the trough, something he wished he'd thought of last night, then got busy mucking the three stalls. When he finished cleaning up, he forked the horses each a fresh flake of hay, gave them a reassuring nose rub and promised them he'd be back that evening to check on them again.

Because based on the rate the snow kept falling, it could be another day or two before roads were passable. He and Chelsea wouldn't get farther than a mile or so if they walked—or trudged, if they didn't have snowshoes for the piled-up snow.

As Jake made his way back to the house, impatience clawed between his shoulders, along with an aggravating sense of frustration. Jake was used to *doing*. Delays and futility didn't rest well with him. Never had. Hell, his need to do something, be something, make a difference were at the root of why he'd left Texas and joined the military all those years ago. Ironic that his first return trip to Texas in a couple years would find him with his hands tied, stranded and champing at the bit.

Jake dug a couple more logs out of the snow covering the firewood Mr. Noble had stacked near the back door, then whistled for Sadie to follow him back inside. He tried to shake off the suffocating feeling of being trapped and ineffective. He didn't want Chelsea to read anything into his restless mood. So far, despite their circumstances, she'd been a trouper, keeping her spirits up, not complaining, and contributing her smart thinking and willingness to pitch in.

He heard water running from the hall bathroom and made his way to the door, which stood cracked open. He knocked softly. "Chels, you okay in there?"

The water cut off, and when he pictured Chelsea sliding into the steamy bubble bath, his pulse kicked, and his groin tightened.

"Better than okay. I found candles, bubble bath and clean towels. I'm in heaven, and I'm not coming out until I'm a prune."

Jake chuckled. "Okay, enjoy. Call if you need me."

"Need you for what? I'm alone in a windowless room. There's nary an evil rubber ducky in here. Feel free to stand down, Spy Guy. This damsel is in no distress."

He pulled a grin. "Not now, maybe, but…what if you need your back washed?"

"Are you volunteering?" He could imagine her coy, teasing grin, the twinkle of mischief in her green eyes.

"I go where I'm needed, help where I can…."

Water sloshed behind the door, and almost of its own volition, Jake's gaze went to the sliver of mirror he could see through the open crack of the door. He caught a reflection of her bare foot peeking up from a mound of bubbles, saw her toes wiggle, watched her hand running a washcloth over her shapely calf. Yowsa!

Down, boy! Back away now, cowboy…. He sucked in a breath, and his nose filled with the scent of lavender bubble bath that wafted into the hall.

"I'll keep your offer in mind," she said, "Right now,

I've got this. But breakfast would good. All that shoveling got me kinda hungry."

He straightened away from the door and gritted his teeth as he tamped down the lust surging through him. "I'll see what I can rustle up."

As he strode into the kitchen, he rubbed his hands on the seat of his jeans. Flirting with Chelsea was all in good fun, but he had to make sure playful banter was where it stopped. He was in no position to start a relationship, and he doubted Chelsea was the sort of woman who indulged in casual flings. She'd been through enough in recent months—not to mention the trauma Brady had put her through yesterday. She was emotionally exposed, and he could never do anything that would cause her more pain or that would take advantage of her vulnerability.

After a breakfast of toast, eggs and bacon—items that would perish soon in the refrigerator after all—Chelsea was beginning to feel human again. She raised her glass of milk toward Jake in a salute. "Here's to gas stoves and men who know how to cook on them. The food was great."

Jake tipped his hat. "Thanky, ma'am."

Nela sauntered in from a back room and sniffed around the plate Chelsea had set aside. Chelsea scratched the cat behind the ears and gave Jake a speculative look. "Want to share what you're thinking? What's the plan for getting help, calling the cops and finding Brady?"

"Well, that old truck out front's not gonna start in this weather, if at all. So we're gonna have to hoof it or—" He lifted an eyebrow in query. "We have Mr. Noble's horses. Can you ride?"

She sent him a confident grin. "I could ride before I could walk. I barrel race. Remember?"

He nodded. "That's right." He folded his arms across his chest and gave her an intrigued grin, flashing those straight white teeth of his.

She let her attention drift to his mouth, his lips. He really had the sexiest smile, and that chipped tooth… How would it feel to—

"I'd love to see that. Are you good?"

She yanked her stare away from his mouth. "Good?"

"Barrel racing."

"Oh, yeah." She wiggled her eyebrows and flashed a smug grin. "I'm great. I have the best horse. George. As in George Strait. George loves to compete. He really gets up for tourneys."

Jake frowned and rubbed a hand across his mouth. "What?"

"Where do you stable George? At your parents' house?"

Chelsea sat forward. "No, at a place across town, nearer my apartment. Why?"

He released a breath and turned up a palm. "Well, if we can ride out on Mr. Noble's horses, then what would stop Brady from riding out if he had access to a horse?"

Chelsea furrowed her brow and mentally reviewed what she knew about nearby farms. "I think the Campbells have a stable. But they're another five or six miles down the highway. Darynda used to have horses, but they sold them when her husband went overseas. It was too much expense, too much work for her, what with the kids and her being pregnant at the time."

"Anyone else?"

"No, except Mr. Noble." A streak of anxiety arrowed

through her. "Do you think Brady might come back for a horse?"

"Well, he's got my truck…damn him." Jake twisted his mouth. "Guess it depends on how far he got yesterday, whether he's waiting out the storm or if he gets impatient waiting for the roads to be cleared." His gaze moved to the window and the stable across the yard. "Bears watching, though. He could come back."

After breakfast, Chelsea curled up in front of the fire and tried to keep her mind off Brady and the possibility of his return. Being stranded by the snowstorm had her edgy, and the relaxing effects of her warm bath evaporated as the morning passed.

She sensed Jake's restlessness, too. Although they shared an easy rapport and pleasant conversation, a thread of tension was palpable in the room. Every noise from outside, every pop and crackle in the grate had him looking out the window or his muscles stiffening, his jaw tightening.

Chelsea did her best to keep the conversation light and teasing. Humor had always been her go-to defense when stress weighed on her. But after hours of idleness, her back had grown stiff from sitting on the floor in front of the fire, and her well of conversation had run dry.

She sighed and rolled her aching shoulders, debating whether to eat lunch or take a nap.

"C'mere." Jake wiggled a finger, motioning her closer.

"What?"

He leaned forward and caught her arm, tugging her across the gap between them. She settled on the floor at his feet, and Jake guided her into position in front of him. "I've got what you need for those sore muscles." He laced his fingers and stretched his hands until his knuckles cracked.

Chelsea thought of every special ops and spy movie she'd ever seen and the lethal skills of the protagonists' hands. Not that she thought Jake was about to snap her neck or pinch her carotid artery. Just the same, a chill shivered down her spine as he swept her hair off her neck and wrapped his long fingers around her shoulders.

He dug his thumbs into the muscles at the base of her neck, working the tissue with deep rubs.

A groan slipped out before Chelsea could stop it. Jake answered with a throaty, sexy chuckle that quivered in her belly. Or maybe it was just the heavenly sensation of Jake's callused hands on her skin, the slow, firm strokes of his massage...the sensual images his caress called to her mind. Her entire body flooded with heat, collecting in a throbbing pulse at her core. *Oh, Texas!*

He moved from her neck down her shoulders and back, paying particular attention to the muscles along her spine. She was putty in his hands and mindless with sweet pleasure when he asked, "Who is Todd?"

She frowned, drawn out of her drowsy fantasies about a naked Jake, and had to work to process his question. Her ex-boyfriend and the pain he'd caused her were not what she wanted to discuss while Jake gave her the massage of a lifetime. "How do you know about Todd?"

"You mentioned him yesterday."

"I did?"

"Yesterday, at the car. You said he told you you were fat."

She swallowed hard and sat straighter, self-consciously tightening her stomach muscles to suck in her gut. "He's my ex-boyfriend."

"Your ex called you fat? What a loser."

She grunted. As much as she didn't want to go down this road with Jake, if he'd keep working her muscles with his magic hands, she'd tell him all her secrets and shameful past sins. "That's why he broke up with me. He said he wasn't attracted to me since I gained weight. Although to be honest, I'd kinda been busy with my mom and hadn't been giving him the attention he wanted. Still, it was a blow when I was already down, and—" she sighed "—it hurt."

Chelsea bit her bottom lip. Why had she added that postscript? She already probably seemed pathetic to Jake without broadcasting how badly Todd's rejection had stung.

"What were you doing with your mom that took so much time?" he asked, his fingers kneading the tendons in her neck.

Chelsea allowed her head to loll lazily to the side, savoring the glorious massage. Somehow, Jake's touch took the edge off the bitter memories she shared. Well played, Spy Guy!

"That was when she was in the hospital with cancer. I spent most evenings after work with her. I ate a lot of fast food and junk from the vending machine during those months. Missed a lot of gym time…and put on like eighteen pounds over six months."

Jake's hands stilled. "So you were dealing with a sick mom, and this Todd jerk broke up with you for gaining weight and not spending time with him?"

His incredulous tone touched her. "That's about the size of it."

A misses size 12–14, to be precise.

Jake muttered a curse. "What an ass! Needless to say, you're better off without him."

Chelsea scowled. In his righteous anger on her behalf, Jake had stopped massaging her shoulders. One more offense she held against Todd.

"What did you see in him to start with?" Jake asked and—hallelujah!—began working her back muscles again.

"He had a good sense of humor and liked a lot of the same stuff I did. We had fun hanging out together. And he was a good kisser."

Jake grunted. Was it her imagination or did Jake's fingers tense a bit at the mention of Todd's kissing skills? Chelsea rolled her eyes at herself. *Right.* Like Jake would be jealous of *anyone,* let alone her ex. And why was she talking about Todd when what she wanted to do was bask in the heaven that was Jake and his magic hands?

"Can we talk about something else?" She searched for a safe new topic. Certainly *not* all of Jake's past girlfriends. Then *she'd* be the jealous one.

"Okay. Why don't you tell me why you have a tattoo of the Chinese character for soup on your shoulder."

Chelsea sat straight. "Soup! The guy told me it meant *harmony!*"

Jake laughed, and the rich sound resonated inside her…despite her disgust with the tattoo con artist.

"Oh, Texas! Are you sure? Of course you're sure. I mean, you're probably fluent in six languages." She huffed. "Maybe I could get my money back…although I'd still have *soup* on my back."

He wrapped her in a hug from behind and kissed the shell of her ear lightly. A dizzying tingle raced through her. She was so enchanted by the brush of his lips on her sensitized skin that she almost missed his whisper.

"Kidding."

She frowned. "What?"

"It says *harmony*. I was teasing."

She huffed a laugh and jabbed him softly with her elbow. "Jake…"

"Although depending on the other characters you use it with it can mean serenity or concord or mediate—"

"Hey, it's all good. As long as it doesn't say *soup*… or *sucker* or *whore* or…"

Jake chuckled again, and she could feel the rumble from his chest against her back. The sensation warmed her from deep in her core. She could stay right there forever, wrapped in his hug, absorbing the heat from his body and savoring the masculine scent of his skin.…

But Sadie, who'd been resting comfortably by her legs, jerked her head up, her ears perking.

"What is it, girl?" Jake said, leaning back, break his hold on Chelsea.

Sadie jumped up and ran to the back window, her fur bristling. She gave a short growl, then started barking at something outside.

Chapter 9

Jake got up and crossed to the window, keeping to the edge and peering through the sheer curtain. "Sadie, what do you see?"

Chelsea joined them, and the sweetness of Jake's soft kiss, his massage and warm hug evaporated in the tingle of anxiety that washed through her. "Is someone out there?"

"I don't know. I don't see anyone." Jake caught her arm and pulled her to the side with him. "Stay clear of the window, just in case."

Sadie continued alternately barking and staring intently at the stable with her ears perked.

"She hears something." Jake scratched his jaw, then moved toward the back door, taking his borrowed coat from the back of the sofa. "It may be nothing, but I'm going to check it out."

Alarm raced down her spine, and she shadowed him

to the door, grabbing the coat she'd worn to shovel. "I'm going with you."

"No, stay here. I won't be long."

She caught his sleeve as he turned. "Call me crazy, but I just feel like we're both safer sticking together until Brady is caught. We can watch each other's backs, work as a team if there's trouble…"

Jake brow dipped as he considered her argument. His gaze raked over her, and she experienced an answering tingle, as if he'd stroked her with his hands. When his gaze connected with hers again, he sighed his resignation. "You may be right. Get some boots out of the front closet. No point getting your feet wet and cold again."

She spun away and quickly retrieved what must have been Mrs. Noble's rain boots, based on the flower design and smaller size. Chelsea slipped them on and even though they pinched her toes a bit, they fit well enough.

"Stay close." Jake opened the back door, a carving knife from the kitchen in one hand and a flashlight in the other, and Sadie squeezed through the opening and bolted out into the snow. The dog hesitated only briefly when she reached the edge of the area Chelsea had shoveled for her before bounding into the drifts. The snow was up to Sadie's chest, and she struggled through the accumulation, making a beeline for the stable.

Chelsea placed her feet in the footprints Jake made as he followed Sadie across the yard. Over the creak of frozen branches swaying in the wind and the ping of icy snow pellets, Chelsea heard the agitated whinnying of the horses. She tugged on his coat sleeve. "Do you hear that?" she said quietly. "Something's upset the horses."

"Yeah, I hear 'em. Let's hope it's just a rat in their feeding trough looking for a free meal."

She grunted. "Yeah. Never thought I'd be *hoping* to see a rat."

As they closed in on the stable, Jake paused and glanced back at her. "Look, Mr. Noble's in there. Why don't you wait out here while I check things out?"

A shiver that had nothing to do with the cold spun through her. She cast a wary glance around the frozen pasture, scrubby trees that lined the property and snow-covered yard leading back to the house. Except for Sadie pawing at the stable door, everything seemed still and quiet, but...

She exhaled, the cleansing breath forming a white cloud between them that dissipated quickly in the icy wind. "All right. I'll keep watch out here."

He tweaked her chin with a gloved hand. "Back in a sec."

Snapping on the flashlight, Jake unlatched the large slide bolt and tugged open the barn door. Sadie wiggled inside as soon as the doors parted. Her barking resumed immediately, and Jake hushed Sadie and whistled for her to heel.

Once Jake had stepped into the dim stable, Chelsea eased back against the weathered wood to wait. She heard Jake crooning softly to the horses, and his lulling tones calmed her, as well.

Deciding she should do more than stand around waiting for Jake, she inched along the front wall of the barn to peer around the corner. Nothing. She continued around the building cautiously and as quietly as she could in the crunching snow. At the next corner, she stopped and peeked around to the back of the stable.

A trail of disturbed snow led from the pasture to a gaping hole where the wind had blown out a large piece of the barn's siding. The tracks didn't appear to be human, but from where she stood, she couldn't tell what had made the trail. She inched closer for a better look, calling, "Jake, there are tracks out here. Some kind of animal—"

Sadie's frantic barking cut her off.

"Sadie, no! Get out!" Jake's shout spiked her pulse. "Go on, you varmint!"

"Jake?" Chelsea had started backing up, retracing her steps, when two gray-brown creatures darted through the hole in the wall of the barn and ran straight toward her.

A short, startled scream escaped her. She backpedaled, slipping on the icy ground, and fell on her butt, knocking the wind from her lungs. When she recognized the animals, another scream hung soundlessly in her throat. Coyotes!

A fresh wave of fear sank to her bones. The carnivores were a menace in the area, known to kill dogs and livestock. Spotting her, the coyotes stopped briefly, eyeing her.

"Chelsea!"

She crab crawled away from the coyotes before finally clambering to her feet. Struggling to catch her breath, she croaked, "Back here!"

Sadie, barking for all she was worth, lunged through the same hole in the stable wall through which the coyotes had escaped.

"Sadie, no!" she cried, her voice stronger now.

Her shout spooked the coyotes. They turned and ran toward the pasture, leaping through the drifts of snow. Sadie started after them, bounding down the path the coyotes created in the snow, and fear for the dog fueled Chelsea's feet, her legs. She ran after Sadie—her movements a sorry, slow-motion imitation of running, bogged down by snow, bulky clothes and ill-fitting boots. "Sadie, come back!"

Suddenly Jake appeared from the front of the barn, his long, powerful legs eating the distance between them in no time. "Chelsea, are you okay?"

Ignoring his question, she pointed to the black-and-white dog. "Stop her! They'll tear her up!"

He turned, loosed a shrill whistle and, in a commanding voice that reverberated to her core, shouted, "Sadie, come!"

Sadie stopped at the edge of the pasture and looked back at them, then again to the coyotes running across the field.

Jake repeated his command, and the dog bounded back through the snow to his feet. Chelsea sagged in relief and ruffled Sadie's fur. "Good girl, yes. You are a good girl, Sadie!"

Jake put a hand on Chelsea's shoulder. "Are you okay?"

She nodded. "Just shaken up. They startled me, then I slipped and Sadie lit after them and…" She huffed out a cleansing breath. "I'm fine."

Jake scooped Sadie into his arms and hitched his head toward the house. "Let's get her back in the house, then I may need your help patching that hole in the wall. We don't need those coyotes or any other critters slipping into the barn again."

She glanced back toward the front door of the stable. "Are the horses all right? Did the coyotes hurt them?"

"Just spooked I think, but I'll check them more carefully after I put Sadie inside."

The repair to the barn took mere minutes and consisted of digging the fallen siding planks out of the snow and nailing them back in place. While Jake hammered, Chelsea cast a wary glance around, keeping an eye out for coyotes, escaped convicts and any other form of vermin that might trespass on the Noble farm.

The rest of the afternoon passed much the way the morning had—conversation laced with an underlying tension about what lay ahead.

Without his saying anything, Chelsea could tell from Jake's expression that he was mentally working through a plan and contingencies for capturing Brady. Her ideal strategy involved staying at Mr. Noble's house with Jake until the snow melted, the power was restored and the police came by to say Brady had been captured and returned to prison.

She rolled her eyes at her wishful thinking. Her plan was about as likely to happen as Jake deciding she was the woman of his dreams and giving up everything to be with her. Oh, well. She had nothing else to do than fantasize, right?

Her fantasies got a shot in the arm that evening when Jake curled against her, spooning, as they had the night before. His arm draped heavily around her and his breath fanned her cheek through a night of little sleep. Having done nothing in particular most of the day, she wasn't tired, and the press of Jake's body against hers left her antsy and flushed and ready to jump out of her skin.

She rose as the sun came up the next morning, to let Sadie out and feed Nela, who'd climbed on Chelsea's legs to sleep in the wee hours. As Chelsea poured the cat's food in a bowl, Nela gave her a dark glare, as if chastising her for being tardy in fixing her breakfast.

While Sadie finished her business outside, Chelsea rummaged in the pantry until she found a box of fiber cereal, which she ate without milk in front of the fire.

Jake stirred and sat up, scrubbing a hand over his face. "Whatcha got there?"

She pretended to read the box. "Sticks and twigs with a touch o' honey."

He flashed a wry smile. "Think I'll finish the Oreos."

Arching an eyebrow, she quipped, "Nutritious."

He shrugged. "So I'll open a can of tuna or chili for protein."

She wrinkled her nose. "For breakfast? Wow, sticks and twigs don't sound so bad anymore."

When Sadie scratched at the back door, Jake shoved off the floor. "I'll get her and take care of the horses, then I'm gonna take a shower, okay?"

An image of Jake, naked with warm water streaming over his body, flashed in Chelsea's mind, and the bite of cereal she was swallowing went down the wrong pipe. She sputtered a cough and wheezed, "Fine."

After letting Sadie in and disappearing to the barn for several minutes, Jake collected a flashlight and headed to the back of the house.

Chelsea took the opportunity to spruce herself up a bit in the hall bathroom, brushing out her hair, washing her face and using the toothbrush she'd scavenged the day before.

Returning to the living room, she pulled a book from Mr. Noble's shelf, a mystery by a popular author she enjoyed. She dragged a chair closer to the window, wrapped herself in the sleeved blanket and used the morning sun to read, hoping to distract herself from thoughts of Jake in the shower.

Several minutes later, Jake strolled down the hall, towel drying his hair and smelling like soap and steam.

He walked to the window where she was reading and

stared out for a moment. "I think the snow has slacked up enough that I can get out now, get to a phone and call for reinforcements."

"We," Chelsea said.

He turned his regard from the window and met her level gaze. "What?"

"You said 'I can get out,' but you meant 'we can get out.'" She arched one eyebrow meaningfully. "Right?"

"Chelsea, I can't let you put yourself in harm's way."

She faced him, scowling, and planted her hands on her hips. "It's my decision, not yours. I'm going with you. I need to check on Darynda and the other neighbors, and I want to get word to my parents that I'm safe. If they got word about the blizzard, they'll be worried."

With a heavy heart, Jake thought of his family, sitting in the hospital in Amarillo, wondering what happened to him. "I need to call my sister and check on my dad, too." He rubbed his chin, thinking. "But all that takes a backseat to finding Brady and contacting the authorities. I don't want you in harm's way if I find Brady at your house."

"And I don't want to be here alone if Brady comes back for any reason…say, to take a horse or get rid of Noble's body, for instance."

Jake's gut soured at the idea of Chelsea facing Brady alone. He grunted his agreement. "What if you stayed with your neighbor while I checked your house?"

She tilted her head, her expression shrewd. "What if we *both* stayed with my neighbor while the *cops* checked my house?"

"I can handle Brady."

"I have no doubt you can, but you don't *have* to. Let the police bring him in. Let them call out their SWAT team or the FBI or whoever they use to catch armed escapees, and you—" She stopped short, as if catching herself before she gave something away.

"And I what? Sit on the sidelines? That's not who I am, Chelsea. I want this guy caught, and I want a hand in bringing him in."

"And I want…" Shadows filled her eyes, and she ducked her head.

"What, Chelsea? Tell me."

"I want you to stay with me," she said softly, almost apologetically, her gaze on the arm of the stuffed chair where she sat as she traced the pattern of the fabric with her fingertip. "You make me feel safe. And…I don't want you to get hurt."

Her honesty touched him, and he covered her hand with his and squeezed, joking, "Shucks, Chelsea. If I didn't know better, I'd say you cared about this ole cowboy."

Her eyes went to their joined hands, then rose to meet his gaze. The tender emotion he saw looking back at him landed a mule kick to his chest and wiped the teasing grin from his face.

A heartbeat later, Chelsea twitched a lopsided grin at him. "Don't flatter yourself, sweetie. It's just nice to have someone with your…um, skill set…around when there's a killer on the loose."

A little jab of disappointment poked him under his ribs, and he sobered, realizing her dismissal of her feelings was the source of his hurt. Over the past couple of days, he developed a fondness for Chelsea that went beyond her pretty face and Marilyn Monroe curves. Her wit, her intelligence, her compassion… Chelsea was the real deal in so many ways.

Of all the women he'd met all over the world, he'd found one of the most intriguing and endearing a mere fifty miles from the home he'd fled ten years ago. The irony didn't escape him. Now that he had the career he thought he needed to make a difference, to give him a sense of purpose, life threw this woman in his path to show him what his life still lacked.

His friends and former black ops teammates Alec Kincaid and Daniel LeCroix had both recently found love and a new level of happiness and direction for their lives. Was that what he wanted? Could he give up his career to settle down, maybe start ranching again?

If his father died, the family ranch would need— Jake cut the thought off unfinished. He refused to think in those negative terms. Dad had to pull through.

"Not that you aren't easy on the eyes and all," Chelsea said, drawing him out of his straying thoughts. "But a handsome mug is really of no use when the bullets start flying. Ya know?"

He flashed her a quick grin and gave her hand a final squeeze. "All right, then, you can ride out with me. But you stay at Darynda's. I'll get the horses saddled."

She pulled a sassy grin as she rose from her chair. "There you go with the 'I' thing again. I can saddle my own horse."

He caught her arm as she turned to leave and cupped her jaw with his hand. "Maybe so, but...you don't need to see Mr. Noble and have that image in your head."

"Oh. Right." The reminder of poor Mr. Noble's body out in the stable turned the food in her stomach to rocks. She swallowed hard to keep her breakfast down. "So do we just...leave him out there? That seems heartless."

"It's a crime scene, Chels. We can't move the body until a forensics team can investigate and collect evidence against Brady."

She bit her bottom lip and nodded. "I know you're right. I just feel so bad for Mr. Noble."

He rubbed his thumb along her cheekbone, then tugged her close enough to kiss the top of her head. "And I love that you care so much."

Her scalp tingled where he'd kissed her, and her thoughts cartwheeled hearing him use the word *love* in a sentence about her. She was still rooted to the spot, savoring the moment, as he headed outside to ready the horses.

"Better wrap up," he called over his shoulder. "The sun is out, but it's still as cold as brass balls out there. One brush with hypothermia is enough, huh?"

She nodded. "I'm on it."

After watching from the window as Jake struggled through the deep snow back out to the stable, Chelsea helped herself to hats and gloves from the front closet. She layered on another sweater and more socks and found another thick shirt and socks for Jake.

Thirty minutes later, two horses were saddled with the third in tow, a lead clipped to his harness. Jake had them waiting by the back door, ready to ride out when she finished gathering the clothes and a thermos of hot tea to take with them. While Jake donned the extra clothes and outerwear she'd set out for him, she asked, "What about Nela and Sadie? We can't leave them here with no one to take care of them."

Jake considered her question as he rebuttoned his coat. "We can send someone to get them once we find a phone."

Chelsea frowned her dissatisfaction with his answer. "Who will we send? The cops? They'll just take them to the pound, and who knows what will happen to them then. Darynda will take them until I know my parents' house is safe. I know she will."

Jake scratched his two-day beard as he mulled their options. "Okay, get a big towel to wrap kitty in. I doubt riding a horse in freezing temperatures is Nela's idea of fun. We'll bundle her up papoose-style to safely immobilize her legs so we can hold her."

"Roger that, Spy Guy." Chelsea grinned, and a warm ribbon of pleasure spun through him.

Accommodating her request had been easy enough, yet her smile made him feel as if he'd accomplished something important. Because he'd made her happy. He rubbed a spot at the center of his chest where the pleasant fullness was centered. A kind and selfless woman like Chelsea deserved to be happy all the time, and he sobered realizing how much he wanted to be the one making her smile.

"We should do the same with Sadie. This snow's too deep for her to walk very far in."

Jake rubbed his hands together. "All right. Two pet burritos coming up."

Chelsea disappeared down the hall for a moment and returned with a bath towel for Nela, then took the throw from the couch for Sadie.

Jake wrapped a squirmy and upset Nela in the towel and held the bundled cat until Chelsea had mounted her horse. "Hold her tightly. She's not a happy camper."

"I bet."

Returning to the living room, Jake scooped the Australian cattle dog into his arms and tucked the blanket around her. Sadie wiggled, unsure about the arrangement, but gave Jake's face a quick lick of trust as they headed into the cold together. He held Sadie under one arm as he climbed into his saddle. "All right, I think we're all here. Lead the way to Darynda's, ma'am."

With a click of her tongue, Chelsea coaxed her horse to set off across the snowy field between the Nobles' house and the Joneses' home.

Being on a horse again felt good to Jake, like spending time with an old friend. Maybe he still had more ranching in his blood than he'd realized. And watching Chelsea in the saddle was a thing of beauty. The lady knew how to sit a horse. Her butt and legs moved in rhythm with her mount, guiding, shifting, tensing or relaxing as needed. Her skill brought sultry images to his mind and ideas of how it would feel to have her riding *him,* her legs wrapped around his hips, their bodies moving together...

Jake gritted his back teeth and shoved the erotic thoughts down. His mission now was to check on the neighbors, deliver Mr. Noble's animals into Darynda Jones's care and capture Brady. He needed to stay focused on that job and not let his desire to test Chelsea's skills in bed distract him. Brady had proven himself deadly, and Jake couldn't afford to let his guard down.

Although...if Chelsea's parents' house turned out to be criminal free, would she be amenable to a little recreational sex before he set out after Brady? The catch was to make sure she understood anything that happened between them was just that...recreational. The last thing he wanted was to hurt Chelsea. If Chelsea misconstrued his intentions toward her and began believing they could build a relationship...

Jake snorted under his breath. Look at him putting the proverbial cart before the horse. Other than a few tender glances and some shared confidences in front of an intimate fire, he had no reason to believe Chelsea felt anything for him other than gratitude and friendly concern. He could have totally misread what he thought was physical attraction.

Jake tried to shove thoughts of tangling limbs with Chelsea aside, but even as they rode up in the Joneses' yard, he couldn't deny the hum of desire still resonating in his veins. Only when he remembered the gruesome carnage Brady had left in his wake at Mr. Noble's did Jake's attention shift fully to the job at hand.

"Let me take the lead, check things out," he warned.

Chelsea shot him a worried look, but she reined her horse and let Jake ride up to the house first.

Chapter 10

Chelsea held her breath, her heart thumping anxiously as Jake rode all the way around Darynda's house before returning to the front yard and nodding his all clear.

After riding up beside Jake's horse, Chelsea zipped Nela more snugly inside her jacket and clutched the cat to her chest. With a hand down from Jake, she swung out of her saddle and slid to the ground.

As Chelsea followed Jake to the front door, she noticed a small section of the yard had been partially shoveled and large dog paw prints filled the area. Jake set Sadie down in the cleared spot, and Sadie eagerly sniffed around and found a place to squat.

Chelsea knocked on the door and called, "Darynda, are you there?"

The thin window covering over the side glass was tugged back, and a young face peered out, followed by a child's shout. "Mommy, there's people here!"

A moment later, the door opened, and a young brunette woman wearing a stained sweatshirt and faded jeans and carrying a baby on her hip glanced warily from Jake to Chelsea and back to Jake. "Can I help you?"

"Hi, Darynda. We need a favor or two."

A large tan dog, some sort of pit bull mix from the looks of him, appeared beside the young mother and barked at the visitors on his porch. Then, spying the other dog in his yard, the pit bull surged past Darynda and into the yard with a "Woof!"

"Dooley, come back! I just got your feet dried!"

"Want me to get him for you?" Jake asked.

Darynda glanced past Jake and worried her bottom lip with her teeth. "I… Oh, he's all right, I guess."

The child they'd seen earlier peeking out the window appeared from behind Darynda. "Who are they, Mommy? Can they come to my tea party?"

"Go finish your lunch, Gabby." Darynda used her free hand to push her daughter back toward the inside of the house, then gave Jake another curious look. "I'm sorry, what did you say you needed?"

Gabby stayed put, staring with big brown eyes at the strangers at her door.

"Our first order of business was to make sure you and your kids are all right. Everybody safe here?" Jake asked, leaving out reference to Brady until he had a chance to feel the situation out.

A tired smile tugged the corner of Darynda's mouth. "How sweet. Yeah, we're doing okay, all things considered—" She glanced to Chelsea and stopped. "Oh! Chelsea, hi! I just recognized you. Geez, it's been a long time! How are you?"

"Pretty well. Can we come in?"

"Of course! I'm sorry. I—" She backed up, opening the door wider and shouting past them, "Dooley! Come on, boy!" She paused and wrinkled her brow. "Is that Sadie? Mr. Noble's dog?"

Gabby clambered forward. "I wanna see the doggie!"

Darynda caught her daughter's shoulder and tugged her back again. "Later, honey. Go finish your lunch like I told you to."

"Unh!" Gabby whined.

"One!" Darynda said, her tone firm. "Two…"

"Okay, okay! Don't count!" Gabby scampered away.

With the doorway clear now, Chelsea stepped inside, then faced Darynda with a puckered brow. "I'm afraid Mr. Noble is dead."

Darynda gasped and pressed a hand to her mouth. "Oh, no! What happened?"

Jake exchanged a look with Chelsea. "Long story. We'll explain everything once we get the animals settled."

"We have his cat, Nela, too," Chelsea added. "And his horses." Darynda's eyes widened as Chelsea unzipped her jacket, and Nela poked her head up. "We need help with all his animals until we can—"

"We have some other business to take care of," Jake cut in. News of a killer on the loose and murdering her neighbors could send the young mother into a panic. He wanted to reassure the young woman she was safe before he dropped such an explosive bomb on her.

"Oh, well…I guess I can help." She peered into the yard at the three horses and frowned. "We haven't had horses in our barn for years, but it's dry and secure. I think we have some hay, but you'll need to bring back some feed if they're going to stay more than a day or two."

Chelsea followed Darynda to a back bedroom, where they settled Nela in and closed the door. Jake spotted a cordless phone on the counter and tested it for a dial tone, although he knew it was likely nonfunctional without power to the base. He was correct.

Darynda noticed the phone in his hand when she returned to the kitchen and shook her head. "Sorry, it's dead. I'd offer to let you use my cell phone, but the battery ran out last night while I was talking to my husband."

"Do you have a car charger?" Chelsea asked. "If your car will start, we can use the car's battery power to make a call out."

Darynda turned up her palms. "I had one. But Gabby was playing with it the other day and now I can't find it anywhere."

Jake scowled. "Can you look for it again? It's important that we get a call out."

Darynda chewed her bottom lip and bounced the fussy baby on her hip. "Is this about Mr. Noble? What happened to him?"

Jake drew a measured breath and said flatly, "He was shot. And we believe his killer is still in the area."

Darynda's face blanched, and she sank onto a kitchen chair. "What?"

Jake and Chelsea took turns explaining the situation to the young mother, who grew visibly more pale and upset as they laid out the events of the past two days. Although clearly shaken by the news of a killer on the loose and her neighbor's murder, Darynda rallied her composure and squared her shoulders. "How can I help?"

"For starters, by finding that car charger. The sooner we get a call out to law enforcement the better," Jake said. "And I want Chelsea to stay here with you until Brady is caught."

"Of course," Darynda said, nodding.

Chelsea shot him a disgruntled look. "Hang on, mister. Don't I get a say? Maybe I want to stay with you."

Jake shot Chelsea a stern look and shook his head. "You know why that's a bad idea. It's too dangerous."

"If it's dangerous for me, then it's more dangerous for you to go alone," Chelsea countered.

He frowned at her skewed logic. "That's not true. I'm trained to deal with this kind of situation. You're not."

"But I can help you." Chelsea flattened her hands on the kitchen table and leaned toward him, an earnest and eager appeal on her face. "I *want* to help you."

He shook his head again. "You'd only be in the way."

Hurt flickered in her eyes, but he refused to back down, even if it meant she was mad at him. Even if she hated him for leaving her behind. Chelsea mattered too much to him to risk her getting caught in Brady's cross fire.

"It's my house, Jake. And I have a personal stake in catching Brady. I have since he stuck that gun in my ribs and carjacked me two days ago."

He shifted his gaze to Darynda. "You want to help? Make her see reason. Explain to her why she can't go chasing armed killers."

Darynda held her hands up. "Leave me out of this."

"Jake," Chelsea said, reaching across the table to take his hands in hers, "I'm willing to take the risk if it means stopping Brady before he hurts anyone else. I can't sit here and do nothing while you risk your life, alone. Surely you can understand that? There's got to be something I can do to help you." Her green eyes bore into his, her stare determined and full of conviction.

The thing was, he could understand her need to *do,* the compelling drive to take action, but for him it mirrored his need to protect her, to right a past failure. He hesitated, not wanting to dig up the past but also unable to avoid it. He had to make Chelsea understand his reasons for keeping her safe, his need to bring Brady down. "I never told you how my mom died."

Chelsea blinked, her posture softening. "No."

Jake dragged a chair out from the kitchen table and sat in it heavily. In his peripheral vision, he saw Darynda ease out of the room, giving them privacy for their heart-to-heart. "The summer after my junior year of high school our church took a group, including my mom, down to Mexico to build houses. My dad stayed home because he couldn't leave the ranch unattended that long, and my sister Michelle was away, working a summer camp. I was supposed to go with my mom but backed out."

Her hands bunched in her lap. "Why?"

Jake's gut rolled remembering his youthful selfishness. "I had a new girlfriend. I wanted to spend time with her, not build houses in the Mexican heat."

She reached for his hand. "Jake—"

"The bus they were on, going to the work site their first day, was attacked by a militant gang involved in the drug wars down there," he said, his tone as flat and empty as the hole the memory left inside him. "They sprayed the bus with machine-gun fire, and six members of our church died. Five were sent to the hospital. My mom was one of the dead."

"Oh, Jake..." she whispered.

"If I'd gone like I was supposed to—"

"Stop right there." She squeezed his fingers hard, her tone firm. "Do not blame yourself for what happened."

"I could have shielded her or protected her somehow." He clenched his back teeth until his jaw ached.

"Or you could have been killed along with the others!" Chelsea sighed raggedly. "Have you been harboring guilt over this all these years?"

"Shouldn't I? I was a selfish prick, more concerned with being with my girlfriend than building houses for the needy or protecting my mother in a violent country." Turbulent emotions gripped his throat and raised his volume. "She went down there to do *good*. And evil people took her from us!"

"Exactly," Chelsea said, her eyes bright and her fingers digging into his. "Evil people killed her. Not you. There will always be evil people in the wor—" She stopped abruptly and sat back in her chair. She drew a trembling breath. "Oh, my God. That's why you do what you do, isn't it? You've built your whole life from that point around fighting the bad guys of the world."

He said nothing. Stared at the floor. His whole body shook with bottled-up energy and emotion. "I have to, Chels. Evil defeated good that day, but I cannot, I *will never,* sit on the sidelines and let the bad guys win, ever again."

Chelsea swiped a tear off her cheek and leaned toward him again. "Never's a long time, Jake. Isn't it time you stop beating yourself up? You had no responsibility for or control over what happened to your mom."

"I let her down."

Chelsea sighed sadly. "Jake…"

He furrowed his brow. "She taught us to be doers. To be involved in changing the world."

"Gandhi's be the change…" Chelsea whispered, "I remember you said it was her mantra."

"And I sat out the mission trip." He clenched his teeth, his fists, still furious with his stupid choice. "I failed her on so many levels."

"She'd be proud of what you've done with your life since then. You have to believe that."

"Yeah, maybe." He scrubbed a hand over his face, then flattened both palms on the table as he leaned toward her. "Chels, I've never told anyone about this before. My family knows the history, of course, and probably guessed at what I was feeling, but…" He shook his head. "The point is, I wanted you to understand why I can't let you put yourself at risk."

"Thank you—" she pitched her voice to an intimate whisper "—for trusting me enough to share your soul with me like this. It means a lot to me."

He nodded and met her damp eyes with a quick half smile, believing the matter was settled.

"Now trust me enough to help you catch Brady."

Jake dropped his chin to his chest with a groan. "Chelsea…"

"I promise not to take unnecessary chances," she pressed. "I can be your backup or a lookout or something. But…I can't sit on the sidelines either. Brady took something from me when he attacked me."

He glanced up at her with a frown.

"I let my fear rule me last time, Jake. I can't let fear win. It's every bit as insidious as evil. Maybe more so."

Jake pulled his hands from hers and pinched the bridge of his nose. He had to be insane to even consider taking her and putting her in harm's way. But he heard himself say, "You can go. On one condition…"

* * *

An hour later, after making an exhaustive and unproductive search for Darynda's cell phone charger and warming themselves with a cup of hot chocolate, Jake shifted his attention to the next phase of his plan. "Can we borrow a few items from you?"

She nodded. "Of course. Like what?"

"Well, most important would be a gun. A handgun preferably, but I'll take a rifle or shotgun if that's all you have."

Darynda glanced uneasily to her children, then back to Jake. She leaned close to him and pitched her voice to a whisper. "I have a .38 in my bedroom closet. Hank wanted me to have it for home protection while he was gone."

"Will you get it for me?" He matched her whisper in deference to the young ears she seemed concerned about. "Along with extra ammo, binoculars…" He rattled off a list of items, and Darynda nodded.

"I'll distract the kids while you gather up that stuff." Chelsea held her hands out to take the baby from Darynda.

The young mother smiled her thanks and passed over the wide-eyed tot. Chelsea grinned at the baby and rubbed her back when the infant whimpered.

Watching Chelsea with the baby, Jake felt a hitch in his chest. She looked so natural with a child in her arms, so at ease…so happy. She would make a great mother one day. With all the love she had to give, her patience and compassion, how could she not?

"Gabby, why don't you show Miss Chelsea your dolls?" Darynda said to her older daughter. "I think it's time for their tea party."

"Yea!" the little girl chirped as she skipped into the living room. "In here, Chessie!"

After Chelsea disappeared into the next room, Jake followed Darynda down the hall to the master bedroom, where she pulled a locked box out of the closet. "Hank cleaned it before he left, but that was a few months ago. It hasn't been fired since then."

She unlocked the storage case, and he examined the weapon. "It's in great shape. Thanks." He stashed the gun in the waist of his jeans and put the box of rounds she handed him in his coat pocket. After she'd rounded up what she could of the other items he'd requested, he packed them in the small pink child's backpack she'd loaned him, and they headed back to the kitchen.

"Keep your door locked, and until you hear otherwise from me or Chelsea, don't open your door for anyone who can't show a valid law enforcement badge. Got it?" he said as he tugged the backpack onto one shoulder.

"Of course." Darynda put a hand on his coat sleeve. "Be careful. Take care of Chelsea."

He nodded and stepped into the living room, where Chelsea, seated at a tiny table with Sadie, a stuffed penguin, a blonde doll and a Raggedy Ann, pretended to sip from a toy cup.

"Mahvelous tea, dear. Simply mahvelous," she intoned with a snooty air, and Gabby giggled.

"Mahvelous!" the little girl echoed, striking a pose and flouncing her hair.

Jake cleared his throat. "Madam, if you are finished with your tea, your coach is ready to leave."

Chelsea turned to Gabby and fluttered her fingers. "I must be off. Thank you for babysitting Sadie and

Nela, Lady Gabrielle. We simply must do this again, dahling."

After a final round of goodbyes and thank-yous, Jake took his cowboy hat off the table and escorted Chelsea out to the horses.

He gave her a hard look as he helped her into her saddle. "It's not too late for you to change your mind and stay here."

She twisted her mouth and raised an eyebrow. "I'm going with you."

Jake pressed his mouth in a tight line of frustration as he jammed his hat on his head. "Anyone ever tell you you're stubborn and a little crazy?"

"Two of my best traits, I'd say," she quipped, and glanced behind him. "Nice backpack, Spy Guy. I like the pink."

He rolled his eyes and swung up on his horse. Without Mr. Noble's pets on board, they set a faster pace going to Chelsea's house. The hum of adrenaline and pre-mission energy flowed through Jake, sharpening his senses. He'd only get one shot at taking Brady by surprise. He had to get everything right the first time.

"Give me the layout of your house." He reined in his horse so they could ride side by side and talk. "For starters, is there an alarm system with battery backup?"

Chelsea snorted and shot him a wry look. "Alarm system? Crime's not a problem out here in the boonies. Why, my dad will tell you, in the thirty-five years my folks have lived in that house, they've never had a minute's trouble with burglars or intruders."

Arching one eyebrow, he sent her an incredulous look. "Irony, anyone?"

She hummed her agreement. "What do you bet, when my dad gets home and hears about Brady, they have an alarm system installed within twenty-four hours? Nothing like closing the barn door after the cow escaped, huh?"

Jake grinned briefly, then focused again on business. "All right. No alarm system actually works to our advantage at this point. No chance I'll accidentally set it off and alert Brady." He furrowed his brow as he thought. "Which rooms have windows facing which direction? Where are the rooms in relation to each other? Is there a basement? An attic? How many doors and where? Do the windows open or are they sealed off by storm glass?"

"Wow. Where to start?" She flashed him a grin, then sobered as she ticked off information. "Basement, check. Unfinished. Small ground-level windows with burglar bars, his one concession to security. Attic, check. The access is in the main hall."

"Brady is most likely in the living room or kitchen this time of day. Which side of the house are they on? We need to approach from the direction he's least likely to look out a window and see us coming."

Chelsea scrunched her nose as she thought, then glanced around as if orienting herself directionally. "Living room windows face east. Kitchen window looks west. It gets the afternoon sun. The blindest side would be the north end where the carport is. There's a small window in the carport door, but it opens into a mudroom next to the kitchen."

"All right, then." Jake tugged the brim of his hat down as an icy breeze swirled around them. "We'll swing wide to the north and approach from the carport side. Is there a landmark you can wait behind, out of sight, until I signal the all clear?"

She shot him a disgruntled look and opened her mouth.

"Don't even start." He cut her off. "Our deal was that you wait for me to subdue Brady if he's there, make sure the coast is clear before you go anywhere near the house."

"Jake—"

He aimed a finger at her. "I will hog-tie you and cart you back to Darynda's if you don't cooperate."

She cocked her head and arched a haughty eyebrow. "Wow, Jake, how very *Fifty Shades* of you."

An image of Chelsea, naked and his willing partner in sexual play, flashed in his mind before he could stop it, and a hum of desire zinged through him. Clearing his throat and shoving the image away, he drilled a hard look on her. "I will. Don't test me."

She heaved an irritated sigh. "I was going to say, there are a couple of scrubby trees at the back corner of our property. Ordinarily they wouldn't hide much, but maybe enough snow clung to the branches or piled up in drifts around them that I'd be hidden. Also, my dad has a toolshed on that side of the house, about one hundred yards from the carport."

"We'll go with the trees for now." He scanned the terrain. "How much farther?"

"Just over this rise." Chelsea plowed ahead, her horse breathing heavily as it churned through the snow. They reached the top of a small hill that overlooked her parents' property, and several of their questions were answered. Jake's truck sat parked near the front door under a blanket of snow, the windows were dark, and a thin column of smoke trailed up from the chimney.

A thread of relief wound through Jake at knowing

he would recover his truck. "Looks like Brady is there, and the power is still out."

Chelsea scowled and shook her head. "It galls me to think of him living in my parents' home. Touching our things and eating our food. I'm going to have to disinfect the whole house before I'll get the image of his—" she pulled a disgusted face as she fumbled for a word "—cooties all over the furniture."

Jake chuckled. "Cooties?"

"It might not be a scientific word, but you know what I mean! He's defiling our house with his evil ectoplasm, his bad karma, his—"

"Forensic evidence." He shot her a stern glance. "Don't wash, vacuum or sweep anything until the police have collected all the evidence they need."

She gave a dramatic shudder, then glanced at him and nodded. "Fine, his cooties can stay until the police are done."

"Come on." He gave his horse a little kick with his heels and rode in a wide arc to the north before heading toward the house. He stopped behind the cluster of scrubby trees, the thick layer of snow adding to the protective cover.

Chelsea rode up beside him and eyed her house with longing. "So close and yet so far..." she muttered wistfully.

"This is your stop until I give you the all clear. Got it?" He waited until she turned to face him, then drilled her with an all-business stare. "You wait here. If I don't signal you within ten minutes, ride to the next neighbor down the road, then the next, until you find a working phone. Stay there with the doors locked until the police come and you're certain Brady is in custody. Got it?"

She dented her brow and twitched a quick pout of discontent. "I understand."

His gaze zeroed in on her full lips. She'd applied a thin layer of lip balm before they headed out from Darynda's, and her mouth looked especially tempting. Dewy and soft, shimmering and sexy. He swallowed hard, shoving the distraction aside in his mind, and he jerked a nod. "Good."

"Jake…" Her eyes softened and concern crept over her face. "Be careful. Please. If it looks too dangerous—"

"Hey…" He reached for her, cupping the back of her head with his gloved hand. "Danger is what I do. I eat danger for breakfast and spit out the bones." Knowing she cared enough about him to fret over his safety touched him. The worry shadowing her eyes burrowed to his core and warmed his soul. "I'll be fine. I promise."

She didn't look convinced, but time was wasting. The sooner he captured Brady and turned him over to the cops, the sooner he could get to the hospital in Amarillo and see his dad.

As Jake snapped his reins and started toward the house, the concern clouding Chelsea's gaze stayed with him. All the impulses and desires he'd been denying and suppressing for the past two days surged up in him and grabbed him by the heart. He yanked back on his reins, stopping his horse and stared at the snowy ground, debating.

With a sigh of inevitability, his pulse thumping with resolve and confidence in his decision, he turned around and rode back to her.

Questions filled her eyes as he guided his horse alongside hers. Pulling off his gloves and nudging his cowboy hat back from his face, he moved in so close that his leg brushed her horse's flank, his knee bumped hers.

"Jake, what is it?"

"Just this." He slid the knit cap off her head so he could run his fingers through her thick silky hair. Then burying his hand in the thick tresses, he cradled the back of her head and pulled her close. Leaned in. Captured her lips.

The startled hitch in her breath only fueled his hunger. He graduated quickly from a polite brushing of lips to a passionate tangling of mouths and tongues. With one hand, Chelsea grabbed the front of his coat while her other hand braced on his thigh for balance as they canted toward each other from their saddles.

Jake molded her lips and angled his mouth, filling himself with her sweet essence. The warmth and gentle suction of her kiss was even better than he'd imagined, and he had to hold himself back to avoid bruising her in his fervor.

A soft moan of pleasure vibrated in her throat and sent an answering tremor through his body. His fingers curled against her scalp, and he angled his head to deepen the kiss. She tasted like hot chocolate and warm woman, and he wanted to continue kissing her in the foreseeable future. He wanted to hold her body against his and imprint her memory in his brain for the long lonely nights he spent while on missions. He wanted the right to kiss her every day, but he knew this moment might be all he'd ever get. If he captured Brady and turned him over to the police as planned, he could be on his way to Amarillo in the next couple of hours. Which made the kiss all the more bittersweet.

When he ended the kiss, he rested his forehead

against hers. As they panted for a breath, a frosty cloud formed between them, swirling and dancing in the cold air before dissipating into the stillness around them.

"What was that?" she whispered after a moment.

He stroked her cold cheek with the back of his fingers and lifted one corner of his mouth. "What do you think it was?"

She pulled back to meet his gaze, touching his jaw with a gloved hand. Her eyes were sad. "It felt like goodbye."

He shook his head. "No, not goodbye. I just seized the opportunity to do what I've wanted to do for most of the last two days."

She blinked as if startled. "Really?"

He gave her face a final caress, dropped one last kiss on her lush mouth and straightened in his saddle. "Watch for my all clear."

With that he tugged his reins hard to the left, turning his horse, and rode quickly toward the house.

Oh, Texas!

Jake had been thinking about, had been *wanting* to kiss her for the past two days? Somehow, that fact didn't compute. Why would a gorgeous, world-traveling special ops soldier who could have any woman he desired want someone as humdrum and everyday as her? And yet she had the proof....

Chelsea touched her mouth, which still tingled from Jake's tender assault, and stared after him as he rode into her parents' backyard and tied his horse to the base of the clothesline pole. Next, he took out a pocketknife he'd borrowed from Darynda and sawed on the clothesline cord. After cutting the line, he unthreaded it from the poles and coiled it around his hand. Another tool in his mission to bring down Brady.

Chelsea squeezed her saddle horn, her body tense as she watched Jake move with pantherlike grace through the snow and into the carport. When she lost her visual of him, she drew a deep breath of icy air and whispered a prayer. "Keep him safe, God. Get us out of this mess in one piece. Please?"

Too restless to stay in her saddle, Chelsea climbed to the ground. Kicking the snow at her feet out of her way, she cleared a tiny patch of dead grass behind the stand of small trees where she could pace without being seen. When her horse snuffled and snorted impatiently, she stroked his nose and cooed softly to calm him, even though she was plenty jumpy herself.

Jake had kissed her. She gave her head a little sobering shake. She wasn't dreaming. He had really kissed her. And not just a friendly wish-me-luck kiss. He'd given her a toe-curling, hot-damn, honest-to-God, now-I-can-die-happy kiss. A tingling warmth filled her chest and brought a sappy smile to her lips....

Until a gunshot inside her house shattered the quiet.

Chapter 11

Jake crept through the mudroom and peered carefully around the corner into the kitchen. Clear. Sidling along the inside wall, he made his way, one silent step at a time, toward the next room. He was almost to the kitchen door when a gunshot blasted through the house, followed by raucous laughter.

"Bull's-eye!" a male voice chortled.

Jake heard the familiar click of a magazine being ejected and reinserted into a pistol. Probably *his* pistol, he thought, grinding his back teeth in fury. He inched farther forward and carefully peeked into the living room. Brady had his back to Jake, his attention fixed on the bookshelf across the room, the pistol aimed.

Jake scowled as Brady fired another shot, shattering a vase perched on one of the shelves. Brady's callous disregard and wanton destruction of Chelsea's family's property gnawed his gut. Easing back a step into the kitchen, Jake fashioned the cord from the clothesline into a lasso and gave it a test twirl. *Just like roping calves with Dad for branding.*

He moved back to the living room doorway and peered into the next room. Brady had his head bent forward and his gaze down as he messed with the gun again. Jake didn't like the idea of engaging Brady while the convict had the pistol in his hand, but he didn't want to waste any time and risk Brady spotting him before he made his move. He surveyed his surroundings, quickly gauging his obstacles, potential weapons, and locating a sturdy place to secure Brady once he'd incapacitated him. His estimations made, Jake tightened his grip on the lasso and prepared to teach Brady a new appreciation for the term *clotheslined.*

Finished fiddling with the gun, Brady set the weapon on the coffee table in front of the sofa and shoved awkwardly to his feet with a grunt.

Time was up. Jake gave the lasso a preparatory spin, then whipped it toward Brady. The cord flew over Brady's head and settled on his shoulders. The convict barely had time to tense in surprise before Jake jerked back on the rope, tightening the noose around Brady's throat and yanking him backward off his feet.

Brady landed on the couch with an *oof* and growled, "What the h—"

The rest of his curse was choked off, as Jake pulled hard again, cinching the clothesline tighter until it strangled his prey.

Brady clawed at the rope, gasping for air.

Jake quickly lashed the cord to a spindle in the half wall between the living room and foyer, keeping Brady from reaching the gun on the coffee table.

When Brady twisted around and met Jake's hard

glare, Jake read recognition in his opponent's eyes. "How did you…get out?" Brady rasped.

Jake pulled Darynda's gun from under his coat and aimed it at the escaped con. "A little ingenuity, some luck and a whole lot of determination to see your ass fry for killing two cops and an innocent old man." He motioned to the floor with the gun. "Now get on the floor with your hands and feet spread."

Glaring his defiance, Brady spat toward Jake and climbed over the back of the sofa, favoring his left leg. The one Jake had shot last time they dueled. With a limping gait, Brady lunged.

Jake was ready, and he used Brady's momentum against him, catching him in a low tackle and easily flipping him onto his back. "Now stay down!"

Brady continued tugging at the rope that cut into his throat, reducing his oxygen supply, but every time he loosened the lariat, Jake jerked it tight again.

"Sonofabitch!" Brady wheezed, scrambling to get up with his good leg.

Jake planted a foot in the man's back and shoved him down again. When he pressed the muzzle of the .38 to the base of Brady's skull, the convict froze. "Give me a reason to save the tax payers the cost of your incarceration. Please."

When Brady had been still for several seconds, Jake stood and took a step back. "Your head is still in my crosshairs, pal." He took another long step backward and untied the rope from the spindle post, keeping the noose tight. "If you so much as twitch, I'll give you the same respect you showed old Mr. Noble."

As he eased back toward Brady, winding the clothesline around his free hand, Jake saw the man's muscles tense. That was all the forewarning he needed.

When Brady sprang up, Jake executed a sweeping roundhouse kick that caught Brady in the kidney.

His opponent doubled over at the waist, clutching his side and wobbling on his injured leg. With an angry growl, Brady glanced up, and his narrowed gaze shot daggers.

"Oh, good," Jake said with a mocking grin. "I was hoping you'd resist."

Brady lunged a second time, head down, shoulder first, and Jake braced his feet. He timed an upward arc of his gun hand so that the barrel smacked Brady in the chin, shoving his head back. Dropping the cord he'd wound on his hand, Jake swung again at Brady's mug before the convict could regain his balance.

When Brady's knees buckled, Jake hooked his leg around the other man's and knocked Brady back onto the floor. Dropping to his knees, Jake straddled Brady and trapped the man's arms at his sides. The cord around Brady's throat had loosened as he fought, and the convict gulped in air, even as he struggled fruitlessly to free himself from Jake's hold.

Brady glowered at him, and Jake couldn't resist punching the smug convict in the jaw once more. "That's for terrorizing Chelsea, you worm."

After blinking and shaking off the blow, Brady grated, "Chelsea, huh? That the fat chick's name?" Brady gave a derisive scoff. "You tapping that c—"

Jake slammed his fist into Brady's mouth, rage pouring through him. "Shut your filthy mouth *now*."

"Go to hell."

Jake's hand flexed as the urge to choke the life out of Brady or snap his sorry neck surged through him. He tamed the savage impulse, though, instead grasping Brady's shoulders roughly and flipping him to his stomach. Jerking the convict's hands behind him, Jake tightened the noose around the man's neck again, then used the remaining length of cord to bind his hands and feet.

"I should have killed you and the bitch when I had the chance," Brady rasped.

Jake gritted his teeth, fighting to keep a level head. "I told you to shut up."

"And I told you to go to—"

Grabbing a fistful of Brady's hair, he pulled the escaped felon's head off the floor, then smacked Brady in the jaw. When the criminal collapsed on the floor, his head hit the hardwood surface hard enough to knock the man unconscious. Brady's body went limp, and Jake felt for a pulse. Reassured his quarry was alive, Jake loosened the noose so Brady could get just enough air to survive. He stashed Darynda's .38 in the waist of his jeans again, then dragged Brady to the center of the living room. He left the convict hog-tied on the floor.

Spying the guns Brady had been using for target practice, he retrieved both his SIG-Sauer and the stolen police sidearm from the coffee table…just in case. He ejected the magazine of the police sidearm. Still empty. His pistol was down to two rounds. Just the same, he shoved the cop's gun in his boot and his pistol in the big side pocket of his coat. At least if Brady woke up, he couldn't wiggle across the floor and get a weapon.

Blowing out a cleansing breath, he picked up his cowboy hat, which had gotten knocked off in the scuffle, and headed back out through the kitchen to signal Chelsea. When Jake walked out of the carport, he looked to the far edge of the yard where he'd left Chelsea waiting behind the scrubby trees. Doffing his cowboy hat, he gave it quick wave.

She appeared from behind the snow-covered trees and waved back, then swung up on her horse and rode toward the house.

He paused for a moment, watching her, and his body hummed with the memory of her kiss. He'd love nothing more than a few days in bed with her to explore the magnetic attraction he felt between them. If they'd met under different circumstances, if he weren't on the clock trying to reach his father's hospital bed, if he hadn't taken a known criminal into custody…

He exhaled harshly. So many damn ifs. Maybe the universe was telling him something. Maybe kissing Chelsea had been a mistake. He had no business giving her false hopes about where their attraction might lead. His life was about counterterrorism and the difference he was making flying missions for the black ops team. No matter how much her kiss fired him up, he had to walk away once Brady was in custody and Chelsea was safe. A pang of disappointment plucking at his chest, he crossed the yard to his truck and opened the driver's door.

Two-day-old blood from Brady's wounded leg covered the seat, spotted the floor mats and was smeared on the steering wheel, door and console. Jake scowled, understanding the sense of violation Chelsea had felt for having the convict in her house. Directing his attention away from the blood, Jake scanned the front seat.

On the passenger side, where he'd left it, sat his cell phone. Heaving a sigh of relief, Jake grabbed it up and checked the screen. Seven new texts and twelve missed calls. He read the texts first. One was a solicitation. One was from an unfamiliar number. Four were from his sister, growing more desperate and asking where he was and if he was all right. Replying to the last text from Michelle, he typed out, I'm fine. Delayed by snow. How's Dad? I'll call ASAP.

The most recent text was from his friend and former black ops teammate, Alec Kincaid. Ur sister called looking 4 U. Sit rep?

One of the missed calls, along with numerous calls from Michelle, was from another former teammate, Daniel LeCroix. Clearly his disappearance had set off more than a few warning bells for his friends and family. He needed to let someone in on what had transpired before Michelle had a stroke....

Chelsea trotted up, dismounted and tied the reins of the dappled gray to the clothesline pole next to the other horse. "What happened?" she asked breathlessly. "Is he restrained?"

Pocketing the phone for the time being, he jerked a nod. "And unconscious at the moment. He resisted, and I punched him in the piehole." He gave her a smug grin. "Felt good, too." He hitched his head toward the house. "Come on in. I want you to watch him, just in case, while I find something stronger to bind his hands and feet. We'll keep him bound until the cops get out here."

Chelsea sent him a concerned look. "What's he tied with now?"

"Your clothesline. But it's kinda old and weatherbeaten. I don't want to risk him figuring a way to loosen or saw through it and get free."

She nodded. "We should have any number of things downstairs in my dad's workbench. Duct tape, cords, wire...take your pick. The basement door is in the kitchen near the refrigerator."

He settled a hand around her shoulders as they walked into the house. "All right. I'll get something and be right back." When Chelsea gave a nervous glance around the kitchen, he added, "Brady's in the living room. I haven't seen your phone yet, but mine was in my truck. I'll call the cops as soon as I have Brady better secured."

She rubbed her hands on her arms and gave him a weak smile. "Okay, I've got this."

Jake stroked her hair, then nudging her closer, gave her forehead a quick kiss. "This mess is almost over, sweetheart. Hang in there." He reached behind him and took Darynda's .38 from the waist of his jeans. "Take this. If he so much as looks at you cross-eyed, shoot him. No second thoughts."

With that, he turned toward the doorway next to the refrigerator and headed down the steps into the dark basement.

This mess is almost over. Chelsea's heart twisted as she walked to the living room. How sick was it that she didn't want this crazy, tragic, scary situation to be over? The end of the crisis with Brady would mean Jake would walk out of her life. Probably for good.

He had a lucrative, exciting career and could have any gorgeous woman he wanted, so he had plenty of reasons to want to put this pain-in-the-butt chapter of his life behind him and never look back. Sure, he'd been sweet to her the past couple days, but taking care of her and protecting her out of his sense of duty was *not* the same thing as building a relationship with her because he wanted to, because he felt something for her.

Guys like Jake Connelly didn't fall for plain-Jane, small-town girls like her. Not when he could crook his finger and have some exotic, size-2 beauty in his bed any night of the week.

Chelsea cast a wary gaze to the man crumpled on

her living room floor and crossed the room to sit on the edge of her parents' couch. The gun Jake had handed her was equally unsettling, and she set it on the coffee table in front of her, within easy reach. She tried to avoid looking at Brady, who'd clearly helped himself to some of her father's clothes. She gasped her dismay when she recognized the shirt Brady wore as one she'd given her father last Christmas. Gritting her teeth, she swept an encompassing look around the room to see what else Brady might have defiled.

Their case of DVDs had been rifled through, empty cans and cracker boxes littered the floor, and the two-hundred-dollar bottle of Cristal champagne her parents had been saving for their next anniversary lay on its side, empty. Fury roiled in her gut. How dare he touch—

A grunt and a twitch from Brady quickly brought her attention back to the man on the floor. Her heart tap-danced as she stared at him. Was he reviving?

She worked up enough spit in her mouth to swallow. *Hurry, Jake! Please!*

Brady made another noise, this one more of a gagging sound. Then his body jerked again. And again, an uncontrolled head-to-toe flinch.

Uneasy with the odd movements and noises, Chelsea rose from the sofa and moved to get a better view of Brady's face, careful to keep her distance.

Brady's eyes were open, but his eyes seemed frozen in a glazed, fixed stare at the ceiling. The clothesline Jake had used to catch Brady was looped around his neck, then wrapped around his hands and his feet. Each twitch of his body tightened the rope around Brady's throat.

As she watched, Brady's face grew red, and he gasped for air.

Chelsea frowned and called, "Jake?"

Suddenly Brady's whole body began violently convulsing. Foamy spittle leaked out of his slack mouth. His wheezy gasps for air grew hoarser and more desperate-sounding as his face darkened from red to nearly purple. The clothesline cut into the folds of his neck, and his eyes rolled back in his head.

"Jake!" Chelsea called, louder this time. "Something's wrong! I think he's dying!"

Panic beat a tattoo in her chest, and her own breath sawed harshly from her throat. She had to do something or Brady would die. Not that she care so much about saving his miserable hide, but neither could she, in good conscience, let him die without doing anything to help him. Wasn't negligently withholding aid as bad as causing harm in the eyes of the law?

"Jake!" she screamed, dropping to her knees and fumbling to loosen the clothesline around Brady's throat. "Help!"

Chapter 12

Jake squinted into the dark cellar, trying to make out the shapes that loomed before him. The small windows, high on the walls, let in pale beams of sunlight from what would be ground level outside. He scanned the unfinished basement. A washing machine, a workbench, cardboard boxes stacked in a corner, a water heater to one side, metal shelving with small appliances, a basket of fabric scraps and sewing supplies, and jars of homemade jelly. The musty smell of mildew filled the air and dust motes danced in the streams of light. The basement at the farmhouse he'd grown up in was much the same as this one. He could almost picture his father standing by the workbench, fiddling with a model airplane.

Nostalgia tugged at his chest. *Hang on, Dad. I'm coming.*

"Let's see," he muttered under his breath. "If I were

a roll of duct tape, where would I be?" Pulling off the coat he'd borrowed from Mr. Noble's closet, he strolled over to the workbench, laid the coat across one corner and checked the top drawers. A lot of clutter but no tape.

The phone in his shirt pocket buzzed, and he pulled it out to check the caller ID. *Daniel LeCroix.* With the press of a button, he answered the call. "Daniel, my man, how's life in Louisiana?"

"About freaking time…your phone!" Daniel's voice was broken by a bad connection. "Where the hell… been? Your sister…of her mind, worrying what hap— you. Which…upset Nicole and Alec's…"

Jake stepped closer to the window, hoping for better reception. "I've been dealing with a little situation involving an escaped convict, no power and almost two feet of snow."

"Escaped con— What the h—" Daniel said. "Do you need backup?"

Jake moved farther into the basement, trying the next window and the next. "I think I have things under control. Thanks anyway. I know better than to pull you or Alec away from your lovely ladies."

He moved through a door, into a storage area at the back of the cellar, and his reception cleared marginally by the last window.

"Well, I owe you one…helping me get Nicole out of Colombia. If…change your mind, I'm a phone call away."

"Thanks, man."

"And I'm sorry about your dad."

Jake's heart seized. What did Daniel know? "Have you talked to my sister? Do you know my dad's status?"

"I haven't talked to her, but Alec has a couple times. He's still in ICU from what I hear."

Chelsea's muffled voice drifted down the stairs. She sounded upset.

"I'll be calling Michelle soon," Jake said, moving back toward the bottom of the staircase to hear Chelsea better, "and I should be on the road a couple of hours from now. I just have to wrap up a few details here."

He glanced at the workbench as he passed it. He still hadn't located anything he could use to secure Brady.

"Jake!" The fear and desperation coloring Chelsea's voice sent a tingle down Jake spine.

Muttering a curse under his breath, he darted toward the stairs. "I gotta go. Something's wrong," he told Daniel as he took the steps two at a time. "I may need that backup after all."

Chelsea's hands shook as she fought to get the cord off Brady's neck. After convulsing for several terrifying seconds, he'd gone limp and motionless.

"Ohgodohgodohgod...don't be dead," she whispered, panic gripping her chest. She slid the clothesline off his throat and loosened the knot at his wrists enough to free his hands so she could roll him to his back. Putting one hand in front of his nose, she tried to determine if he was breathing. She didn't feel any air moving out of his nose or mouth, and his eyes were mostly closed now. Next she palpated his carotid pulse, but her hands were shaking and her own heart was hammering so hard that she couldn't tell whether he had a pulse.

"Jake!" she screamed again and scrambled mentally to recall her CPR training. Bending over Brady, she pressed her ear to his chest to listen and feel for his heartbeat.

The thump of footsteps hurrying up the basement stairs signaled Jake's return.

But before she could do more than recognize the noise, Brady surged off the floor, knocking her backward on her butt. Chelsea screamed as the scene, which passed in seconds, unfolded like a slow-motion horror movie.

Brady lunged for the gun she'd set on the coffee table. Raised the pistol. Aimed for the basement door.

Jake appeared at the top of the stairs, his cell to his ear. A loud crack splintered the air, and Jake jerked, then stumbled backward, dropping his phone.

Brady fired again. And again. Drywall flew as those shots pocked the wall near the stairs.

Jolted from her shock, Chelsea sprang toward Brady. "No!" she yelled, throwing herself on his back and swinging at his gun arm.

Jake crashed against the wall behind him before losing his balance and toppling down the stairs, out of Chelsea's line of sight. He'd left a smear of blood on the stairwell wall.

Icy fear clamped around her heart. "Jake!"

With an angry roar, Brady bucked, throwing her off him. All the air whooshed from her lungs as she crashed to the floor. She wheezed in vain, trying desperately to suck in the precious oxygen she needed to fuel her fight, keeping her eyes trained on Brady.

Snarling a cruel epithet at her, he swung the weapon toward her head. Reacting more than choosing her next move, she rolled to the left, feeling the heat of a bullet streak past her ringing ears. As Brady clambered to his feet and took aim again, Chelsea swept her leg toward him as hard as she could. Her foot hit him in the back of his knees, and his legs buckled. Brady fumbled for his balance, juggled the gun.

Seizing her chance, Chelsea bolted for the stairs. She gasped for a breath as she staggered in a zigzagging path toward the basement door. Another shot whizzed past her and splintered the wood frame of the cellar door.

Grabbing the doorknob as she darted past, Chelsea slammed the heavy basement door and slid the first of three barrel bolts into the lock position. With trembling hands, she fought the other bolts into place. When a bullet slammed into the heavy door, making it shudder, she dropped to a crouch, then scrambled down the steps, out of the line of fire.

Jake lay at the bottom of the stairs, clutching his shoulder, his face twisted in a mask of pain. Blood bloomed on his shirt near his collarbone.

"Jake!" she cried, hurrying to his side. "How bad are you hurt?" She started unbuttoning his shirt and carefully tugged the fabric back to examine his wound.

"Can you…lock that door?" Jake asked. His voice sounded weak.

"Already did. We installed slide bolts to secure the door in case of tornado." She gave a nervous scoff. "As if a few bolts would make a difference against wind strong enough to drive a straw through a tree. But they made my mom feel safer."

He groaned and shut his eyes.

"Do you think you broke any bones when you fell? Are you shot anywhere else? Oh, God! Tell me what to do!" Her words rushed out as panic spiked her pulse.

Jake caught her hand, squeezed. "Breathe."

His voice sounded strained, full of pain, and her worry ramped higher. "You can't breathe?"

"I mean...you. Breathe. Calm down." He drew a ragged breath as if to prove he could and clutched her hand tighter. "I need you...not to fall apart...on me."

She bobbed her head. Tears pricked her eyes and blurred her vision. She forced herself to inhale deeply and blow it out slowly. "There. I promise not to fall apart, but—" her fingers curled into his shirt "—I need you not to *die* on me."

Even though his brows were furrowed in pain, his cheek twitched. "Deal. Now...we gotta find something clean...to stuff in the bullet hole. Stop the bleeding. I think the bullet passed clean through. So you'll...have to pack the exit wound, too."

With a grunt, he rolled onto his side, and sure enough, a bloody exit wound marred the back of his shoulder near his armpit. Nausea roiled in Chelsea's gut. Not because of the blood—she saw enough of that on the job at the blood center—but because of how close she'd come to losing Jake. That scared the hell out of her because, deal or no deal, he could still die. Blood loss, infection, dehydration—the enemies were numerous, and it would be her job to keep him alive.

The doorknob at the top of the stairs rattled, and the door shuddered as Brady crashed into it, trying to get through. "A locked door ain't gonna stop me! You're dead, cowboy! You and the girlie are not going to turn me in!"

More gunshots blasted at the top of the stairs, the bullets slamming into the locked basement door. Adrenaline, already stringing her tight, kicked her blood pressure even higher.

Bullets hammered the door, and splinters of wood

sprinkled on them from the top of the stairs. She needed to move Jake out of harm's way, needed to stop his bleeding, needed to pull herself together if she was going to keep Jake alive.

Using her adrenaline-fueled strength, she gripped Jake under his arms and dragged him back from the foot of the steps, toward a pile of dirty laundry heaped on the floor next to the washing machine. Jake cried out in pain as she moved him, his face wrenched in a grimace.

"Sorry, sorry, sorry," she repeated through her tears, her stomach rebelling at the notion of the pain he had to be in. Once she'd situated him on the bed of dirty clothes and spread his coat over his lower body for warmth, she scanned the basement, her hands shaking and her heart racing. Surely she could find something clean enough to tend his wounds.

Her gaze hopped from the workbench to the dusty shelving, back to the dirty laundry and...laundry!

She spun toward the dryer and snatched open the door. The load of her delicates she'd washed the night before the snowstorm hit was still waiting to be folded. Chelsea plunged her hand in the pile and pulled out the first thing she grabbed: a cotton jogging bra.

She bit at the back seam, chewing through a few threads, then yanked hard to rip the bra into usable pieces. "Jake Connelly—" she knelt beside him and rolled the first piece of bra into a tight plug "—you are going to owe me a new wardrobe of bras when this mess is over." Her voice warbled as she worked, her hands unsteady. "You already destroyed my best underwire, and now my favorite sports bra is going to stop up your bullet holes."

His gaze rose to meet hers. The pain and fading light in his eyes scared her spitless.

"Bra shopping… It's a…date."

Her fingers trembled as she poked the rolled fabric into the gaping wound in his back. "At Neiman's…"

He grimaced and growled in pain, and she swallowed the last of her teasing parry.

"Stay with me, Jake. Please…"

He tugged on the coat she'd spread over him, grappling with it until he withdrew a pistol from the pocket. He shoved it at her. "Keep this close. Just in case."

"Oh, Texas…" she muttered, her gut flip-flopping. If she never saw a gun again in her life, it'd be too soon.

"Two shots left," he rasped, curling her hand around the weapon and drilling her with a piercing stare. "Make 'em count."

"Don't shoot till I see the whites of his eyes?" she quipped feebly, her stomach rebelling. She sucked in a slow breath and swallowed hard to keep her lunch down.

"You'll know when. Just aim and…squeeze the trigger."

She exhaled through pursed lips and set the gun aside. "Right."

"Now…my phone…" he said, his voice growing thready.

His phone? Chelsea's hands stilled as she flashed back to the seconds right before Jake was shot. He'd held his cell phone to his ear when he appeared at the top of the stairs. She swiped at the tears blurring her vision. Heart racing with new hope, she glanced toward the foot of the steps where Jake had fallen. Nothing.

The stairs. Nada. Where could his phone have landed?

When he tried to move and groaned in pain, she abandoned her search for his phone and pressed a hand to his uninjured shoulder, holding him down. "Whoa, Spy Guy. Lie still. The more you move, the more you'll bleed. I'll find the phone once I get you fixed up."

"Daniel…"

Chelsea frowned. "Who is Daniel?"

"On the phone…can help…"

She rolled a piece of her torn bra in a tight plug and poked it in the seeping wound in his shoulder. When he cried out in pain again, she winced in sympathy and remorse. "Sorry, I know it hurts, but I have to."

He met her eyes and nodded. "I know. Do it."

She tried again to plug the bullet hole, her heart raw as he gritted his teeth against the pain. Dear God, this was her fault. If she hadn't fallen for Brady's act, if she hadn't untied the cords binding Brady, the wretched man wouldn't have shot Jake, wouldn't have them trapped in the basement….

You'd only be in the way.

Swallowing the lump in her throat, she struggled for her composure. She'd promised not to fall apart and, damn it, she wouldn't. She owed Jake that much and a whole lot more. Maybe if she could distract him… "Who is Daniel?"

"Former member…of my black ops team." Jake drew a shallow breath and screwed up his face in agony as she rolled him on his back to address the entry wound. "Got injured. Then engaged. He's retired, but he's still…one of the best."

Chelsea finished packing the exit wound with strips of fabric from her bra, and only then did Jake's explanation replay in her head and sink in. "Black ops? So… that's what you do?"

His gaze darted to hers as if he hadn't realized what he'd said.

She twitched a smile. "Don't worry, your secret is safe with me." She lifted her eyebrows as she folded a camisole from the dryer into a small square to hold against Jake's wound. "As if anyone would believe I was rescued by a black ops agent who looks like Chris Hemsworth and kisses like—"

She stopped herself, avoiding Jake's eyes. Her skin flashed hot remembering the soul-shaking caress of his lips on hers. They hadn't had a chance to talk about their kiss. What it meant. Assuming it meant anything to him. He'd said he was just acting on an impulse. Maybe that was all it was. *Probably* that was all. She didn't dare believe it was more, couldn't risk involving her heart when she knew he'd be leaving her as soon as—

"Kisses like?" he prompted, his voice still a rasp.

She forced a teasing grin. "Digging for a compliment, Spy Guy? Oops, my bad. Black Ops Guy." Her voice trembled with the unspent adrenaline still roaring through her, and her hands shook as she pressed the camisole firmly against the gunshot wound. "I've heard of black ops. Real top secret. Very dangerous. All off-the-record for deniability. Sometimes sketchy legality…"

She'd known for days that Jake did dangerous work, but somehow knowing the volatile nature of his missions, the secrecy surrounding his work, the danger involved, sent a shudder to her core. The thoughtful, charming hero she'd gotten to know the past few days didn't jibe with her conceptions of a black ops soldier—ruthless, lethal, hard-edged.

He knocked her hand aside as he took over holding

the camisole compress against his wound. "We save lives. Stop terrorists." He dragged in another shallow breath. "If we cross a line…the ends justify…the means."

Her mouth dried, and an apology rose in her throat. She hadn't meant to imply she questioned Jake's ethics. "Jake, I…"

Before she could put together a coherent response, he hitched his head toward the stairs again. "I've got this. Find my phone."

She sat back on her heels, wiping her hands on the khaki pants she'd borrowed from Mrs. Noble's closet. Blood smeared on the legs of the pants. Jake's blood. *If Jake died…*

Her stomach rolled, but she battled down the flutter of panic that tried to return. *Keep it together. For Jake.*

Pushing to her feet, she put a lock on the nerves that could only hamper her ability to think, to facilitate their escape, to help pull Jake through his medical emergency. He was counting on her, and she wouldn't fail him.

She searched the area at the base of the steps, then up the stairs themselves. Finding nothing, she walked up the unfinished stairs, slowly, peering through the open back of each step to the basement floor below. Finally, as she neared the top, she found a piece of the phone's casing, the cover to the battery compartment, in a crack between the stairs and the wall. Peering through the gap at the back of the unfinished step she spotted Jake's phone below her in a dark corner of the basement floor. In two more pieces.

"Oh, no." Her heart sank as she scurried back down and retrieved the parts. With the compartment door broken off, the battery had fallen out of the cell phone, and the screen had a large forked crack. "It's broken."

Chelsea carried the pieces back to Jake's makeshift bed on the pile of laundry and showed him the damage. "I can try to put the battery back in, but based on the crack in the screen…"

"Try it. Even if we can't get a call out—" he paused and inhaled carefully again "—it might still emit a GPS signal."

"What good would that do us?"

"Daniel."

"Your former black ops teammate?"

He nodded. "I had him on the line…when I was shot. He'll come. Or send help."

Chelsea straightened her shoulders, the knot in her chest loosening. "You're sure?"

She saw the subtle flicker of doubt that passed over his face. The merest of hesitations before his features firmed with confidence. "Daniel won't let us down."

She wrapped her fingers around Jake's wrist and held his gaze. "Maybe we should make a plan of our own, a strategy we can start working on *now*. Just in case."

Jake's jaw firmed, and he nodded his agreement. What went unspoken between them was a truth that chilled her to the bone.

Jake's friends might come to their aid. But in his condition, Jake didn't have time to wait.

Chapter 13

Brady glared at the bullet-pocked basement door and lowered the smoking gun in his hand. He'd fired at the locked door until the pistol answered his trigger pulls with an impotent click. He hurled the empty gun aside, frustration and fury boiling over.

Stupid, stupid to let the cowboy sneak up on him! Even if he had thought the two were dead, he should have been paying more attention, been prepared for someone to approach the house.

Brady returned to the living room, kicking at the ropes the cowboy had tied him with, and dropped onto the couch to brood. To plan.

If Cowboy and Chelsea had made it here from the Cadillac, it stood to reason the roads were passable now. And if the roads were plowed, did that mean the cops had found the Cadillac? The car had been shot up in his firefight with Cowboy, and he'd bled at the scene. The snow should have covered the stains on the road, but the car floor and backseat would have been covered in his bloody DNA.

Even if the cops hadn't connected him to the abandoned Cadillac, had Cowboy and Chelsea found a way to place a 9-1-1 call before busting in on him today?

Brady's pulse hammered. Cops could be converging on this house even now. He needed to move. He needed to dig out Cowboy's truck and get the hell out of Dodge while he could.

Damn it!

Brady snatched up the men's coat he'd taken from Chelsea's front closet and limped toward the back door. His tussle with Cowboy had his leg throbbing again, and Brady clenched his teeth in disgust. He'd really love to plug that bastard for screwing up his getaway and giving him this frickin' gash on his leg.

He slammed through the door to the carport and stormed out into the cold air. He'd seen a shed of some kind at the back of the property when he arrived and guessed that would be where he'd find a shovel. Assuming Chelsea's folks had a—

Movement near the shed caught his eye, and Brady jerked to a stop, tensing. *Hold the phone...what was that?*

Two horses, both saddled, had been tied to the clothesline pole. So that was how Cowboy and Chelsea got here. That was why he hadn't heard a car engine.

Brady sent an encompassing look around the property. Should he take a horse and be gone? No. Traveling by horse was too slow, wouldn't get him far enough, fast enough, and was far from inconspicuous. And horses stank. Brady rolled his lip in a sneer, thinking of his misspent youth and the days he'd spent mucking stalls for minimum wage. He snorted. Was it any wonder he'd turned to armed robbery and petty theft?

Taking a horse was a good backup plan if he needed an emergency contingency. He marched through the snow, checked out the horses and decided which one he'd take. In a pinch. For now he'd dig out Cowboy's truck. If the roads were clear, he could be in Mexico by morning.

Chelsea glanced at her watch. "Two-thirty. We've been down here an hour."

Jake nodded, concentrating on taking slow, even breaths. Anything to take his mind off the burning pain in his shoulder. Chelsea had found an almost-full bottle of acetaminophen tablets in a drawer of her father's workbench and given him a couple. For a gunshot wound, the pills were kinda like spitting on a wildfire, but still better than nothing.

A little while earlier, the bleeding had finally stopped, and since then he'd been bracing himself for what he knew needed to happen next.

"Things are quiet upstairs," Chelsea said. "I wonder what evil deeds Brady's up to. Probably going through my mother's jewelry looking for valuables to pawn."

"Chels…"

She looked over at him, her expression reflecting the strain of their situation. She flashed him a brave smile despite her obvious worry. "I'm babbling, I know. I do that when I'm nervous."

He held her gaze, knowing she wouldn't like what he was about to tell her any more than he did. "You need to stitch me up…close the wound…"

He gritted his teeth as a sharp ache sliced through him when he moved his arm.

Chelsea's gaze widened and darted to his. "Come again?"

"You told me you quilted as a hobby. You know how to stitch."

"Cloth scraps, not people!" Panic flared in her eyes. "Besides that, where am I going to get—"

"Look in there." He aimed an unsteady finger at the box of fabric scraps on the metal shelving.

Chelsea glanced toward the shelves, then met his gaze again with resignation and acceptance of her task written on her face.

"You can do it. I trust you." He squeezed her hand, and tears filled her eyes.

"I don't want to hurt you. We have no way to deaden the pain."

"Let me worry about that. Find me something to bite down on."

She scanned the room, then went to the dryer and retrieved a pair of her clean panties. Arching an eyebrow and shooting him a devilish smile that didn't reach her eyes, she quipped lightly, "Wanna sink your teeth in these, Spy Guy?"

He gave her the best teasing grin he could, considering the throbbing in his shoulder and his skull. "You gonna be…in them?"

She rolled the panties up and laid them on his chest. "Not this time, sugar." She swiped at a tear that dripped onto her cheek. "But you pull through this, and I'm all yours, handsome."

The tremble of fear and grief in her voice belied the sultry promise in her flirting and tugged at Jake's heart.

Chelsea pushed to her feet and took the box of sewing scraps from the shelf, setting it on the floor to rummage through the contents. Digging deep into the bits of fabric, she pulled out a small wooden box. "We're in luck." She opened the lid of the wooden box and tinny, tinkling music wafted through the basement.

"'Love Story,'" he said, identifying the song. "My mom's favorite movie."

Chelsea removed a spool of thread and packet of needles from the box, closed the lid and returned to his side, frowning. "Why? The woman dies! I need a happy ending. There's enough sadness in the world without watching movies where true love is cut short by tragedy."

"Two words." He watched her unwind a length of thread and snap it off. "Ryan O'Neal. My mom made no secret of her…crush on him." He scowled at the spool. "Purple, huh?"

"Sorry. It was this or a horrid green. And this is official TCU purple, Spy Guy. You should feel honored."

"Really? Not so much. I went to A&M for a year before I joined the Air Force."

She gave him a quick side glance and grunted. "If you ever meet my dad, don't lead with that. First impressions are important, and he's a Horned Toad through and through." She pulled out a needle, threaded it, then twisted her mouth in thought. "Hang on."

She scurried over to the washing machine, retrieved the jug of bleach, and dunked the needle and thread in the sterilizing liquid. The thread came out a strange shade of pink.

"So much for official TCU purple, huh?" she said, then gave him a reluctant look. "Ready?"

He nodded. "Do it."

She moved close, stuck the rolled-up panties between his teeth and peeled back the dressing she'd made for the wound earlier.

Drawing a deep breath, she bit her bottom lip and carefully pinched together the edges of his wound. A sharp pain, disproportionate to the poke of a needle, sliced through his shoulder as she started. Likely drips of bleach on his open wound. He bit hard on the cloth roll, and a hiss of pain escaped him, despite his best effort to endure the ordeal silently. Chelsea was stressed enough without knowing just how much he really was hurting.

Her hands stilled, and she raised apologetic eyes to his. "Sorry. I wish there was some way to make this easier on you."

He was lucky the bullet had passed through, though. With the plugs in the wound to stop the bleeding, followed by a quick stitch-up job, he'd be good as new... in a couple of months. Meantime, he could still move his arm, even if it hurt like hell, and with a couple of hours to rest, he'd be back on his feet, finding a way out of this cluster eff.

He removed the bite roll and took a cleansing breath. "I'll be okay. Better if you work quickly...get it over with."

She nodded but didn't start back to work. Her brow furrowed, and she nibbled her lip as she cast a glance around them. "Something..." she muttered under her breath, then froze. Her gaze darted back to his, and she wet her lips.

"Chels?"

Her expression modulated, and she set the needle and thread on his chest. One sculpted eyebrow arched, and a grin twitched at the corner of her mouth. "What you need is something to distract you."

"Like wh—" His question stuck in his throat as she

grabbed the hem of her shirt and whipped it and her bra off in one smooth motion.

Jake's breath caught in his lungs. His attention zeroed in on the two perfect breasts and peaked nipples that greeted him. "Chels…" he croaked.

"Enjoy, Spy Guy." She stuck the rolled panties back in his mouth and set back to work. As if nothing were different. As if she hadn't just offered up the most tempting and luscious pair of breasts he'd ever had the pleasure of viewing. *Geezums*… He'd been shot through the shoulder, but he wasn't dead!

A rush of heat flooded him, settling in his groin. Damn, she was hot. Even without makeup, her cheeks splotched red from crying, her hair mussed from the wind and her eyelashes spiked by tears, Chelsea was something to behold.

Sure, he'd seen women with more perfect features, more classically beautiful faces and model-thin bodies, but Chelsea had something those women didn't. *Realness* was the only way he could put it. Warmth. Life. Passion.

The sting of the needle didn't recede as she continued stitching him up, but her distraction worked. Gritting his teeth and focusing on the nearly naked woman hovering over him, Jake shut out all but the worst pain. Rail-thin models didn't have the full, rounded cleavage a man could wrap his hands around and fondle at leisure, savoring.

Jake lifted a hand toward Chelsea's bosom but stopped himself before touching her. Blood stained his shaking hand, and the notion of defiling her pale skin and rosy nipples seemed profane. But as he withdrew his hand, Chelsea wrapped her fingers around his and pressed his palm to her breast.

She met his gaze and gave him a timid grin. "It's okay. Whatever you need to keep your mind off the needle."

He moved his hand to her cheek and stroked her flushed skin with his thumb. Pushing the bite roll out of his mouth with his tongue, he whispered, "You're beautiful, Chels. Don't ever doubt that."

Her eyebrows twitched as if in denial, but rather than reply, she ducked her head and poked him again with the needle.

He grunted and pulled a cleansing breath through his nose. He focused again on her bared chest and cupped the nearest breast in his palm. When he flicked the pebbled tip with his thumb, she sucked in a quick breath and tensed. He paused, briefly, then circled the nipple again before pinching it lightly.

A soft moan escaped Chelsea's taut lips, and the sexy sound shot fire through his veins.

"Almost done," she said, her voice unsteady. She tugged on the thread, tying off her last stitch, then set the needle aside. Her brow puckering in concentration, she examined her handiwork. "I think that should h—"

She stopped midsentence when he squeezed her breast again, molding it with his palm.

Digging her fingers into his arms, she closed her eyes. "Wow."

Lust spiked inside him, and his body grew rigid, vibrating with need, his stinging shoulder forgotten. Jake curled both hands around her butt and guided her leg over him so that she straddled his hips.

As she settled into the new position, she grazed the swollen ridge behind his fly. He bucked, firming his grip on her hips, and she gasped. Her legs tensed on either side of him, before slowly relaxing and settling on him, their sexes fitted intimately.

Jake's heart tapped a hard staccato beat, and his breath sawed from him in shallow pants. "C'mere."

Sliding his hand into her hair, he pulled her head down and caught her lips for an openmouthed kiss. He moved his mouth greedily against hers, but instead of slaking the flare of heat that surged in him, the fire inside him burned hotter, higher.

Chelsea braced her arms on either side of his head, clearly trying to keep her weight off him, but the position allowed her breasts to brush his chest. The sensation of her taut nipples grazing his skin drove him crazy, coiling the need in him tighter.

"I want you…" he said between kisses, his tone more growl than murmur.

With a sigh, Chelsea pulled back, just far enough to look into his eyes. Her pupils were large black pools of desire. She licked her lips, and her throat convulsed as she swallowed hard. "I promise, my intent was not to seduce you. I just thought if you had something else to think about—"

He cut her off with another blistering kiss. "If you don't want to, just say no."

"Oh…no! I mean, yes… I mean…oh, my God, Jake…" More tears puddled in her eyes. "Yes…"

Chelsea stared at Jake for a few stunned seconds, waiting to wake up, waiting for him to flash her a lopsided grin and tell her he was kidding. Instead, his blue eyes held hers while a smoky desire swirled in their depths. He tugged her close for another devastating kiss, and her head spun, muzzy with sweet sensation. Her breasts skimmed across his chest, and the light friction made her nipples gloriously achy and hypersensitive.

"Y-your shoulder—"

"Is fine for now." Skimming his hand down her bare back, Jake's fingertips trailed along her spine and sent electric sparks shimmering through her. His hand nudged her as he wedged it between their bodies, fumbling. She was so lost in the heady pleasure of his kiss that it took her brain a moment to process his groping. At the button on her pants. And his zipper.

Oh, Texas…he truly wanted her. He was undressing. He was…

With a tremulous breath, she rolled off him, taking over the job of stripping her pants down her legs and tossing them and her panties aside. When he sat up to shove his jeans down to his ankles, he grunted and winced in pain.

She sent him a concerned look, opening her mouth to call a halt to things, but he silenced her with a look and a shake of his head. "I'm fine. Just…give me a hand with my boots?"

With a nod, she helped him tug off his boots—and, *sheesh,* found another gun tucked in one. She set them aside as he kicked off his jeans.

Facing Jake, she drank in the sight of him, and her mouth dried. He was everything she'd expected a man of his powerful build, his rugged appeal, his alpha soldier hotness would be. And then some.

Her breath stuttered from her in a fluttery exhale, and she reached for him, stroking her cool fingers along his heated flesh. His moan startled her, and she snatched her hand back.

"No, don't stop," he rasped. "That feels wonderful."

She met his gaze, saw the affection and pleasure that

lit his smile, and her heart twisted. Could she make love to him and not become emotionally attached to him? "Jake…"

"Don't overthink it, Chels. If this isn't what you want, it's okay. If it is, then—" he reached for her "—kiss me."

She didn't have to weigh the matter. She wanted him more than she could bear. Turning toward him, she caught his lips with hers and savored the welcoming warmth of his kiss. She might be dreaming. She might just be a convenient and willing body to satisfy an itch for him, but at that moment she didn't care. She wanted Jake in a way that was way beyond sexual hunger and hovered dangerously close to her heart. Her soul.

The crazy impossibility that she, Chelsea Plain-Jane Harris of Small Town, Texas, was in the arms of a prince among men, a sexy warrior god, a hero worthy of a Hollywood spy thriller, only made her cherish the moment all the more. She knew how rare and special making love to Jake was in the big picture. She was one lucky girl, and she wasn't about to argue with fate or karma or whatever happy power had brought her to this moment.

She wrapped her fingers around his arousal and gave him a few long, tender caresses. Jake caught his breath, and his body bowed off the bed of laundry.

"Oh, Chelsea…" he said, the sexy rumble of satisfaction in his voice stirring a heady confidence in her. She smacked another fervent kiss on his mouth before swinging her leg over to straddle him again.

With his hands on her hips, he helped guide her descent as she sank down, taking him deep within her, savoring the glide of his heat inside her, filling her. She let her head fall back, thrusting her chest forward, and clinging to his arms as she rode him.

He sat up enough to draw her nipple into his mouth and roll the tight peak with his tongue. Ribbons of tingling sensation unfurled in her, puddling at her core and building the sweet frenzy scrambling inside her. She explored his skin with her fingers, then her lips, learning every inch of his chest, arms, neck. When his tongue dueled with hers, she met his parry and thrust, their mouths mirroring the motion of their bodies.

Eyes closed, she hovered near the edge of her climax, savoring every second of their union and the sensual experience. She'd have been happy to stay in that moment forever, but Jake slipped a hand between them to caress her highly sensitive flesh. Just one stroke of his finger shot her into the stratosphere, shuddering and deliriously swamped in pleasure. A ragged cry escaped her, and Jake responded with harder thrusts, which sent her higher, drew out her pleasure and made the heady sensation more intense.

Soon his moans joined hers, and she felt the tremor that shook him as he buried himself deep inside her. When she opened her eyes, she found him watching her, his eyes bright and penetrating. The intensity of his gaze hit her with a jolt, and a different sort of quiver tumbled through her. She could almost believe, looking back at him, seeing the fierce power of his expression, that he shared the emotions that tangled inside her.

But believing that was folly. Chelsea released the breath she held. Jake had no room in his driven, top secret, danger-filled life for a relationship. He'd said as much, and one lightning-hot roll in the hay—or laundry pile, as the case may be—didn't change that fact.

A sharp pang sliced through her, and she quickly

shoved it down, not wanting anything to spoil the moment, the tingling afterglow of incredible sex. With the man of her dreams. Chelsea raked her hair back from her face with one hand and carefully moved off him, rolling to his side in utter exhaustion.

Jake put an arm around her, lightly strumming his fingers along her arm, but for several minutes neither said anything. Huddled against Jake's chest, she could feel and hear the thump of his heart beneath her ear.

"So…I guess we should talk about the obvious," he said finally, his voice soft.

She frowned. "The obvious?"

He sighed. "We didn't use protection."

Her gut tightened. "Oh. Right." She swallowed hard. Good grief! How could she have gotten so caught up in the moment that *that* got by her? "Wow." Angling her head back, she met his gaze.

"For my part, you're safe. I'm always careful." He scowled and grunted. "Well, present circumstance aside."

"'Kay." She nodded. "Same here. In fact, the only other guy I've slept with was my ex-boyfriend."

"Todd the Jerk?"

"That's the one." She sat up, found her clothes and started dressing. Now that the heat of the moment had passed, she was awkwardly aware of her less-than-seductive love handles.

Jake, on the other hand, seemed perfectly content to remain naked. Her pulse spiked again as she cut another glance down his toned warrior body. Oh, Texas!

He stroked a knuckle along her forearm. "Which leaves us with…"

She met his gaze. "The pregnancy question."

"Yeah."

Settling back down beside him, Chelsea chewed her lip and tried to remember where in her cycle she was. "Wrong time," she said, mixed feelings swirling through her. While she wasn't ready to have a baby, had no money to support a family, the idea of carrying Jake's child, having a tiny bundle of life with his eyes and his smile made her heart melt. "It's the wrong time of the month for me. I know it's not foolproof, but my Catholic friends swear by—"

He caught her mouth in a kiss. "You'll let me know either way?"

She dragged a finger down his chin and sent him a reassuring grin. "Of course."

But even as she promised him, she wondered if she'd be able to find him, get a message to him if he was on one of his top secret assignments, undercover somewhere. And what would he do if she were pregnant? Would he leave the job he loved to help her raise a child? Could she ask him to make that sacrifice?

She stared up at the unfinished ceiling and chuckled her disbelief. "Well, that was...certainly more fun than I ever thought I'd have in my parents' basement."

Eyes closed, Jake only hummed an acknowledgment.

Chelsea's gaze drifted from her father's workbench to the metal shelves stocked with her mother's canning and partially finished sewing projects. "When I was little, I used to come down here and play princess. I'd pretend I was locked in a dungeon and my only escape was through that window." She pointed to the window above the dryer, and Jake opened one eye long enough to look. "I discovered the burglar bars on that window weren't bolted securely, and by climbing on the dryer, I could open the window and push the bars out far enough to wiggle my eight-year-old self through the gap."

Jake's eyebrows drew together, and he rolled his head to the side to look at her. "Wait a minute. That window's bars aren't secured?"

Her pulse kicked, seeing where he was going. "They weren't as of ten years ago when I sneaked in that way late one night because I'd forgotten my key. I don't think I've tested them since then."

His blue eyes drilled hers. "If you could get out through that window, you could ride to the next nearest neighbor and call the cops."

She propped on an elbow and held up her free hand. "Whoa, whoa, whoa. I'm like three dress sizes bigger now than I was at fifteen for starters. And even if I could squeeze my breeder's hips through that little opening, we already know Darynda's phone is dead—"

"Hey…" He caught her fingers in his and kissed her palm.

Chelsea's heart leaped, and a lump swelled in her throat. "Besides…how can I leave you like this? You're hurt. I—"

"I'll be all right. You can do it." He started to sit up but stopped short, grimacing and grunting in pain.

"See? You can't even sit up!"

"Don't go to Darynda's. Keep heading south," he persisted. "Head out to the road. Maybe you'll intercept a snowplow or power company truck."

"Don't ask me to leave you, Jake." A familiar chill crawled through her, the fear she'd experienced every time she'd left her mother's hospital room, the tiny voice of doubt that asked, *What if she takes a turn for the worse while you're gone?* Fresh tears filled her eyes. If Jake needed her, if his condition worsened and she wasn't here… "I n-need to take care of you. You've lost blood and…" Her stomach pitched, remembering the duty she'd already neglected while she ravaged an injured man. "And—oh, geez!—I still need to sew up your exit wound."

Chelsea, you idiot! What were you thinking? she scolded mentally as she crawled to her knees to check his wound.

"Chelsea, honey—"

"Can you roll to your stomach? I'll help." She put her hand on his shoulder and encountered a warm dampness. But in this cold basement, the old blood should be— "Oh, no! This is new blood." Panic climbed her throat, squeezed her chest. "You're bleeding again!"

"So we'll stop it, and you'll stitch it closed like the entry wound."

Acid guilt bit her gut, and she moaned. "Oh, God… instead of sewing you up like I should have been, I was shagging you like some wanton—"

Jake grabbed her wrist and shook her arm lightly. "Chels, quit blaming yourself. Do you really think I couldn't have stopped us anytime if I'd wanted to?"

"I threw myself at you."

He pulled a face. "Yeah, guys hate that."

Somewhat appeased by his teasing, she foraged through the basket of clean laundry and found a cotton nightgown. With shaking hands, she folded the gown to make a compress. "I'm just saying—"

"Chelsea!" He huffed an exasperated laugh. "Are you hearing me? I take responsibility for what happened. I have no regrets."

She held out the nightgown compress. "Roll over."

He caught her wrist and locked a steady gaze on her.

"I wanted to make love to you, Chels. I'd gladly bleed out for another chance to be with you."

She shook her head, tears spilling onto her cheeks. "Don't say things like that! You are not going to die! I won't let you!"

"No, I won't. I promise." He cupped his hand behind her head and dragged her close for a kiss. "Don't cry, sweetheart."

Pulling away, she shook the gown at him. "Are you going to roll over or not?"

"Fine, but help me get my clothes on first. I'm getting cold."

With her help, he wiggled back into his jeans, and she repositioned the coat on him like a blanket.

"Thanks." He firmed his mouth, the muscles in his jaw flexing as he gritted his teeth, and, growling his pain, he flipped carefully to his belly. "Have at me, darlin'."

Gnawing her bottom lip, Chelsea leaned close to better study the wound and what she needed to do first. She plucked the saturated bra strip from the wound and gently wiped the skin around the bullet hole. When she reached for the bleach to sterilize the area, he groaned. "I think I saw some hand sanitizer on the workbench. Could you try that instead?"

"Sure." She stroked a hand over his hair and kissed his cheek before pushing to her feet and finding the disinfectant. She used a squirt on her own hands and set to work cleaning his wound, stanching the bleeding, then sewing closed the ragged gap.

As she worked, Jake's hands fisted in the bed of laundry, his knuckles white with tension. Her heart twisted every time he'd flinch or hiss in misery.

"So this Todd person," he said when she was half-way through stitching him up, "where does he live?"

Her hands stilled briefly. "Why do you ask?"

"I thought I might look him up, break his nose for hurting you the way he did."

"Who says he hurt me?"

"You slept with him, and he dumped you for selfish reasons when you needed him most. You have cause…"

"True, but…" She forced the ache in her chest down. Now was not the time to examine the lingering pain of Todd's rejection. "I'm over it," she lied.

"Are you?" He shifted his head to look back over his shoulder at her.

She pressed a hand against his back. "Hold still." She concentrated on her next stitch, then sighed. "Look, the truth is I *had* gained weight from all the junk food and lack of exercise while my mom was sick. I'd been mopey and tense and putting him off to be at the hospital, just like he said. He was right. I wasn't the girl he'd started dating anymore. *He* had cause."

He huffed. "That's crap."

"Jake…"

"No, don't defend him. You deserved better. He was selfish and shallow, and if I ever meet him, I *will* bust his chops for the way he treated you."

Jake's vehemence on her behalf brought a new sting of tears to her eyes. "Well, let's hope you don't ever meet him, then. He's the sort who'd press assault charges, and I don't want you going to jail. He's not worth it."

"Yeah, but you are."

Chelsea's breath stuck in her throat. The sweet words, the touching sentiment were heart-wrenching enough without her being in an overwrought state because of Jake's injury and the threat of Brady's looming presence upstairs. She blinked hard to clear her vision and tied off the last stitch on Jake's wound.

"Well, it's not pretty." She sat back on her heels and let her hands lie limply in her lap. "If you don't get to a doctor soon so they can sew it up properly, you'll have a rather ugly scar."

"Won't be my first." Jake dragged in and exhaled a couple ragged breaths, his face pinched with pain.

After wiping her hands on the dirty laundry, she smoothed Jake's hair back from his face and bent to press her cheek against his. "You are the bravest, most extraordinary man I've ever met."

He grunted softly. "I haven't done anything any other man worth his salt would have done."

"Don't underestimate yourself," she whispered, her voice catching. "You've gone far above the call of duty for me more than once. I hope you know how much your sacrifice means to me."

"Anytime, beautiful." His reply was quiet, his breathing slowing and growing a little deeper.

Chelsea closed her eyes, thinking of all Jake had suffered because he'd stopped to help a stranded motorist, because he'd walked unwittingly into her nightmare. How could she do any less for him? Time was crucial. Jake needed a doctor, and if she could do anything to bring him help sooner, she had to try. Like she'd told him earlier at Darynda's, she couldn't let fear win. "I'll do it, Jake. I'll get out that window somehow and ride for help."

Chapter 14

A loud scraping sound jolted Jake from a combat nap. When he jackknifed to a seated position, white-hot pain seared his shoulder and pulsed through his head. Gritting his teeth against the pain, he scanned his dark surroundings, orienting himself.

Staircase. Workbench. Washing machine and... Chelsea stood atop the dryer, her arm stretched through the open basement window.

"Chels?" His throat was raw and dry, and his voice sounded gritty.

She spun around so fast that she almost lost her footing on the dryer and had to grab the window frame for balance. "You're awake! Thank goodness. You scared me when you got so still and quiet, but I knew you needed rest after what your body had been through."

Jake pressed a hand to his shoulder and found she'd tied a bandage on him that looped under his arm and over his shoulder, covering her handiwork on both the entry and exit wounds. He knew he was lucky as hell the bullet hadn't hit bone or the upper lobe of his lung. He had some painful physical therapy ahead of him, working his shoulder back into shape once the tendons healed, but he was alive, and that was what mattered.

And he had no doubt Chelsea's quick attention to his wound had kept him from bleeding out.

She jumped down from the dryer and unwrapped a shirt from around her hand. "I got the window open, finally, but the snow piled against the window is keeping me from pushing the burglar bars out of the way like I used to do. They're too big to come in the window without turning them, but I can't turn them either…again, because of the snow."

Jake smiled. Chelsea's nervous chatter had grown on him in the past few days, soothing him the way white noise lulled one to sleep.

She flexed and balled her hand, and even in the fading afternoon light he could tell her fingers were red. "I've been digging out the snow, dumping it in that can." She pointed to an old coffee can under the window. "My dad had nails in there, but I thought if I melted some snow, we could drink it."

Considering his tongue felt like cotton and his throat was parched, a drink of water sounded heaven-sent. "Good thinking. I'll take a sip of that."

She brought him the coffee can and helped him tip it up for a drink. "I'm making progress digging out, but it's slow going. If I don't get the snow cleared enough for me to move the bars in the next hour or so, I might run out of daylight before I reach Mrs. Posey's place. She's the next house down the road. A divorcée, lives alone, kids are grown, but she's bound to have a cell phone or working landline." She frowned and added in a mumble, "Please, God…"

Jake didn't comment on the fact that Chelsea had clearly had a change of heart about riding out for help. He also kept silent about his true purpose for getting her away from her parents' house. They were sitting targets if Brady found that basement window. She would be safer somewhere else. The sooner she was gone, the better.

Knowing how frightened she must be at the idea of sneaking away from the house undetected, leaving him injured and facing the snowy miles alone on horseback, her decision filled Jake with pride. She was a tough cookie, stronger than she gave herself credit for.

When he finished drinking, she set the can aside and tipped her head as she studied him. "You know, I could make an ice pack for your shoulder. It would reduce the swelling and numb the pain some."

"Brilliant," he said with a nod. "I think I love you."

She snapped a startled glance toward him, and he realized how his quip sounded. "I mean…I love the way you think… That you…"

Clearly flustered, she shook her head. "I know what you meant. Let me fix you up."

He kicked himself mentally. The last thing he wanted to do was hurt Chelsea, lead her to believe they had any future together. Her scummy ex had done a number on her already, and she didn't deserve more heartache.

Yet when he thought about telling her goodbye and returning to the front lines of black ops work, a hollow ache filled his chest. She'd gotten under his skin. He'd miss her smile, her sense of humor, her compassion and common sense. And her heat, the passion she poured in every kiss, the electricity that crackled between them with every touch, every glance.

Damn it! Don't fall in love, Connelly. Your place is with the black ops team. You have a duty to do something, make an impact in the world. That kind of difference and change doesn't happen without sacrifice. His mom had paid the ultimate price the last time he'd put his love life first. He had no right to indulge himself with a relationship while there were still terrorists to defeat.

Jake watched Chelsea roll a handful of snow in a T-shirt, and his heart kicked. He'd never had a problem with the idea of giving up a relationship and starting a family before now. Before Chelsea. Maybe it was because of his father's heart attack, but he'd spent a lot of time these past few days thinking about his life, what he'd done with it. And what he hadn't accomplished yet. Giving his dad grandchildren, taking that father-son trip to the Super Bowl, finishing his college degree.

He rubbed his eyes. *Geezums,* he was getting maudlin.

"Here." Chelsea placed the ice pack behind his shoulder, and he glanced up at her.

"How long was I asleep?"

"Not too long. About thirty minutes." She adjusted the bandage she'd wrapped around him to hold the snow pack in place.

"Any noise from upstairs?"

"A few bumps. Nothing that worried me." She gathered another shirt. "I'll make another pack for the entry wound. Are you warm enough? I can cover you up with some of the laundry if you want."

"I'm good," he assured her before an involuntary shiver raced through him.

She frowned and started spreading shirts and towels over his legs and torso. "Don't try to be a martyr about this, Jake. If you're hurting, take more Tylenol. If you're cold, cover up with more laundry. You don't get extra points for needless suffering."

He grinned and stroked a hand along her cheek. "Yes, ma'am."

She caught his fingers in her cold hands and pinned a hard stare on him. "I mean it. I'm going to be worried enough about you when I leave. Promise me you'll take care of yourself, that you'll be careful and not take unnecessary risks."

"I will, if you promise the same."

She nodded. "Of course."

He gripped her hand harder. "When you leave, we have to be sure Brady doesn't see you. Stay quiet. Move quickly and look carefully before you cross an open space. Know where the next protective cover is in case you have to use it."

The color drained from her face, but she nodded.

"When you're ready to move out, I'll create a diversion for you, try to draw his attention away from the yard."

Worry dented her brow. "Jake…"

"I'll be fine." He tugged up his cheek. "I'm a trained special ops agent, remember?"

"But you're not bulletproof."

"I'll be armed," he lied, nodding to the second gun he'd stashed in his boot. "I plan to get off the first shot." She didn't need to know the gun was out of rounds. He still had in his coat pocket the box of ammo Darynda had given him for her .38—the gun Brady now had. Irony seemed to be the theme of the day.

But as soon as Chelsea was safely away from the

house, he'd catch Brady with his guard down. He had enough resources to recapture him…but only after he knew Chelsea was out of harm's way.

His power nap had recharged him somewhat, and between the ice pack and the acetaminophen, his pain was manageable. Sitting around this basement doing nothing, waiting for Chelsea to send law enforcement, waiting for Daniel or his team, was unacceptable, unthinkable. Not gonna happen.

As soon as Chelsea was gone, Jake would put an end to Brady's reign of terror…one way or another.

Using a shirt wrapped around her hand to protect her from the cold, Chelsea finished scooping out the snow and muscled the burglar bars out of the way. The window she'd climbed through so easily as a kid looked dauntingly high and small now.

As much as she wanted to stay put and take care of Jake, she knew she had precious few hours of daylight left to reach Mrs. Posey's house. The last thing she needed was to cripple her horse or get stranded by riding into an unseen hazard.

She glanced around the basement one last time, making sure she'd left everything Jake would need within his reach. She'd taken a few of the acetaminophen pills for herself, sipped some more melted snow and eaten half of a candy bar she'd found in her father's not-so-secret candy stash, leaving the other half for Jake, and stuffed the pistol Jake had given her in the pocket of her coat. *Two shots. Make 'em count.*

Taking a deep breath for courage, she faced Jake. "I guess that's it. I should go."

He sat up and waved her to him. "One more thing."

She crossed to him and knelt beside him, nervous energy buzzing inside her. "What?"

"Just this." He cupped the back of her head and drew her close for a kiss.

In that moment, she realized she had no way to know what would happen once she left, how long it would take to contact the police, when she would see Jake again. *If* she'd ever see Jake again. Her throat clogged with emotion and trepidation.

His lips were warm and gentle, his kiss thorough and deep. She wound her fingers in his thick hair, savoring the taste of him, locking away memories of the heroic and handsome warrior who'd rescued her. She may not get happily ever after with Jake, but she'd never forget the fairy-tale days she'd spent with this man of her dreams.

When he broke the kiss and rested his forehead against hers, she sucked in a shaky breath.

"Hey," he whispered, "still not goodbye. Just good luck."

Her throat was too tight to answer.

His fingers curled against her scalp. "I have faith in you."

Don't die. I love you, she wanted to say but didn't dare.

She nodded and pulled away before she lost her nerve. Climbing on the dryer, she said a silent prayer that after his sweet goodbye kiss that she didn't embarrass herself by awkwardly clambering out the window or getting stuck in the small opening.

Hoisting herself up and pushing off the wall with her toes, she got the top of her body through without problem. Because of her bulky coat, wiggling the rest of her body through the window made her feel like Winnie the Pooh in the honey tree. But she did it. She wedged through the opening and crawled onto the snowy ground of her parents' side yard.

"Chelsea!"

She dropped to her knees and peered back into the basement. Jake had struggled to his feet and leaned against the dryer, holding his injured shoulder.

"What are you doing?" she scolded. "You're supposed to rest!"

"I'm going to create a diversion. Wait until you hear me yelling before you cross the yard to the horses."

She hesitated. She didn't like his plan but knew the basement door was locked. Jake's relative safety or jeopardy level would remain the same in that respect. "All right."

"Last thing…" he said, his gaze intense. "Once you get away from here, once you reach safety, send law enforcement." She opened her mouth to tell him his request was obvious when he added, "And don't, for any reason, come back here."

Jake pulled the window closed to conserve what little heat was left in the basement and heaved a sigh. The hurt that had crossed Chelsea's face when he ordered her to stay away made him feel as if he'd kicked a puppy. Even though he'd done what was in her best interest, she'd clearly felt rejected, wounded.

And what did you think would happen when you left her to return to work with the team, Connelly? You can't make love to a woman like Chelsea, who gives her whole heart to relationships, and not expect her to suffer when it ends.

He watched through the window as Chelsea eased along the wall of the house, headed toward the backyard where they'd tied the horses. He sent up a quick prayer for her safety, then prepared for his part of the plan.

Jake gritted his teeth against the pain that assailed him as he crossed to the staircase and slowly climbed to the locked door. His shoulder throbbed as he moved, but a different sort of ache sliced through his chest, squeezing his heart.

Focus, Connelly. He had a job to do. Keeping Brady's attention distracted from outside for the next several minutes was essential to Chelsea's safe escape.

Jake slammed his fist against the locked door. "Brady! You want a piece of me? Come get it, you worthless sack!" He listened for a moment to see if he detected Brady's footsteps. "Do you hear me, you jackass? You're going down!"

No sound answered his shouts. A tingle of apprehension skittered down Jake's back. Where was Brady?

Chapter 15

Brady stuck his shovel in the pile of snow he'd mounded beside the driveway and stretched his back, rolled his aching shoulders and rubbed his throbbing leg. Despite the frigid temperature, he'd worked up a sweat. He wiped his brow with his gloved hand and looked back at the progress he'd made. He'd cleared at least fifty feet. Not bad…except he still had another effing two hundred feet or more to go to reach the highway. Why the hell did houses out in the sticks have to be built so far off the road?

Brady huffed his disgust. The work was exhausting and back-breaking, and at this rate he wouldn't finish shoveling until tomorrow. Hell! He needed to be outta here today. Now. Hours ago!

He'd seen a snowplow lumber down the highway a while ago, and that meant the cops could get out this way if the cowboy had managed to get a call out.

Brady glanced back at the house. He needed another of Marian Harris's oxycodone pills and maybe something hot to drink before he finished clearing the driveway. Leaving the shovel where it was, he headed back toward the house. As he neared the house, a commotion in his peripheral vision caught his attention. Someone was in the yard!

He tensed and dropped to a crouch behind the cowboy's truck. Damn it! Had the cops arrived without his knowing? His heart slamming against his ribs, Brady peered out, narrowing his gaze on the figure headed to the back of the property.

Long, thick, brown hair spilled out from under the person's knit cap. It was the woman—Chelsea! But he'd shoved the refrigerator in front of the basement door. How had she gotten out?

Had the cowboy moved it? Was the cowboy still alive?

Brady watched Chelsea approach the horses tied to the clothesline pole and quickly sorted through his options. He couldn't let her get away. That much was certain.

When she swung up on the gray mare, he bit out a curse. "Oh, no, you don't, girlie."

He dug the gun out of his coat pocket and, leaning across the hood of Cowboy's truck, he aimed. Fired.

Chelsea had just gotten in the saddle when a gunshot shattered the quiet. She gasped, flinched. The horses startled, and the gray mare she rode reared up on her back legs. Chelsea held on, crooning calming words to her mount, even as adrenaline jacked through her. Jerking a glance around the yard and toward the house, she searched for the source of the gunfire.

Immediately, a muzzle flash and the cracking boom of another shot drew her gaze to Jake's truck. Brady stood near the hood, aiming a gun at her. Her stomach swooped, and she reflexively hunched down against the horse's neck.

In the next second, Brady fired again, and a tug on her coat sleeve told her the bullet had grazed her. Where she was, she had no cover other than the horses, but she knew a moving target was harder to hit.

"H'yah!" She tapped her heels in the mare's ribs and slapped the reins.

The nervous horse bolted forward, stumbling through the snow as quickly as she could. Brady fired again, and the gray tossed her head and bucked.

"Come on!" Again Chelsea urged her skittish horse forward.

Whinnying nervously, the mare loped behind the house, out of Brady's line of fire. Chelsea stayed hunched low to make herself a smaller target. Gathering the tattered edges of her wits about her, she headed toward the highway as fast as the horse could go in the deep snow. She had a job to do, and she refused to let Jake down.

When the first gunshot rang out, ice streaked to Jake's core. He stopped pounding the door and jerked his head up, his senses on full alert.

Chelsea!

By the time the third shot faded, he had the slide bolts on the basement door unlocked. He ripped open the door only to find the doorway blocked by a massive refrigerator, clearly Brady's attempt to keep them trapped in the basement.

Biting out a curse, Jake raced back down the stairs

and was halfway to the window when he saw Chelsea ride the gray mare past the window. Relief spun through him so hard and fast that his knees buckled. Or maybe it was blood loss, he acknowledged as black spots danced in front of him. He braced a hand against the washing machine until his head quit spinning and his vision cleared. Climbing onto the dryer, he shoved the window open. He was about to squeeze himself out the narrow opening when the rattle of reins and a male voice called his attention to the back corner of the house.

"Hold still, you stupid animal!" Brady clambered into the saddle of Jake's horse and, with a yank of the reins, set off in the same direction Chelsea had gone.

Following her. Another cold wave of fear washed through him.

Stop him, his brain screamed. He had to buy Chelsea time to get away, had to keep Brady from tracking her down. He had to end this debacle. Now.

Jake ducked his head and shoved his good arm out the window. Gritting his teeth against the pain, he pulled himself through the tiny opening and rolled out into the snow. "Hey!" he shouted. "Over here, you bastard!"

Brady turned his head, his gaze searching before locating Jake at the ground-level window. His expression hardened as he raised his weapon and fired a shot toward Jake. The bullet pocked the siding inches from Jake's head. Then…*click.*

Jake jerked his head up at the telltale sound. Brady was out of ammunition. Jake's heart accelerated as he shoved to his feet and lumbered through the snow toward Brady.

Growling his disgust with the empty gun, Brady

threw the weapon aside and kicked the horse. "Go, damn you!"

Jake swiped his good arm toward the bay, hoping to catch Brady's leg, a corner of saddle blanket, the horse's tail. Anything to prevent Brady from escaping again. To no avail.

His heart sank as he watched Brady ride away. Jake was stranded, unarmed and hindered by an injury, but somehow he *would* stop Brady. Failing Chelsea was not an option.

The plows had cleared the road at some point, which was good. But the road-clearing process had piled huge quantities of heavy snow at the edge of the highway, which was bad. The mounded snow was too deep to ride through without risking injury to the gray or getting the horse stuck.

Chelsea reined the horse and studied the long ridge of mounded snow along the road. As she debated how to get across the snowy hill, she replayed the moments as she escaped the house and rode away under gunfire. A shudder rolled through her, the fading traces of adrenaline, and she began second-guessing herself. Because Brady saw her leaving, he had to have figured out how she got away. Her escape gave Brady the information he needed to reach Jake. And kill him.

Should she go back and help Jake, or hurry to Mrs. Posey's and call the police?

Don't, for any reason, come back here….

Her heart wrenched, knowing Jake was trying to protect her, but his order stung anyway. It felt like a rejection.

Quit it! She inhaled the frozen air and sobered. *Get your head together and do your job. Find help.*

But first she had to figure a way over the snow mound. She swung down from the gray and stomped through the snow to the pile. She tested the edge of the chest-high pile with her foot. Her borrowed boot sank deep into the road debris. She stomped again, next to the first footprint…and an idea settled over her. She had no way to move the snow, but could she pack down enough to make a path through it?

She stomped again with her foot and packed the snow into a hard, icy layer. Packing the snow down one footprint at a time would take forever. Jake didn't have that kind of time. She needed another way, something like…*snow angels!*

Turning her back to the pile, she flopped backward and sank into the drift. Then clambering to her feet, she did it again. Each time, her body impression packed another few feet of snow. The progress was slow, and she was getting thoroughly chilled, but she kept throwing her body weight into the snow and packing the impression with her boot. Several minutes later, she'd made an initial narrow pass but needed to widen it and pack the base firmer.…

In the stillness, a noise reached her ears—the jingle of reins.

Holding her breath, praying the sound meant help was nearby, she raised her head. But her fear was confirmed.

Brady had followed her.

Jake knew he couldn't catch up to Chelsea and Brady without a horse. Knew that Noble's third horse was at Darynda's. Knew Darynda's cell phone only lacked a working battery. Those factors made his next step a logical choice, even if his heart wanted to go to Chelsea *now*.

With no time to waste, he slogged through the drifts to his truck and found his car charger. Pocketing it, he headed back toward Darynda's on foot, retracing the path the horses had made in the snow coming over.

His shoulder ached, but he ignored the pain, trying to keep his arm immobile as he waded through the snow. Already weakened by blood loss, he tired quickly. Fatigue pounded at him, and his muscles quivered. More than once he stumbled and fell in the icy drifts, only to shove back to his feet and plow on. He closed his mind to anything but reaching Darynda's. Saving Chelsea.

He put one foot in front of the other. Again. And again.

His feet grew numb in the cold. His shoulder throbbed. His head spun.

Drawing labored breaths of frozen air into his lungs, he staggered on.

Pulse thundering, Chelsea swung up on the gray and clicked her tongue. Brady had seen her and was closing in.

"Come on, girl!" She urged the horse toward the narrow path she'd made through the snowplow's pile. The gray balked. "Please, girl. We gotta go!"

She kicked her horse again, and finally the gray took a few tentative steps on the packed snow, picking her way through. The gray's hooves sank into the snow up to her fetlocks, but she squeezed through the gap in the snowy hill.

Chelsea cast a glance over her shoulder, monitoring Brady's progress. Despite the deep snow cover, he'd pushed his horse to close the gap between them, and the bay was breathing hard, acting jittery.

"Go, you dumb animal!" Brady shouted, fighting the reins, clearly inexperienced in handling a horse.

Chelsea seized on what might be her only advantage, whispering an apology to the bay under her breath. As the gray's flanks brushed the snow pile on either side, Chelsea scooped a handful and formed a snowball. Twisting in her saddle, she lobbed the snowball at the bay's head and hit the horse on the neck. The bay shook his mane, confused. Chelsea followed with another snowball that hit the bay's nose.

"What the h—" Brady's shout ended abruptly as his horse reared, throwing him.

Her own mount slipped on the packed snow, but Chelsea crooned to her and coaxed her through to the road. On sure footing again, the gray bobbed her head and set off at a trot down the highway. Knowing she had to make the most of her lead, Chelsea bent low over the gray's neck and squeezed the horse's ribs with her knees. "Come on, girl. Let's fly."

"That's got to be the place. The coordinates we triangulated for his phone match up," Daniel LeCroix said, glancing across the helicopter cockpit to his former black ops partner.

Alec Kincaid pointed through the windshield. "That looks like Cowboy's truck parked in the drive."

"Yep." Daniel set the GPS locator aside and twisted in his seat to retrieve two Kevlar vests.

"I'm gonna set her down in that pasture." Alec shot a side glance to Daniel. "You ready to move out?"

"Let's do this."

Within minutes of his abruptly ended phone call

with Jake, Daniel had Alec on the phone and had a plan to assist Jake in the works. The cell phone connection Daniel had had with Jake may have been spotty, but the sound of gunfire at Jake's end had been clear. His buddy's reference to an escaped convict and the past three hours of radio silence from Jake told Daniel all he needed to know—his former black ops teammate needed backup.

Alec had met him at an airstrip in Amarillo minutes earlier, having flown down from Colorado the same way Daniel had gotten to Texas from Louisiana, via private jet.

As the helo settled on the frozen ground, Daniel shoved a Kevlar vest at Alec. "Suit up, man. You're a daddy now, and I promised Erin I'd return you in one piece."

The mention of the two loves of his life—his wife, Erin, and their infant son, Joey—brought a smile to Alec's lips. "How did you convince Nicole to let you come?"

"Just told her Jake needed my help. Because Cowboy was instrumental in her rescue last year, she couldn't say no." He double-checked the magazine of his pistol, then stuffed the earpiece to his two-way comm with Alec in his ear.

"How's your knee? You up for this?" As he strapped on his vest, Alec nodded toward the knee Daniel had had a full joint replacement on months earlier.

Daniel jerked a nod and opened the helicopter door. "All healed up and ready to go to work."

"You want to take point?" Alec asked, adjusting his lip mic.

"Roger that." Daniel climbed out onto the snow-covered field and ran toward Jake's truck while Alec covered him from the helo. Once he reached the truck, Alec made his move, joining Daniel behind the protective cover of Jake's vehicle. Daniel rose enough to peer inside the truck. "We've got blood in here. Looks old."

Alec looked for himself, then pointed out a bullet hole in the back panel. "He took fire."

Daniel exchanged a grave look with Alec. "I've got a bad feeling about this."

Alec arched an eyebrow. "Ditto, Obi-Wan."

Hitching his head toward the house, Daniel crept toward the carport door. Tested it. When the door swung open, he stood aside and peered around the frame, weapon poised. Signaling Alec, he waited until his partner was at his six, then moved inside, leading with his gun.

"Clear," he said, moving through the empty mudroom into the kitchen. Together they quickly scoped the kitchen for occupants before fanning out to check the rest of the house. Daniel eased into the living room, noting the disarray and debris while focusing on canvassing spots where a person could hide for an ambush. Seeing no one, he called, "Living room clear."

Daniel was mentally cataloging the bullet holes in the walls, the tangled clothesline cord on the floor, the shattered vases near the shelves and blood spots on the carpet and sofa when Alec appeared from the hallway. "Back of the house is clear."

Alec swept his gaze around the room and grunted. "Not good."

"Did you notice the refrigerator as we came through the kitchen?" Daniel asked.

Alec's eyes narrowed. "The fact that it had been moved from its normal spot? Yeah."

"Let's go see why."

Alec followed Daniel back into the kitchen and helped roll the refrigerator back to its proper place. Rubbing a hand over his jaw, Daniel surveyed the bullet-riddled door and frame. A knot of dread sat in his gut.

Alec muttered a curse. "I believe we've found Alice's rabbit hole."

Stepping to the side, Daniel waited until Alec was in place on the other side of the door before testing the knob. Locked.

"The hinges are on the other side," Alec noted, meaning they couldn't remove the barrel from the hinge and take the door down. "And that wood looks pretty sturdy. We won't be able to kick it in."

"Let's scout the perimeter of the house. If this door goes to a basement like I think it might, there may be a ground-level window or outside storm entrance."

Alec nodded and headed back out the way they came in. In the yard, they took turns covering each other and carefully scanning the terrain in case the escaped convict Jake mentioned was hiding on the property, waiting to ambush them. Almost immediately they spotted the trail of disturbed snow from the carport to the back of the property.

"The footprints are different sizes, different shoe treads," Daniel said.

"Yeah, I see at least three different prints." Alec glanced up at him. "Jake and the convict, but who's the third person?"

Daniel scowled. "Homeowner? The information I found on the house earlier said the property belongs to a family named Harris. So where are the Harrises?"

Alec heaved a sigh. "Oh, God, don't let them be massacred in the basement."

Daniel gritted his back teeth. "Only one way to find out."

As they moved toward the back side of the house, Alec hesitated, his gaze snagging on something new. "Hang on. There are more tracks out there."

Daniel followed Alec as his former partner plodded through the deep snow drifts into the side yard. They stopped to examine the prints in one of the trails of disturbed snow, and Daniel grunted. "I'll be damned. Are those horseshoe prints?"

"Looks like it." Alec moved to another trail. "Same here."

"So someone rode out of here on horseback." Daniel turned three-hundred-and-sixty degrees, scanning the horizon.

"Lafitte." Alec's voice was somber as he addressed Daniel.

Daniel faced his partner, then sent his gaze the direction Alec pointed.

"Those prints lead to that basement window." Alec tramped through the snow, then dropped to his knees beside the open ground-level window. He stayed close to the wall of the house, his gun ready, and glanced inside.

Daniel joined him, crouching on the other side of the window. *Well?* he asked with a look.

"Too dark in there to see anything," Alec said. "Cover me. I'm going in."

Daniel moved to a better position, while Alec crawled headfirst, gun leading into the basement. After a moment, Alec called, "Clear!" then, "Crap. More blood. This isn't good. Lafitte?"

Holstering his gun, Daniel slithered through the window and dropped into the basement.

Alec was crouched next to a pile of bloodstained laundry. "This looks much more recent than the blood in the truck."

As his eyes adjusted to the dim light, Daniel took in the other clues something bad had gone down in the basement. Bullet holes pocked the wall beside the stairs and the door at the head of the steps. Additional crimson-stained clothes littered the area near the foot of the staircase. And more ominous, a large red streak painted the wall at the top of the stairs.

"You said you heard gunfire before you lost contact with Jake?" Alec said, rising to his feet to study the damning evidence that their former teammate had been shot.

Daniel's gut twisted. "Yeah."

Alec huffed a sigh. "As bad as this looks, we have to remember, there's no body. If Cowboy *was* shot, evidence seems to show he survived and got out of here somehow. Probably through that window."

"The escaped con's gone, too. Possibly on horseback." Daniel narrowed a sharp look on Alec. "My guess would be Jake went after him, but he's injured."

Alec jerked a nod. "Then let's get the bird in the air and see if we can find them. He's gonna need backup."

Chapter 16

"**D**arynda!" Jake shouted as soon as he stumbled through the fence at the edge of her yard. Every muscle in his body was stiff from cold and fatigue, and his gunshot wound stung like fire, pain blazing down his arm. "Darynda!"

The front door squeaked open, and the pit bull, Dooley, charged out and bounded through the snow toward Jake. The dog planted his paws on Jake, nearly knocking him over.

"Dooley, come back here!" Darynda shouted from the stoop. When her gaze found Jake, she gasped. "Oh, my God! Jake, what happened to you? Where's Chelsea?"

Jake trudged the remaining steps to the front door, his breath sawing from him. "Need...horse."

"What you need is to sit down and rest." Darynda shoved a shoulder under Jake's good arm and dragged him toward the front door. "Good God, Jake, you can barely stand!"

He shoved away from her and fished in his pocket for the car charger for his cell phone. "Take this. See if it will…fit your phone. Can you crank your engine… long enough to call 9-1-1?"

She took the cord and studied it. "I don't know. It looks close, but…"

Before she finished, he turned and, clinging to the railing, he staggered back down the stairs. Darynda followed, grabbing his arm to stop him.

"Where's Chelsea?"

He hissed in pain when she tugged on his injured shoulder. He clutched his throbbing arm, and her eyes widened in dismay. "You're hurt!"

"I'll live. Have to help Chelsea."

"Jake, what happened? Where's—"

From his pocket, he pulled out the .38 he'd collected from where Brady discarded it, and shoved it at her. "Reload this."

"Jake?"

"Have it ready when I…come back around here." Without waiting for an answer, he plodded toward the barn behind the house where he'd left the other bay. Mr. Noble's third horse stood nibbling on the hay Darynda had provided, and Jake bridled him quickly. He didn't waste time saddling the horse, but led the bay out through the snow to Darynda's porch. He didn't have the energy to climb onto the horse's back without assistance, so he guided the horse next to the front porch steps, climbed the stairs and clambered onto the horse's back from there.

Darynda reappeared at the front door with the gun and a frown. "I couldn't find any more ammunition."

He sighed. "Thanks anyway. See about using that charging cord…to get a call out."

"Jake, you're in no condition to ride or to confront a killer."

"No choice."

"You do have a choice! Please stay here and let me—"

"I have to go." Fisting one hand in the bay's mane to steady himself when a dizzy spell swamped him, he kicked his heels into the horse's ribs. "Chelsea's in trouble."

The bay lurched forward, and with his fading strength, Jake tugged the reins, directing the horse toward the highway.

Chelsea didn't bother looking over her shoulder. She could hear the jangle of reins, the clop of hooves. Brady was behind her. She knew her only hope was to go faster, to reach Mrs. Posey's house and get inside. When she reached the end of Mrs. Posey's driveway, she reined her horse and swung down. She clambered over the snowplow pile at the edge of Mrs. Posey's property and hurried across the untouched snowfall to her neighbor's house.

Mrs. Posey's car wasn't in her carport, nor was there any evidence a car had been driven out since the snowstorm started two days ago. Chelsea shoved down the niggling panic that the woman, her best hope, wasn't home. She reached the empty carport and charged toward the door.

"Mrs. Posey!" Chelsea banged her fist on the closed door. "Mrs. Posey, are you there? Please!"

She noticed the note then, taped above the doorbell. Chelsea ripped it down and read, *Dear Rose—Power*

out. Drove into town to stay with Hillary and the kids.
Call me next week. Frances P.

Chelsea crumpled the note in her fist, her stomach sinking. Cupping her hands around her eyes, she peered through the window in the top half of the door. Across Mrs. Posey's kitchen, Chelsea spotted a wall-mounted telephone. A landline.

She debated her options for, oh…three seconds. Picking up the broom leaning in the corner of the carport, Chelsea smashed the door window with the broomstick and knocked away the loose glass shards. As she pulled her fist back in the sleeve of her coat for protection, she prayed Mrs. Posey had an alarm system that she'd just triggered. Police showing up at the house would be ideal. She poked her arm through the broken glass and twisted the latch, unlocking the door, then shouldering it open.

At the road, she could see Brady nearing the spot where she'd abandoned her horse. She slammed the door closed and slid a chair over from the table, jamming it under the knob. Skittering across the broken glass, she rushed to the phone and snatched up the receiver.

And was greeted by a dial tone.

She nearly wept with relief as she punched in 9-1-1.

"What's your emergency?" an operator asked.

"Brady is here! The convict that escaped…he took me hostage, and he's been living at my parents' house during the storm."

"Ma'am, I need you to calm down and take a breath. What's your name and address?"

She swallowed her impatience and answered, "Chelsea Harris," then gave the woman her parents' address.

"But I'm not there anymore. I'm at Frances Posey's, and Brady's right behind me."

"What's the address of your location?"

"I—I don't know. Can't you trace the call?"

"Can you hold, please?"

"No! Listen to me! Brady is here *now!* I need the police. And Jake's been shot. He needs an ambulan—"

The door crashed open, and Chelsea screamed.

The chair she'd propped under the knob clattered uselessly to the floor, and Brady marched into the kitchen.

"He's here! He's here!" she shouted at the operator as terror climbed her throat. "Send help!"

Brady yanked the phone from her hand, then back-handed her hard enough to knock her to the floor. Pain streaked through her jaw, then jolted up her spine when she hit the floor, butt first.

Chelsea crab-crawled away from Brady as he ripped the phone cord from the base and yanked a large knife from the butcher block on the counter.

Her coat pocket thunked against the floor as she scurried into the living room, away from the killer. *The gun!* A fresh spurt of adrenaline spiraled through her. *Two shots left,* Jake had told her. *Make 'em count.*

The hardwood floor vibrated as Brady stomped in from the kitchen, glowering at her. "You shouldn't have done that, girlie."

After days of been terrorized by Brady, his condescending attitude grated on Chelsea's last nerve. "*You* shouldn't have done a lot of things. Kidnapping me, shooting Jake, killing Mr. Noble! Where should I begin?"

"Shut up!" Brady barked, stepping closer and shoving the knife toward her. "It's because of stupid women like you that I ever went to prison! My bitch ex ratted me out to the cops, and my slut of a mother wouldn't back up my alibi." His eyes narrowed menacingly. "I will slice you to bits before I go back in the joint."

Her hand shook as she dragged the gun from her pocket and aimed it at him. "Don't come any closer. I *will* shoot you, if only to pay you back for hurting Jake!"

Brady hesitated, eyeing the weapon in her hands, and Chelsea realized he hadn't produced his own gun. Had he lost it? Her heart thumped a wild cadence, and she inhaled deeply, trying to calm herself, trying to steady her hands enough to aim.

"Go ahead, girlie." Brady took another step, and the floorboards creaked. "I'd rather die here than go back behind bars like some caged animal."

"You are an animal," she muttered through clenched teeth.

"But if you shoot," he taunted, taking another step, "you better hope you kill me, 'cause I hear getting cut up is a bad way to die."

Acid rolled through her gut. She lined up the sights on the barrel.

A gloating smile spread over Brady's face, and he took another step. "I knew you didn't have the—"

Chelsea held her breath…and squeezed the trigger.

"Down there!" Daniel pointed through the windscreen of the helo to the lone horse and rider galloping down the plowed highway. "I'd know that black cowboy hat anywhere."

"Is it just me or is he slumped over?" Alec asked, bringing the helicopter lower and in line with the horse and rider.

"You're right." Daniel replied, nodding. "So where's the convict?"

"Good question. See a place to set down?"

Below them, Jake craned his head back to look up at them, then waved one arm, directing them down the road, pointing ahead.

"Seems he has a destination in mind. Follow the highway and keep your eyes peeled for trouble."

Alec jerked a nod. "Meantime, put a call in to get an ambulance and police support out here."

Daniel lifted the helicopter's radio mic. "Roger that."

The recoil of the gun blast reverberated up Chelsea's arms and kicked the barrel toward the ceiling. Her shot flew wide, and the bullet lodged in the wall across the room. For a breathless second, neither she nor Brady moved. He seemed to be assessing, deciding if he'd been hit.

Immediately Chelsea regrouped. *One shot left.* She had to try again, had to account for the recoil of the powerful weapon. She tightened her grip, aimed for center mass.

But Brady lunged, growling like a rabid dog. He knocked her arm aside and tackled her with a breath-stealing impact.

Stunned by the move, Chelsea gasped for air, instinctively fighting to keep the gun out of his reach. He grabbed her wrist and smacked her arm to the floor. The blow jarred the gun from her hand and sent it skittering across the hardwood planks. Chelsea's heart sank, and she stretched her arm, groping for the weapon.

Metal flashed as he raised the knife.

When he reared back for leverage, she twisted

hard to the left. The blade swooshed past her ear and thunked as it stabbed the floor. Using the surge of adrenaline that shot through her to fuel her strike, she swung her elbow backward, jabbing Brady in the gut. She followed with an instant swipe at his face, cracking her balled fist into his jaw.

He rocked back, away from her blows, and clutched his cheek. Angling a malevolent glare at her, he snarled, "You'll pay for that, girlie."

Mentally she scrambled for her best defense. Did she try to get the gun? Did she try to disarm him? Did she fight him? Try to injure him so she could wiggle free?

Straddling her hips, he gripped the knife between his hands and lifted his arms over his head. Her gaze zeroed in on the blade, her most immediate threat. *Get it away from him....*

Chelsea tensed, preparing to evade his next strike, deciding how to liberate the blade from his grip.

But Brady froze, his gaze snapping toward a window, his expression confused.

Then she heard it. The *whoop, whoop, whoop* of an approaching helicopter. Someone was outside! Flying low, by the sound of it.

Chelsea changed strategies. She channeled her energy on wrenching free, whatever it took. She had to get outside, had to flag down the helicopter.

She bucked her hips up, hard, and planted her hands in Brady's chest as he reeled. While he groped for balance, she rolled to her belly. Using her toes, she gained purchase on the hardwood floor and scrambled to her hands and knees. Brady grabbed her hair and yanked. Her head snapped backward, and a thousand pinpricks of pain burned her scalp, making her eyes water. But she fought back with every ounce of strength. She had to get away, get outside, flag the chopper...

On her knees, she turned toward Brady, clawing at his eyes, blocking his arm when he swiped at her with the knife. The blade hit its mark once or twice, and she felt the sting of the cut to her skin. Knowing she needed a bold and decisive move to get free of his grip and his superior strength, Chelsea dropped to her bottom, sacrificing altitude, giving Brady the advantage he needed for a fatal strike....

But also giving her the angle she needed to bring her knees to her chest and kick out with all the power of her barrel racer's thighs. Her feet hit Brady square in the chest and sent him sprawling backward, his head thumping against the hard floor.

Chelsea didn't waste a second. She sprang to her feet and sprinted toward the door. Brady swiped at her foot as she darted past him, making her stumble, but she didn't stop. Throwing open the carport door, she ran out into the snow, searching the sky for the helicopter. When she spotted it, swooping low over the highway, she waved her arms, screaming, "Over here! Help me!"

With her attention focused on the helicopter, she didn't see Brady closing in behind her until he'd bowled her over, knocking her face-first into the snow. He pinned her down, holding her head in the drift. Snow filled her nose and mouth when she tried to draw air.

"Not so fast, girlie. If I'm going down, you're going with me."

The hard, cold kiss of steel jammed against her skull.

Stark panic sluiced through her. He'd found the gun. With one shot left.

But at point-blank range, one was all he needed.

* * *

Jake watched the helicopter swoop over the small house and circle around. Having backup boosted his confidence that Brady would be taken down or brought in within minutes, but he hadn't seen Chelsea yet, and that fact ate at him.

The hike to Darynda's had worn him out far more than he'd expected it would. Just staying atop the horse as he galloped down the snowplowed highway took most of his remaining strength. Every pounding step the horse ran jarred his shoulder and sent paroxysms of pain rolling through him. He stayed conscious through sheer willpower. He couldn't, *wouldn't* surrender to the pain and exhaustion until he was certain Chelsea was safe.

Her horse and the bay Brady had stolen were wandering aimlessly on the road near Mrs. Posey's house. They spooked and ran a bit when the helo flew over, but thanks to the snow mounded on either side of the highway, the horses were corralled to some extent on the highway.

The helo flew past the house, banked left and came around.

As his horse ran nearer the house, Jake searched the grounds. Where was—

Chelsea ran out from the carport, her head tipped skyward as she waved to the helicopter. The pressure in Jake's chest eased, knowing she was safe…only to wrench tight again when Brady stumbled out behind her, a gun in his hand.

Brady tackled Chelsea, and Jake had seen all he needed. Adrenaline spiked in his blood, and he kicked his horse to run faster. He charged toward Mrs. Posey's yard, compelling his mount to jump the snow piled at the edge of the road. They landed awkwardly, but his horse staggered forward through the snow, across the yard, toward Chelsea.

Gripping the horse's mane, Jake swung his leg over the animal. Sighted his target.

As the horse raced past the bodies lying in the snow, Jake leaped and landed on Brady's back. As Jake used his momentum to roll, pulling Brady with him, the gun fired. The concussion of the blast thundered in Jake's chest, and the noise rang in his ears. The impact of the jump jolted him to his bones. White-hot pain ripped from his shoulder through his body. But he clung to Brady, dragging him away from Chelsea.

"Sonofabitch!" With a sharp twist, Brady wrenched free of his grip and staggered to his feet.

Jake rolled to his back, mustering his strength for the battle ahead.

Swinging his hand up, Brady aimed the gun at Jake's chest.

"Jake!" Chelsea screamed.

Brady pulled the trigger, and the pistol clicked, its magazine empty.

Fury and frustration darkened Brady's face, and he flung the weapon away.

"Chelsea?" Jake called, his gaze seeking her as a deafening rumble approached.

"I'm okay!"

The helicopter buzzed past, kicking up a swirl of stinging snow as it settled on the lawn a few dozen feet away.

Brady jerked his gaze from the helo to the road, then spotted Jake's horse trotting restlessly at the far side of the lawn near a fence. He took off, his pace a slow-motion run through the deep snow.

Grunting in pain, Jake shoved to his feet, staggering after him.

"I got this," a familiar voice called as a tall, dark-haired man sprinted past him. *Alec Kincaid.*

Jake altered his course, veering toward Chelsea. She clambered to her feet and rushed toward him.

"Are you all right?" Her hands were everywhere—his face, his chest, his hair, his arms—as she assured herself he was in one piece.

Exhaustion swept through him, and he sank to his knees, pulling her down with him and into a firm hug. "I'll…live," he panted. "Are you…hurt?"

He pushed her to arm's length, drinking in the sight of her, visually assessing her condition. "Your arm's bleeding."

"He cut me, but it's not deep." She smiled through her tears. "I'll live, too, thanks to you."

Daniel LeCroix reached them and paused long enough to drop a first aid bag in the snow beside Jake. "Are we good here?"

Jake glanced across the yard in time to see Alec overtake Brady and drag him down. "Go on. Help Alec subdue that SOB. Don't let…that bastard get away again."

Daniel jerked a nod and headed across the lawn to add his muscle to Alec's.

And the spots at the edges of Jake's vision closed in, blanking his vision as he collapsed in the snow.

"Jake!" Chelsea's heart lurched as Jake's eyes rolled back, and he blacked out. She huddled over him and patted his cheek, trying to rouse him. "No, Jake! Don't do this. Don't you die! You promised!"

The dark-haired man who'd dropped the first aid kit beside her hurried back to them. "What happened?"

"He passed out!" Chelsea felt Jake's throat for a pulse. "He was shot earlier and lost a lot of blood. He needs a hospital. Fast!"

The man, whose swarthy good looks were on par with Jake's golden perfection, nudged her aside. "Let me have a look."

"Are you Daniel?" she asked as she scooted aside, giving him room to check Jake's pupils and pulse for himself.

He lifted a startled look before opening the first aid kit and rifling through it. "I am, and that's Alec Kincaid. We're friends of Jake."

"Former black ops teammates."

Another startled look. "And you are?"

"Chelsea Harris."

"Harris. That's your house down the road. Where Jake's truck and the blood are." A statement. Not a question. She didn't bother to ask how he knew. Jake was her priority at the moment.

"Will he be all right?" she asked as Daniel opened Jake's coat to examine the gunshot wound. "Can you take him to the hospital in the helicopter? He needs blood. Soon."

Maybe blood she drew... The stray thought hit her like a fist, stealing her breath.

Don't sell yourself short, Chelsea. What you do is important, too, she heard Jake saying their first night together. Her heart stuttered as something inside her shifted.

"Did you do this?" Daniel asked, pointing to the crude stitches on Jake's shoulder.

She nodded stiffly.

Daniel's eyebrows lifted. "Good work." His gaze narrowed on hers, his expression darkening. "I don't want to lose him either. We'll take good care of him."

The wail of sirens filtered through the frozen air, and Chelsea glanced to the road as a sheriff's department cruiser skidded to a stop with an ambulance close behind.

"Looks like the cavalry's here," Chelsea said, her voice shaking with fatigue and emotion. As she watched in a daze, the lights on the ambulance and sheriff's cruiser strobing red and blue on the snow, Daniel waved an EMT to help with Jake, and two sheriff's deputies snapped handcuffs on Brady and dragged him up from the ground where Alec had pinned him. She stared numbly as a backboard was carried across the snow from the ambulance and Jake was strapped onto it. She answered questions like an automaton, first for the EMT who bandaged the cut Brady had inflicted—no, she wasn't hurt anywhere else—then for the policeman—Brady had carjacked her at gunpoint two days ago. Jake had stopped to help....

Movement in her peripheral vision called her attention to Brady as he was hauled toward the waiting cruiser. Brady narrowed a malevolent glare on Chelsea and curled his lip. "You better be looking over your shoulder every day. I'll be comin' for you, girlie. This ain't over."

Chelsea shuddered. She knew she'd be seeing Brady's dark eyes in her sleep for months to come.

"That's enough!" the sheriff's deputy beside Brady barked, shoving his head down and guiding the convict into the backseat.

"Chelsea?" Daniel's voice snapped her from her trance, and she turned. "He's conscious."

Holding her breath, she hurried to the side of the backboard and grabbed Jake's fingers as the EMTs lifted him. "Jake, I'm here."

His eyes found her, and his cheek twitched with a grin. "Hey, brave lady."

"Hey, yourself. You gave me a scare, passing out like that. Hang on, okay?" She shifted her attention to the nearest EMT as they started through the snow, carrying Jake away. "Where are you taking him? Which hospital?"

"Depends on the roads."

"Put him in the helicopter," Daniel said. "We'll fly him. Does the county hospital have a helo pad?"

"County doesn't. Nearest one would be—"

"Amarillo," Jake interrupted. "Take me to Amarillo. I need to see my dad."

While Daniel and the EMTs had a brief discussion about whether Amarillo by helicopter or the county hospital by ambulance would be faster, Chelsea bent to press a kiss on Jake's cheek. "I'll meet you at the hospital. Okay?"

"No." He grimaced in pain before adding, "The cops will need you to…answer questions. Take them to Mr. Noble."

She nodded. "All right. But then I'll come. I'll drive your truck up to you."

He frowned. "Can't. It's evidence."

"Amarillo, then," Daniel said as he ended his conversation with the EMTs and signaled Alec, who was talking to a deputy. "Let's roll!"

Before she could say any more to him, Jake was carried toward the helicopter. She trudged through the deep snow, feeling unsettled, trying to keep up with the EMTs, wanting more time to tell Jake what was in her heart.

She hovered close by as he was loaded in the helicopter, needing just a moment with him. *I love you* only took seconds.

But as Alec jumped in the cockpit and an EMT climbed in next to Jake for the ride to Amarillo, Jake's gaze found hers. "Wait," she read on his lips over the whir of the turbines.

She crowded in close to his side and leaned close to hear and be heard. "Jake, I—"

"Don't come, Chels."

She blinked, not sure she could trust her ears. "What?"

"I'll be all right. And we…" He paused and took a breath, his expression grave. "I hate long goodbyes."

"Is that what this is? Goodbye?" Her throat grew tight with tears.

"I'm sorry. But my work…" He looked away for a moment before finishing. "I can't give you what you need."

A fist of despair squeezed her chest, even though she'd known deep in her heart this was how they'd been destined to end. He could sugarcoat it to spare her feelings, but she recognized the truth. She wasn't the sort of woman a man like Jake fell in love with, gave up his career for.

"No, you're right." She nodded and smiled bravely. But she hated the idea of Jake spending his life alone because of the guilt he felt over his mother's death, so she added, "But while I'm not the one for you, don't deny yourself the chance to love and be loved when the right woman comes along. If you let guilt over your mother's death keep you from sharing your heart with some lucky girl, it only means the evil that won that day is still winning."

Jake's eyes widened, and his cheeks grew a shade paler.

Drawing a breath for courage, she stepped back and gave a wave to the pilot.

"Chels…" he called over the ruckus, but she didn't want to hear his rebuttal. She was having a hard enough time fighting back the tears, and she refused to cry in front of him, let him see how much his leaving hurt.

Daniel closed the side door and climbed in the cockpit with a wave. Kicking up snow as the rotors whirled, the helicopter lifted off…and was gone.

Chapter 17

Jake's sister met the helicopter on the roof of the Amarillo hospital and let him know his father was still alive, improving slightly, but still in critical condition. With that knowledge, Jake was taken for tests and treatment before he was allowed to visit his dad from a wheelchair.

Although he was relieved to be with his father and hear that the doctors were hopeful his dad might pull through, a pall hung over him. The pain in Chelsea's eyes as he'd said goodbye haunted him, and her parting words replayed in his head. *I'm not the right one for you.*

Was that really how she felt? The emotion in her eyes as they'd made love had seemed real, but...

Hell, the demands of his job made it a moot point.

As he went through his own recovery and held vigil at his father's bedside in the days that followed, he missed her wry humor, her peachy-floral scent, her soul-stirring smiles. Telling himself he'd done what was best for her didn't ease his guilt or the empty ache in his chest. He'd bought a replacement cell phone and had been tempted many times to call her just to hear her voice. But what would he say?

He texted her once, just to let her know he was healing and that his dad was holding his own, but she never replied.

A week later, though, while sitting in his father's hospital room playing cards with Michelle, his cell phone buzzed. He'd checked the incoming text, and his heart rose in his throat. *Chelsea.*

Sheriff's office called 2day. Ur truck is ready @ impound. Chels

Jake frowned. The terse message lacked the warmth and vibrancy he'd come to associate with Chelsea. Was her cold, all-business message a reflection of her hurt, of where they now stood?

"Who was that?" Michelle asked.

"Chelsea. The cops have released my truck." Jake had told his dad and Michelle about what had happened to delay him, beyond the snowstorm, including the amazing woman he'd met.

"Are you going to see her again?" Michelle asked now.

He grunted. Making love to Chelsea in her parents' basement had given him fodder for restless nights of longing in the months to come, but he knew that wasn't what Michelle meant. "No," he said. "A long-distance relationship would be too difficult and, because of my job, would ultimately go nowhere. She deserves better."

He was about to set his phone aside when it buzzed again.

P.S. I'm not pregnant.

He stared at the message, knowing he should feel relief, but instead feeling...disappointed...and not knowing what to do with his reaction.

"What wrong, Jake? Bad news?"

He should be glad Chelsea wouldn't have to deal with an unplanned pregnancy, shouldn't he? So why—

"Jake?" Michelle said, louder.

"No, it's...good news actually." He paused, reading the words again, then hedging, "Kinda, I guess."

But his heart was unconvinced.

"What the— She's not *pregnant?*"

He shot his sister a disgruntled look as he hid the screen against his chest. "Hey! A little privacy?" He frowned across the small table at Michelle, confused. "Wait. How did you know?"

"Same way she's been reading your cards all evening," said their father, his voice thin. "The refection in the window behind you."

Jake turned his head to the night-darkened glass behind him, then stood to lower the blinds in a huff. "Michelle, you brat..."

"This baby Chelsea's not having... Yours?" his father asked, a note of disapproval in his tone. "Yet you had no plan to see her again?"

"If there'd been a baby, things would be different." Was that the root of his disappointment? Had he been looking for an excuse to see Chelsea again, some way to hold on to what they'd shared for a few sweet days?

He shook his head and divided a scowl between his father and sister. "But there's not, so drop it."

"Geez, Jake, I never knew you were the love-'em-and-leave-'em sort," Michelle said. "I'm disappointed in you."

He sighed and shot his sister a scowl. "And I never knew you cheated at cards." He tossed his phone on the table. "My job doesn't leave room for a relationship."

"So...the job means more to you than Chelsea does?" his father asked.

"I..." Jake frowned, not wanting to answer the question or examine his feelings too closely. "I don't know that I'd say that. But...the work I do is important. It's a critical part of this country's security, and I'm good at what I do. I'm making a difference. How can I walk away from that?"

"Your work *is* important, son. And I'm proud of what you're doing, but..." His father's brow furrowed. "You can fight terrorists till the end of the age, and it still won't bring your mother back."

Jake sat back in his chair, stunned by his father's comment. "I know that."

"Do you?" His father stacked his hands on his chest and took a wheezing breath. "I've watched you struggle with your mom's death for the last twelve years. I understand what you're doing and why you're doing it, but I can't see where it's bringing you any closure."

Jake stared at his father silently for several stunned seconds, gathering his thoughts. "Maybe...closure isn't my end goal. Maybe there is no end goal. Maybe I just want to live the kind of life she'd have been proud of. Maybe I want to be on the front lines fighting the kind of viciousness that took her from us, the malignance that is too prevalent in the world."

"And you have," his father said.

"Is this some kind of survivor's guilt thing?" Michelle asked.

"No. My job gives my life purpose and meaning. Direction."

"Are you happy?" his father asked.

Jake blinked. "Happy? Dad, I'm a counterterrorist agent, not a clown. My work is dark and stressful most days. But I have a feeling of accomplishment when we finish a mission. I have a pretty good life."

"But are you happy?" His father's eyes narrowed on him. "I may not have a lot of time left on this earth—"

"Dad!" Michelle protested. "Don't say that!"

Their father raised a hand to silence her. "The one thing your mother and I wanted for you two was for you to be happy. That's why I didn't stop you when you left the ranch. If ranching's not for you, I don't want you spending your life doing something you don't love."

"It's not that I didn't enjoy ranching, Dad. I just felt a need to do something…" He fumbled for the right word.

"Redemptive?" his father supplied.

Jake opened his mouth to refute his father's assertion but couldn't. He had been hoping to find some absolution along with restoring some order to the chaos of a world where a mother doing mission work could be killed for no reason.

"Chase terrorists if it makes you happy, but if it doesn't, stop trying to right a wrong that can never be changed. Your mother would never want you to give up what makes you truly happy because of what happened to her."

Jake plowed both hands through his hair, reeling from his father's challenge, trying to make it fit with his reality. "But how do I justify putting myself and what I want over a job where I stop the scum of the world from hurting innocent people? Mom wouldn't condone a selfish agenda."

"No, she wouldn't. But foreign countries haven't cornered the market on evil. You got a taste of the local brand of miscreant scum last week and saved a nice young lady in the process."

"I have a commitment to my team..." Jake hedged, but his father had given him a lot to think about. As Chelsea had.

Don't deny yourself the chance to love and be loved.

"It's your choice. Your life," his father said, settling back against his pillow with a tired sigh. "Don't live a life that leaves you with regrets, son. Your mother would have hated that."

"Hi, Mom," Chelsea sang out as she entered her parents' kitchen one day that spring. "How are you feeling?" She stooped to pat Sadie, who rushed over to greet her with a wagging tail and full-body wiggles.

"Depends," her mother replied, pulling a casserole from the oven. "Are you asking in a rhetorical, polite greeting kind of way or are you still playing the worrywart daughter waiting for your poor mother to relapse?"

"Sue me. I care." Chelsea slung her purse down on the counter and cast a furtive glance toward the basement stairs where Jake had been shot. She suppressed a shudder the memory still caused, even though her parents had repaired the house and obliterated any evidence Brady had ever been there.

"I'm fine, sweetheart. You're the one who's losing weight." Her mother stripped off the oven mitts and gave her daughter a considering glance. "Do you feel all right?"

Other than the hollow ache in my soul and feel-ing like my heart's been ripped out, you mean? "The weight loss is intentional. I'm trying to get back in my old clothes by summer."

Her mother waved a dismissive hand. "Buy new things. You deserve a treat after what you went through."

Chelsea shrugged and sat on a stool behind the coun-ter. New clothes wouldn't fill the Jake-shaped hole in her life, so she'd better find a way to move on and stop agonizing over what she'd lost.

Sadie nuzzled her leg, looking for more attention, and she gave the dog another ear scratch.

"Speaking of 'what I went through—'" She drew quotation marks in the air. Her mother found it hard to name the violence Chelsea suffered, much the way Harry Potter's friends refused to speak Voldemort's name. "I got a letter today from Jodi Israel, an assis-tant in the DA's office. I'm supposed to go in to her of-fice Monday for a deposition. I'll be the star witness in the state's prosecution of Brady later this summer."

Her mother frowned and stepped close to put her arms around Chelsea. "I know why you have to tes-tify, but I hate that you'll have to relive all the horror in order for the state to convict that man."

"The trial's a formality. Due process and all that. I'll do whatever I have to if it'll keep Brady behind bars." Chelsea's cell phone rang, and she wiggled free of her mom's embrace to dig the phone out of her purse.

The name on the caller ID stopped her cold.

Jake Connelly.

"Um, I'm gonna take this in the other room," she told her mother as she hurried toward her old bedroom for privacy. As she hustled down the hall, she answered the call. "Hello?"

"Hey, Chelsea. It's Jake. I, um… How are you?"

She shook from head to toe, both elated to hear from him and terrified what it could mean. "I'm, uh…" *Missing you like crazy. Heartbroken. Can't sleep at night because of nightmares about Brady killing you.* "I'm okay."

Nela was curled up, asleep on her old bed, and she sat down beside the cat, taking a deep breath for composure. "And you?"

"I'm good. Busy. The bad guys never take a holiday, so neither do we."

"Hmm. Damn inconsiderate of them, I say."

He chuckled, then she heard him sigh. "God, I miss that."

"What? Vacations?" She stroked Nela's soft fur, and the feline stretched out, offering her belly for a rub.

"I miss your dry humor."

Her hand stilled on Nela's tummy. He missed something about her? That he even thought about her was more than she'd hoped. She, on the other hand, missed everything about Jake. Right down to his chipped incisor. "Oh."

Jake cleared his throat. "Anyway, I called because I got a letter today from the state district attorney's office."

"Yeah, me, too." Her spirits lifted. "Does that mean you'll be coming back to Texas to give your deposition?"

"Well, probably not. She's arranged for me to be deposed here via Skype or videotape because of the distance, the nature of my job and all."

Chelsea's heart sank. "Oh."

"I'll probably submit my testimony for the case that way when it goes to court, as well."

"Well, that's…certainly a lot easier for you." She curled her fingers in Nela's thick fur, swallowing against the emotion that tried to clog her throat.

"This Jodi Israel who caught the case is pushing for me to come back for the trial. Live testimony goes over better with the jury."

Chelsea mentally clamped down on the hope that fluttered in her chest. *Don't set yourself up for disappointment.*

"So…why did you call?" She didn't mean to sound so cool and dismissive, but she didn't want Jake to know how much she missed him. It wasn't his fault she'd fallen so hard for someone with a career that put him completely out of reach. She wouldn't lay a guilt trip on him because she'd let herself fall in love with the wrong man.

"I was thinking about you and just wanted to see how you were," Jake said. "What happened to you was…traumatic. Are you coping okay?"

His concern for her touched her, made the raw ache inside her oddly better and more painful at the same time. "I have bad dreams sometimes, but—" *Missing you is the hardest.* "But I'm handling it all okay. It helps knowing Brady's in custody and can't hurt anyone anymore. How's your shoulder?"

"Better every day. I'm back in the field, flying missions. Before I left Texas, I had physical therapy to regain my range of motion, and I have exercises I still do to stay loose." His tone warmed. "I do have an interesting-looking scar. But I kinda like it. It reminds me of a special lady in Texas and her…unorthodox way to manage pain."

Chelsea grunted, and her cheeks flushed. "Unorthodox. Is that what you'd call it?"

She closed her eyes, holding back tears. She replayed their lovemaking, the way Jake felt beneath her, inside her, every night. She longed to feel his body curled around hers, keeping her warm the way he had at Mr. Noble's.

"No, I'd call it…hot…." The low, sexy rumble in his tone curled Chelsea's toes, and heat flashed through her. "Seductive…awesome… Chelsea, there aren't enough words. You left your mark on me. In more ways than one."

Just not the way that mattered. He didn't love her.

"Jake, I—" A loud buzzing sounded on his end of the connection, and he cursed under his breath.

"Sorry, I gotta go. Duty calls."

"Right. Of course." She infused her tone with a cheer she didn't feel. "Be careful. Thanks again for everything you did for me."

He was silent for a couple of seconds, though the buzzing continued, telling her the connection hadn't been broken. "Chels, I—" He fell silent again, then, "Look, I'm not able to talk very often, but you can email me if you ever need anything. I promise to answer as soon as I can."

He gave her his email address, and she wrote it down, knowing she'd not likely use it. What was the point of dragging out her one-sided crush on him? Better to move on. Put him behind her with the rest of the heartbreaking events from January.

"Got it," she said.

"Okay. So…bye."

And he was gone.

Chelsea looked at the address she'd written, her

heart stinging, then ripped the sheet off the pad, crumpled it and tossed it in her wastebasket.

Jake hung up with Chelsea and hurried out to the tarmac where his team had assembled on a helo, ready to deploy to the next hot spot, the next mission, the next undetermined stretch of weeks. Going black, going undercover, being completely out of touch with his family. And Chelsea. More than ever before, the distance and disconnect necessary for black ops work chafed something deep inside him.

Hearing Chelsea's voice again had revived the stir of emotions he couldn't ignore, no matter how hard he tried to untangle his heart and focus on his job. Being with Chelsea, even for so few days, had given him a glimpse of what he was missing. Roots. An intimate connection with someone special. Love and compassion. He saw so much darkness and depravity on the job, but Chelsea had been a breath of fresh air after too many months smelling the stink of humanity's cesspool.

Spending time with his father at the hospital had given him a chance to reflect on the choices he'd made, both in the past and for his future. As much as he wanted to be with his black ops team, doing the work he'd trained for, sacrificed for, he wanted more from life.

He climbed in the pilot's seat of the helicopter, the last of the team to arrive, and glanced across the cockpit to his copilot, Bruster.

Bruster sent him an impatient look. "Glad you could join us."

Jake shoved his cowboy hat in place, as he did before

every mission, flipped a few switches and glanced over his shoulder to the team leader. "All systems go, sir."

"Take her up," the team leader replied.

Jake lifted off smoothly and headed toward their next mission. As they neared their destination, enemy fighters on the ground opened fire on them, shooting machine guns and launching small rockets at the helo. Jake tensed, dodging the small arms and praying a stray bullet didn't reach the fuel tank. An ominous clang told him a round had hit them and crippled the turbine.

"We're hit! Prepare for emergency landing, boys and girls!" he shouted over the blast of his team's returned gunfire.

An image of Chelsea flashed in his mind along with a clarity he'd never had before. He didn't want to die. He wanted a future. With Chelsea.

If he survived this mission, he prayed he could convince her to trust him with her heart.

Chapter 18

October

Brady drew an *X* over the box for that day on his cal-
endar and ground his back teeth together. Every day
behind bars was agony. Tonight, one way or another,
would be his last day in this hellhole.

"Would you sit your ass down? You're bugging the
hell outta me." Brady glared at his cell mate as the other
man paced their tiny cage.

"Can't help it. I'm edgy. Somethin' don't feel right.
There's gonna be a fight."

"You don't know nothing. Sit down." Brady stacked
his hands behind his head and stared up at the ceiling.
"I go to court tomorrow, and I got planning to do."

"What kind of planning?"

Brady sent his cell mate a flat look. "You'll see.
Rather, you'll hear about it—" he curled his mouth

in a gloating grin "—when I don't come back tomorrow night."

"You're gonna make a break for it again? How the hell you think you're gonna do that?" His cell mate folded his beefy arms over his chest and stared at him.

Brady didn't answer, but he conjured a picture of himself sitting on a beach in Mexico, free as a bird. Another image came to him. Chelsea Harris. The bitch was the reason he was back in custody, starting with her crappy car running out of gas. She owed him.

Brady grinned to himself. He'd need a human shield to get out of the courtroom alive tomorrow. Chelsea Harris would fit that part real fine. Tomorrow was payback time.

Chelsea climbed the steps of the old courthouse and smoothed her sundress down when it ruffled in a warm autumn breeze. She'd taken extra care when choosing her clothes and fixing her hair and makeup this morning on the off chance that Jake showed up to testify. Chances were he wouldn't be at court today. But if he did come in person, would her new appearance make a difference to him?

She clenched her hands in fists and castigated herself for harboring that thin hope. She'd lost weight and gotten back in shape for herself, for her health. Whether Jake noticed or approved of her new look shouldn't matter. Didn't matter.

She huffed her frustration. Who was she fooling? As she'd prepared herself mentally for today, she'd been more nervous about the possibility of seeing Jake again than she had been over the certainty of facing Brady across the courtroom. Because no matter how she tried to convince herself otherwise or talk herself out of it, the simple truth was, she'd fallen hard for Jake last winter. Over the months since he'd been loaded into the helicopter and left her standing in the snowy field, that fact hadn't changed.

She sighed. *Pitiful.*

Snap out of it! said a voice in her head that sounded a lot like Cher, à la *Moonstruck.*

The call last spring had been the last she heard from him, a clear indication that she was clinging to a fantasy, hoping that someday he'd see her in a new light, that he'd deem her worthy of huge changes in his life. Even if he'd cared about her a little bit, he'd obviously weighed the choice between her and his career and she'd lost. The guilty mind-set over his mother's death was hardwired in his brain and had shaped his life the past twelve years. How did she compete with that? And did she want him to forsake his career for her? His heroism and courage were a large part of what made him the man she loved.

Disgusted with her one-track, pipe-dream train of thought, she pulled open the courthouse door. She had to find a way to move on, as Jake clearly had. With a shaky hand, Chelsea removed her sunglasses, surveying the line of people waiting to go through the security check. Several of the men wore cowboy hats, and her stomach performed a forward roll as she scanned each one. Just in case.

No Jake.

Moving to the shortest security line, she set her purse on the counter to be searched, then showed the security guard her subpoena. "Do you know where I'm to report?"

He directed her to the stairs that led to a waiting area outside the courtroom on the third floor. After thanking him, she made her way up the steps, then paused before leaving the stairwell.

She pressed a hand to her newly flat stomach as she drew a fortifying breath. Time to collect herself and remember the directions ADA Israel had given her last week. God, she'd be glad when this was over. Brady had stolen enough of her life.

Maybe once the trial was over, she could truly put the events from January and everyone involved behind her, make a fresh start. Squaring her shoulders, she opened the stairwell door and stepped out into the corridor. She cast a searching gaze down the long hall, spotted the double doors to courtroom number three and studied the faces of the people already waiting on the hard chairs lining the wall.

No Jake.

Her heart gave a painful throb as she ambled to an empty chair and took a seat. She shouldn't be surprised he wasn't there. He had an important job. He had lives to save. He was probably deep undercover and couldn't blow his cover to fly back to Texas. He'd told her he couldn't have a relationship. It was time her heart accepted the truth, and she moved on.

Crossing her ankles, she pressed her thumbs together, trying to burn off nervous energy. She needed to get her thoughts together, organize herself in preparation for testimony. While the state had a solid forensic case without her, she gave the jury the all-important human angle. Her job was to personalize the charges against Brady and make the jury identify with the trauma she went through.

She had to keep her recounting of events succinct. Stick to the facts. Displays of emotion were fine and played well with the jury as long as the sentiment was genuine and kept under control. Don't be afraid to look at Brady, but make the jury your focus. Make eye contact. Don't mumble or ramble. If she got nervous and chattered too much, she might give the defense an opening to discredit her testimony. She had to remember to—

"Hello, Chelsea."

Her heart lurched, and she jerked her head up at the sound of the familiar baritone voice. Unable to contain her pleasure at seeing him, she smiled so broadly that her cheeks hurt. "Jake!"

He gave her a cursory appraisal, his own heart-stopping grin in place, before he took the seat next to her. "You haven't changed a bit."

Her smile faltered. "I haven't?"

Her mother had told her she could see the weight loss in her face, her cheekbones being more prominent. She'd hoped even if her dress hid her flatter stomach and slimmer hips, that at least he'd notice the changes in her face.

Instead, he shook his head and gave her a wink. "Nope. Same beautiful smile I remembered. How are you?"

Beautiful smile? Didn't that fall in the same backhanded-compliment category as "But she has a great personality"? Disappointment pierced her bubble of hope and brought her crashing back to reality.

Shoving down the lump that tightened her throat and chafed her edgy mood, she worked to keep her expression upbeat and her voice even. "I'm well. I got a promotion at the blood center. I'm the shift manager now."

He lifted his eyebrows and gave a nod of acknowledgment. "Hey, that's great."

"Thanks." She smiled politely. Her promotion was

good news for her, but it seemed so pitiful compared to raiding military compounds to rescue political prisoners or topple dictators. Her life and Jake's would never be in step, and she had little to offer that could compete with the glamour, excitement and challenge of black ops work. She saw that now, and her heart sank a bit lower.

"How are your parents?" he asked.

"Good. Mom's still in remission, and they're thinking about taking another cruise next spring. This time to Alaska."

He nodded again. "Alaska is beautiful. They'll love it."

God, listen to them with the banal, awkward niceties after the intimacy and connection they'd had in January. Maybe all they'd shared had been an illusion on her part and this stilted formality was all they really had. That thought made her chest ache with a sharp grief.

Conjuring a smile, she sent him a side glance. "How is your dad?"

Jake face fell. "He died last month. Another heart attack."

She placed a hand on his arm, sympathy twisting her heart. "I'm so sorry, Jake."

"Thanks." He cut a quick look toward her, then glanced down the courthouse corridor. "I was out of country. Again. On a six-month assignment." He inhaled deeply and blew it out slowly. "Michelle couldn't reach me, and I missed the funeral." His shoulders sagged, and the guilt and grief etched on his face wrenched inside her. "I only found out about it last week when the mission ended."

Her fingers curled into the sleeve of his dress shirt, and she bit her tongue as empty platitudes sprang to mind. Nothing she could say would make up for what he'd missed. The best she could offer was her unconditional friendship and moral support, and if he didn't already understand he had that, then there was more distance between them than she'd imagined. And the connection she believed they had was a farce.

He rubbed a hand on his chin, as if scrubbing out the bad memory, and gave her a tight grin. "So…what else is new? You adopted Sadie and Nela, right? What happened to the horses? How's Darynda doing?"

His change of topic signaled he was through discussing his father…even if she could still see shadows of unresolved doubts lingering in his eyes.

"Um, my parents took in Nela and Sadie, and they're thriving. Mom spoils them. Mr. Noble's children auctioned the farm, and the buyer bought the horses, too. My mom says they're nice folks, but I haven't met them. Kinda hard going back to that house." Though not for the reasons he might think. Seeing Mr. Noble's house was just too painful a reminder of how she'd fallen for a man who could never love her the same way she loved him. A sharp ache pulsed in her chest, and she cleared her throat as she searched her memory for more updates. "Oh, yeah, Darynda is pregnant again." Chelsea smiled, remembering the last visit she'd had with her parents' neighbor. "Her husband's tour ended, and he came home two months ago. They're over the moon."

Chelsea's heart gave a little twist of envy. Seeing how happy and in love Darynda and her husband were only made her longing for the same bliss a sharper ache.

He gave her a smiled acknowledgment. "That's great. When you see Darynda again, give her my best. Okay?"

"Sure." She fingered her purse strap, mentally

scrambling for the next item of small talk. But idle chatter felt like such a waste of time. Jake was *here*. "I thought you were going to submit your testimony by video."

"I'd thought I might have to. My last mission was complicated and lasted longer than projected. But—"

The squeak of a door opening at the end of the long hall interrupted him and drew both of their gazes. Two uniformed police officers stepped into the corridor, followed by a dour man in an ill-fitting suit. *Brady.*

Instinctively, she reached for Jake, putting a hand on his arm.

Chains shackled Brady's hands to each other, then to a sturdy belt fastened around his waist. The steel links of the chain clattered as Brady shuffled toward Chelsea and Jake.

She tensed, her heart rate picking up as the trio— guards and prisoner—walked toward them. Her grip on Jake's arm tightened, and she sent him an alarmed glance.

Jake sat straighter, raised his chin, set his jaw. His left hand slid over to cover hers where she squeezed his right arm.

As Brady shuffled down the corridor, his gaze zeroed in on them, and his expression darkened. Malevolence blazed in his eyes.

Acid rolled through Chelsea's stomach, but she kept her head high, her stare level and her mouth set. She wouldn't show Brady the anxiety he still stirred inside her. She had the upper hand now. He couldn't hurt her. And she had a role in seeing that justice was served.

Drawing a slow breath through her nose, she thought of Brady's victims—the two policemen, Mr. Noble. Remembering whom she was speaking for bolstered her conviction and her courage.

When Brady reached the area where she and Jake sat, his feet slowed, and he focused his attention, his wrath on Chelsea. "I'm comin' for you, girlie. This ain't over."

Her gut jerked into a knot, and her pulse kicked higher, but she kept her expression even, schooled.

One of the guards jerked on Brady's arm. "Let's go, Brady! Keep moving."

"Sorry about that, ma'am," the other guard said as Brady was hauled away. "The usual prisoner entrance is closed for construction."

Chelsea acknowledged the guard with a halfhearted smile, then dropped her gaze to her lap as she gathered her composure.

"You all right?" Jake asked as Brady was led inside the courtroom.

She suppressed a shiver, not wanting Jake to know how Brady's taunt rattled her. "Sure. He can't hurt me. He's in custody. I'm going put him away for life with my testimony. He's the one who should be scared, right?"

Jake twitched a cheek, flashing a grin that caused a flutter behind her ribs. "That's right."

"So…funny story about the construction the guy mentioned." She kept her tone as even as possible, hoping her commentary would convince Jake she was calmer than she might appear. "The steps in that stairwell were like a quarter of an inch off regulation height for stairs or something…not much at all, but strangely, enough that people kept tripping and falling. A real liability issue apparently, so the city is having to rebuild those steps."

Jake quirked an eyebrow, clearly amused by her nervous chatter. "You don't say?"

"Yeah. It was in the newspaper the other day. Weird, huh? Quarter-inch off."

Shut up, dummy! Stop prattling....

"Hmm," he grunted in response.

She cleared her throat. "You were saying...you thought you'd have to video your testimony bu-u-ut..." She drew out the last word, leaving it open for him to finish the sentence.

"But...I told my team I had to be here. We'd just wrapped up an assignment a couple of weeks ago, and the team has other pilots, so I told the team leader I had official business." He squeezed her knee, and when she glanced up at him, he held her gaze. "Besides, I wanted to see you again."

Chelsea blinked. "Me?"

He laughed. "Why do you sound so surprised? I sure didn't come to see Brady's ugly mug."

Chelsea shifted in her seat to face him, trying to keep her runaway emotions in check. Just because he wanted to see her didn't mean he returned her feelings. He could have come to tell her goodbye. Or tell her he'd met someone else. Or to tell her he was going deep undercover and wouldn't be able to call her for the next two years. Or... "Why?"

Jake's brow furrowed. "Why what?"

She narrowed a cautious look on him, afraid to acknowledge the bubble of hope welling inside her. "Why did you want to see me?"

He snorted and pulled an incredulous face. "You have to ask after all we went through together? We survived some rough stuff, and I thought we'd formed a...friendship."

Pop. The *F* word pierced the bubble of hope. It was the classic relationship kiss-off. *I hope we can stay friends.*

Disappointment left her feeling sick to her stomach, but she bit the inside of her cheek, desperately trying to hide her dejection from him. After all, this was what she'd expected all along.

His gaze penetrated hers, and his smile dimmed. "That word bothers you."

"No, I understand. We can only be friends. Because of your job. Because I'm not—" To her horror, her voice cracked, and her eyes filled with tears.

"Chelsea Harris."

Jake's gaze darted from her to something past her down the corridor.

"Chelsea Harris." It took a moment for the new voice to register. Another couple of seconds to realize what was happening.

Numbly she turned, and her gaze followed the sound of her name to the guard standing just outside the court-room doors. She was being summoned to testify.

Her fingers curled around the armrest of her chair, and she dug deep for the strength to stand despite shaking legs, the willpower to walk away from Jake.

He stood when she did, and he caught her arm.

"We'll finish this later. Okay?" Jake's eyes were hard to read, and her stomach bunched. With an encouraging smile, he stroked her hair and leaned in to kiss her forehead. "Good luck. You've got this."

Chelsea nodded and walked stiffly behind the guard as he led her up the aisle to the front of the courtroom. She heard the hollow thud as the heavy doors to the chamber closed behind her. Heart scampering, she cast a sweeping gaze around the courtroom. The judge, a thin older man with a scraggly comb-over covering his bald pate, gave her a friendly smile.

Assistant District Attorney Jodi Israel wore her hair scraped back in a clasp at the nape of her neck and bobbed her head once, giving Chelsea a confident look clearly meant to reassure and inspire her. Spectators, many of them journalists with notebooks and laptops poised before them, gave her curious glances. The jury box had been filled with the expected mix of young and old, male and female of various races, all watching her intently.

And at the defense table, Brady sat next to a portly man in a gray business suit, with thick black hair and an ingratiating smile. Brady stared flatly, almost appearing apologetic and kind now that he was before the jury. But his hissed warning replayed in Chelsea's head, and she shivered.

This ain't over.

He'd said as much as he'd been dragged away by the police from the snowy field months earlier.

He can't hurt you. You're the one in control now.

Spying the witness stand next to the judge, Chelsea headed for it, but was cut off by the bailiff who blocked her path and shoved a book in front of her. A Bible. "Raise your right hand."

She did.

"Do you swear to tell the truth…" Chelsea watched the bailiff's lips move as he spoke, but her head was spinning in so many directions, the words became a muted drone as adrenaline caused the blood to whoosh past her ears.

I'm comin' for you, girlie.

I wanted to see you again.

"Miss Harris?"

Her attention snapped back to the bailiff. "Oh, I…"

"We need a verbal response for the court record in order to proceed," he prompted.

"The truth, yes. I'll tell the truth."

The bailiff arched a judgmental eyebrow, chastising her for her inattention, then nodded his head toward the chair on the witness stand. "Take a seat."

"Thank you for being here today, Miss Harris." The judge gave her another smile before turning to the prosecutor. "Ms. Israel, you may begin."

"Thank you, Your Honor." Jodi Israel stood and approached Chelsea, smiling kindly, her eyes saying, *Remember what we rehearsed.*

"Hello, Miss Harris. You are here today to testify about the events of January sixteenth of this year and the ensuing days. Correct?"

"Yes." The word croaked from her, and she paused to clear her throat. "Yes, ma'am."

"In your statement to the police you said that the defendant, Mr. Brady, kidnapped you at gunpoint when you stopped to buy gasoline for your car. Is that right?"

"Y—"

"Objection!" Brady rattled the chains that bound his hands. The shackles that had been attached to a belt at his waist were now threaded through a hasp on the defense table. "She wasn't kidnapped. She willingly offered me a ride."

Chelsea's jaw dropped. "What? That's bull!"

The judge pounded his gavel. "Mr. Brady, sit down. You'll get your chance to testify. Mr. Janesky, please advise your client not to interrupt the proceedings, or he'll be held in contempt of court." He faced Chelsea. "Same for you, young lady. You're only to address the court. And only when asked a question by one of the lawyers or myself. Understand?"

Chelsea nodded, her heart pounding. "Yes, sir."

"Good. Please answer Ms. Israel's question."

"Yes," she said, facing the jury and scanning their faces. "Mr. Brady *kidnapped* me from the gas station. At gunpoint."

"Will you please recount for the court in your own words what happened, starting from the moment you arrived at the gas station?" ADA Israel asked.

Chelsea glanced to Brady, whose eyes were riveted on her. A tiny leering grin tugged at the corner of his mouth. A leer she remembered well. He was trying to get in her head, rattle her, shake her composure.

Gritting her back teeth, Chelsea shoved down her agitation and consternation over Brady's interruption. She fisted her hands in her lap and tried to clear her mind of all but the day in question. "I was driving my mom's Cadillac, Ethyl, and I was down to fumes. I knew I wouldn't make it to my parents' house without filling up, so I stopped at my usual place...."

Jake couldn't sit still. His foot tapped the floor, and his fingers drummed on the armrest until his restlessness finally propelled him from the hard chair to pace.

Damn it, he'd fumbled the exchange with Chelsea and managed to hurt her again. She'd clearly been bruised by his lack of communication in the past months—not that he could have done any differently, due to the circumstances surrounding his last assignment—but the new distance between them scared him. Was he too late? Had he lost his chance with Chelsea by putting her off and holding her at arm's length all these months?

*I understand. We can only be friends...Because
I'm not—*

Her unfinished thought and the tears that choked
her up sat heavily on his chest. It pained him to think
she believed any of the distance he'd put between them
had been due to anything she lacked. Had he unknow-
ingly led her to believe she didn't measure up somehow? He thought of the jerk who'd dumped her when
her mother was in the hospital. Todd the Ass had made
her feel less than worthy of complete, unconditional
love. As bright and compassionate and beautiful as
Chelsea was, she still measured herself according to
some unrealistic standard and discounted the unique
and wonderful aspects that made her who she was—
the woman he loved.

Jake dropped back into a chair and groaned. *Of
course* she'd have protective walls around her heart,
guarding her from more heartache. He clenched his
teeth. At his soonest opportunity, he had to assure her
that he loved her and that his love didn't come with
conditions.

Chelsea needed a man who was steadfast and de-
pendable, but he'd disappeared for long, silent months.
She needed a love she could trust not to be snatched
away on a whim, yet he'd put his guilt concerning his
past sins over her needs. She needed someone to cherish her for who she was and make her a priority, but
he'd picked his job over her.

Both Daniel and Alec had retired from active duty
with the black ops team to be with the women and fami-
lies they loved. When he thought of building a life with
Chelsea, he knew he could walk away from the black
ops team without regret. In the past months, something
had changed for him. Maybe he'd come to terms with

his mother's death, or maybe he'd realized his personal mission of redemption came at too high a price.

A stabbing grief shot to his core when he thought of missing his father's funeral.

Don't live a life that leaves you with regrets, son.

Jake swallowed hard. He regretted a lot about the way things had transpired between him and Chelsea. Today, he needed to right those wrongs and beg her for a second chance.

Chapter 19

"I never saw Mr. Noble's body. Jake found him in the stable and told me about him," Chelsea told the jury. She'd had the jury's attention through most of her testimony, but now the gazes of a few members drifted toward the defense table.

"Jake wouldn't let me go out to the stable. He shielded me from the scene so I wouldn't have that image in my head." Chelsea cast a curious glance toward the defense table as more jury members' eyes shifted that direction. "And he wanted to preserve the crime scene."

Brady shifted restlessly in his seat, tugging at the front of his shirt, then leaning over to whisper to his attorney. The chains of his shackles rattled and thumped on the defense table.

Irritation flared inside her. She wouldn't put it past Brady to be intentionally distracting the jury from her testimony. She glanced at the judge, but he seemed not to notice. His head was down as he made notes… or perhaps doodled on a pad at the bench.

"Did you or Mr. Connelly report Mr. Noble's death to the police?" the prosecutor asked.

Flicking a quick glance to the defense table, Chelsea noticed Brady lean forward, his hands pressed to his chest. His behavior agitated her. "Not right away."

The prosecutor frowned her displeasure with Chelsea's inattention. "Why not?"

"Um…" Again, Chelsea glanced toward Brady as his antics grew noisier and more dramatic. "The power was out, and the landline phones in Mr. Noble's house wouldn't work without power to the base unit."

A murmur passed through the courtroom, and Chelsea raised her voice to be heard over it, determined not to let Brady derail her train of thought. "Like I said before, neither of us had our cell phones. We were stranded because of the storm and couldn't get to a working phone for several days."

The ruckus at the defense table grew louder, and with a scowl, Chelsea turned to glare her disgust with the interruptive tactic.

Brady was clutching his chest and gasping for breath. A tingle of alarm shot up her spine. What was happening?

The defense attorney jumped to his feet, shouting, "I'm sorry, Your Honor, but we need to request a recess. My client is ill and—"

Before Janesky could finish, Brady yanked hard on his shackles, giving a loud wheeze, then collapsed dramatically and began writhing in his chair. "Can't… breathe!"

The courtroom gave a collective gasp. Janesky

stooped over to assist Brady, and the closest bailiff edged forward to monitor the situation. As he convulsed, Brady slumped from his chair to the floor, though the shackles kept his arms stretched toward the locked hasp on the table.

Chelsea gritted her teeth, remembering how Brady had duped her into freeing her from the cords Jake had tied him up with. He'd been convincing then…*as he was now.* The hair on her neck stood up. *I'm comin' for you, girlie.*

Around her, the courtroom came alive, a beehive of activity and noise.

The judge banged his gavel, shouting, "Order! Bailiff, please take the jury out of the room."

The uniformed guard closest to the jury directed the group to stand and follow him out, even as several members of the panel craned their heads to see what was happening.

"We need a doctor! I think he's having a heart attack!" Janesky shouted, tugging to loosen the Windsor-knotted tie around Brady's neck. "He needs air!"

Chelsea divided her gaze between Brady and the judge, trying to get the latter man's attention. "Your Honor, he's faking! Don't fall for it!"

"My…hands…" Brady raised his cuffed hands, even as he bucked and wheezed, his face turning red.

"Unlock his hands!" Janesky demanded, grabbing the bailiff's arm. "My God, man, he's dying! Unlock the cuffs so we can lay him flat on the floor!"

"No!" Chelsea leaped up from the witness chair. "No, don't unlock him! It's a trick!"

Her shout was drowned out by the voices from the gallery, the clanking shackles, the defense attorney's cries for help.

The judge pounded his gavel. "Clear the courtroom! Bailiff, what's happening over there?"

Panic swelled in Chelsea's chest. This was wrong. She had to stop them, had to convince them Brady was faking! "Listen to me!" she shouted into the din. "He's done this before! He's faking!"

She clambered down from the witness stand and tried to push through the gathering crowd of people around Brady. She gasped in horror as the bailiff took a ring of keys from his hip and applied one to the locks at Brady's wrists.

"No! Stop!" Chelsea's gut pitched. This couldn't be happening!

With his hands free, Brady clutched at his throat for a moment, still sucking in raspy-sounding breaths. But an instant later, he snatched the ink pen from his lawyer's breast pocket and thrust it into the bailiff's neck. In the split second of shock, as the guard grabbed for his punctured throat, Brady seized the officer's sidearm.

As if in slow motion, although really a matter of seconds, Brady swung the gun in an arc that smashed his lawyer's face, and fired a shot in the bailiff's chest that knocked the guard onto his back.

Ice flooded Chelsea's veins. *I'm comin' for you, girlie.*

Sounds of a commotion drifted from behind the closed courtroom doors, dragging Jake out of his self-recriminations and regrets. He exchanged a curious look with another witness waiting to testify and rubbed his hands on the legs of his pants. Something was wrong. A courtroom should be quiet.

He slid to the edge of his chair, debating what to do…until a gunshot echoed from the courtroom.

Chelsea!

Jake bolted from his chair. He yanked open the heavy double doors only to be met by a tide of humanity fleeing the scene of the shooting. "Chelsea!"

Her breath suspended in her lungs, Chelsea backpedaled away from Brady. Screams filled the courtroom, and chaos ensued as people ran for exits or dived under tables. Climbing to his knees, Brady swung the gun left, then right, firing at anyone who came near him. The people who'd gathered close to help Brady—defense team clerks, reporters and even Janesky, whose nose and throat dripped blood—all scrambled away, seeking protection from the gunfire.

Trembling, Chelsea crouched behind the court reporter's desk with the woman who'd been transcribing the proceedings.

"Jake…" she whispered.

She glanced toward the double doors at the back of the courtroom where people fled en masse. Her heart was torn, both wanting Jake to come help her and praying he'd stayed safe outside the courtroom. Shifting to her knees, Chelsea peered cautiously around the corner of the desk to monitor Brady's activity.

A man from the gallery approached Brady from behind, tackling him, and tried to wrestle the convict to the ground. Brady elbowed the hero wannabe in the gut, then slammed his head back into the other man's nose. The man slid to the ground, cradling his bleeding face in his hands.

The bailiff who'd led the jury from the room ran back in through a side door, his gun poised to shoot.

But Brady spotted the returning guard and picked him off with a shot that struck the pudgy man's head.

Suddenly, Brady's gaze locked on Chelsea, and an evil sneer, full of intent, twisted his mouth. She cast a quick glance from one door to the next, trying to determine her best escape route. Every door was jammed with people filing out of the courtroom. Except one— the side door that was barricaded and marked with yellow caution tape and a sign reading Closed for Construction. She pushed to her feet and took two running steps before a hand closed around her arm, jerked her backward. She turned her head as she stumbled and met Brady's gloating grin.

He pressed the gun into her neck and hauled her up against his wiry frame. "Hello, girlie. It's payback time."

Jake assessed the scene in seconds. Brady firing into the room. One bailiff down, another shot in the face as he watched. Keeping low, Jake made his way up the aisle in the gallery, moving against the stream of people who shoved their way out of the courtroom. Through the throng of bodies, he caught a flash of pink, the color of Chelsea's dress, near the court reporter's desk. Was that her or had she already escaped through another door?

In all the missions he'd undertaken with the black ops team, he'd never felt the edge of fear he did now. Even though lives had been at stake in all of those assignments with the team, he hadn't had the personal stakes on the line that he did now. Because he hadn't been in love with any of the people at risk.

Knowing he needed to focus, he shoved down the anxiety that rose inside him. He zeroed in on Brady and hurried toward his target. Dodging spectators who'd huddled behind the railing between the well and the galley, Jake drew close to Brady...just as the convict charged across the well and grabbed—

"Chelsea!" Jake's heart seized as Brady jammed the pistol into Chelsea's throat. "Chelsea!"

Her gaze darted to his, even as Brady dragged her across the courtroom toward a barricaded side exit. Her mouth formed his name, and even though he couldn't hear her for all the raised voices around them, Brady clearly did. Brady followed the path of her gaze and stiffened when he spotted Jake. With a dark grin, he snaked his arm around Chelsea's waist and shouted, "You want her, hero? Come get her!"

Brady fled toward the blocked exit, dragging Chelsea with him and barreling through the warning-taped door.

"Jake!" Chelsea cried, struggling to free herself, fighting her captor despite the muzzle pointed at her.

Heart pounding, Jake scrambled after them, taking the service weapon from the felled guard by the jury room door as he rushed toward the side door. He burst through the side entrance and found himself in a stairwell littered with bits of plaster, metal scraps and sawdust from construction work. The door swished closed behind him, shutting out the cacophony in the courtroom.

The scuffle of feet, a feminine gasp, and Brady's barked, "Damn!" called his attention to the stairs.

Jake darted to the railing and looked down. "Chelsea!"

Brady had made it down one flight of steps to the landing at the turn in the stairs. Beyond the landing was an open maw. The steps to the floors below had been demolished, leaving a two-and-a-half-floor drop to the ground level. Brady had nowhere to go except back up the steps toward him.

"You're at a dead end, Brady," he shouted, the bailiff's service weapon poised in his hand. "Let her go."

Brady's chin jerked up, his gaze finding Jake at the top of the stairs. "No chance. She's my ticket outta here. You drop your weapon, or she dies."

The convict jammed his gun in Chelsea's ear, and Jake's heart lurched. He inhaled slowly. Exhaled. Forced training to the forefront. He steadied his aim, didn't blink.

Brady scowled. "I said drop the gun!"

Behind him, the courtroom door burst open, and Jake darted a glance over his shoulder as a man in a suit ran out. "Can I help?"

Jake swallowed a curse. He waved the man away. "No, get back! Get inside, and don't let anyone except law enforcement through that door. Got it?"

"No tricks! I will kill her!" Brady shouted. Swinging his weapon toward Jake, he squeezed off a shot. Bits of plaster rained down from the wall behind him.

"Jake!" Chelsea cried.

Jake dropped to a crouch behind the marble newel post at the top of the half flight of stairs, the only protection available to him. The man in the suit protected his head from the falling debris and rushed back through the courtroom door.

With a two-handed grip on his pistol, Jake took aim at Brady's head. But with Chelsea in front of the convict, he didn't have a clear shot.

The convict jerked his arm up from Chelsea's waist to her throat, anchoring her in a choke hold, and Jake's heart thundered as he scrambled for a plan.

His thoughts kept circling around to one fact. He loved Chelsea. Losing her would destroy him. During the short, intense time they'd had together, the smart, compassionate, witty spitfire had become the center of his universe. The hollow ache that had gnawed in his chest the past nine months gave a painful throb.

Almost as an afterthought, his brain registered the distant voices, the squawk of police radios coming from the floors below. Backup.

If he could keep Brady locked in this standoff a little longer...

Chelsea clawed at Brady's arm, struggling to get air. Jake drew slow deep breaths, trying to calm his racing heart, control the adrenaline pumping through him. He needed a steady hand, perfect aim.

The sounds of approaching guards grew louder. *Hurry!* Jake wanted to shout. *She can't breathe!*

Brady clearly heard the commotion of the guards floors below drifting up the empty stairwell, as well. He glanced nervously toward the gaping maw where the unfinished construction loomed. The cops couldn't reach him from that direction, but he was vulnerable from his position on the landing. Brady must have realized this, too, because he stumbled back a few more steps.

"I'm not going back to prison, man!" Brady shouted. Jake heard the rising desperation in his tone. *Not good.*

"Let Chelsea go," Jake repeated, his voice firm and flat.

"No!" Brady growled. He swung wildly toward Jake and fired again. "Get outta my way! I'm getting out of here one way or another if I have to kill you both to do it!"

Then a memory shifted to the front of Jake's thoughts like a gift from the beyond.

"Chelsea," he called, "do you remember what I told you about the stray dog in Afghanistan?"

Chelsea lifted a startled look to him. "What?"

"Stop it!" Brady scowled, the gun in his hand waving wildly in his agitation. "I'm not playing games here!"

"Chels?" Jake watched her face intently for indication she understood what he was asking. Her furrowed brow eased, and her gaze held his.

"Rex?" Her voice rasped as Brady tightened his hold.

He nodded. *Good girl.*

Taking aim at Brady again, he waited, watched....

As Brady shuffled back another step, his arm loosened on Chelsea's neck. She gasped a deep breath of oxygen...then ducked her head and bit the fleshy part of his forearm.

"Ow! You bitch!" Brady barked, yanking his arm away from her.

Jake tensed, ready to fire.

Before Chelsea could take the needed step away from Brady for Jake to take his shot, Brady backhanded her—hard—across the cheek. The blow reverberated in the stone staircase, and Jake saw red, his body twitching as rage rolled through him.

Chelsea reeled. Stumbled. Fell.

Jake took his shot. And missed.

The split second in which he'd reacted to Brady's strike had been enough to throw him off. But as he readied for another shot with his next heartbeat, the momentum of Chelsea's fall carried her to the ragged edge of the drop-off. Her legs slipped into the maw, and a bone-chilling horror flooded his veins. "Chelsea!"

Brady shifted his attention to Chelsea, who was scrabbling on the smooth marble floor for purchase. A gloating grin spread Brady's lips. He stepped over to her and kicked her hard in the ribs.

With a cry of pain and panic, she slid farther over the end of the construction.

"Chels, hold on!"

"In here!" a voice shouted from below.

Brady aimed his gun into the gaping hole, toward the lower floors.

Jake lunged to his feet and squeezed off three more shots in rapid succession. Brady jerked, then toppled back, crimson stains blooming on his chest. Without hesitation, Jake ran down several steps, then leaped over the handrail to the unfinished landing.

Chapter 20

Chelsea's breath sawed from her in ragged, shallow pants. She was afraid to move, even to take a deep breath, scared that she'd lose the tenuous grasp she had. Terror clawed at her, and tears stung her eyes, filled her sinuses. Around her the world seemed to explode. The deafening blasts of gunfire echoed in the stairwell and pounded her eardrums.

"Jake…" she rasped, her throat raw, her voice windless.

She clung with one hand to the broken edge of the marble floor. With the other hand she clutched an exposed rebar that jutted through the jagged concrete at the edge of the demolition. Her legs dangled helplessly over the empty space, three floors above the lobby landing.

Voices came from below, but she didn't dare to look. They couldn't help her anyway.

Adrenaline fueled her muscles, but her arms, her fingers were quickly weakening, cramping. Her sweaty hand slipped on the slick marble, and her grip faltered.

She was going to fall. Oh, God, she didn't want to die!

"Jake!" The scream ripped from her throat as her fingers lost purchase on the marble and scraped down the rough concrete. She grabbed another rebar and squeezed her eyes closed as a sob of terror surged up her throat. *Please, God!*

Her arms shook. Her fingers ached. She held her breath. Slipping... *No!*

"Chelsea!"

Firm hands grabbed her wrists, and she jerked her gaze up.

"Jake!" Her cry was raw, full of tears and heavy with relief.

"Hold on!" Fear filled his handsome face. His eyes were wild with emotion, and panic creased his brow. "I've got you, honey."

"Brady—" She gulped.

"He can't hurt you anymore."

A shiver of relief rolled through her, but the pain in her arm muscles screamed she wasn't safe yet.

Jake held her gaze. "Chels, I'm going to try to pull you up, but first you have to let go and grab my arms."

"Let go?" Her voice squeaked with fear.

"You can do it, sweetheart. I won't let go. I promise I won't. I...won't ever let you go again." His voice cracked with emotion and sent an answering ripple through her.

Below them, someone shouted, "Where's Brady?"

Jake's gaze shifted to the people on the lobby level. "Dead, or close to it."

"Hang on to her! We're sending help up now, and someone's getting a construction tarpaulin for us to catch her, just in case."

Jake's focus returned to her, and he drilled her with an urgent look. Clearly he knew the physics of the situation as well as she did. A tarpaulin would be little good if she fell.

The fatigue in her arms was a physical ache, the muscles tested beyond their limits. She swallowed the whimper of pain that tried to escape. She refused to quit, wouldn't give up.

"Grab my arms, Chels. Come on, honey," Jake coaxed. "Please trust me. I won't let you get hurt."

His calm voice and the resolve in his eyes filled her with the will to shove her fear aside and try to shift her grip.

She released the first rebar, and when she turned her hand to seize Jake's wrist, a knifing pain shot through her shoulder. She cried. Having been thrown from her horse once and suffering a dislocated shoulder in a barrel racing competition, she recognized the searing pain. Based on the look that crossed Jake's face, he could tell what had happened, as well.

"Damn, honey, I'm sorry. I know it hurts."

Blinking back tears, she shifted her other hand to his wrist.

"I'm going to try to pull you up now. Ready?"

"Hurry!"

She felt the muscles in Jake's arms quiver, and he tugged her up a couple inches, but not nearly enough to get her onto the landing.

With a barked curse, he stopped pulling, and closed his eyes. Huffing a deep breath, he returned his gaze to her, his eyes apologetic. "I'm slipping toward the edge.

I have nothing to brace against, no leverage to pull you up. This marble is providing no traction at all."

"Then how—"

"A little help here! Hey! Somebody!" he shouted, angling his head toward the stairs. Glancing back at her, he coaxed, "They'll be here any second, honey. They said they were sending help up. Don't give up on me."

Her eyes locked on his. Had he intended the double meaning she heard in his tone? The emotion filling his gaze sparked a light deep in her soul. "I won't."

The slam of the courtroom door preceded the sound of pounding feet on the stairs.

"Grab his legs! Pull him back!" The guard who'd shouted the order dropped to his belly beside Jake and caught Chelsea's hand. "On three! One, two, three!"

Clinging to Jake's wrists, she gritted her teeth against the pain as the men pulled her up and onto the landing. The jagged edge of marble and concrete scraped her stomach through her thin dress and the tugging on her injured shoulder sent paroxysms of pain through her arm.

"Watch her shoulder!" Jake said, pushing the other men aside as she lay back on the cold marble floor. "Hold her still while I work the joint back in place. Sorry, sweetheart, but this will hurt." Strong hands pinned her down, and Jake twisted and tugged her arm until it popped back in the socket. Almost immediately the writhing agony stopped, replaced with a tolerable ache, and Chelsea shuddered with relief.

As the men around her stepped back, she cut her gaze around the landing and spotted Brady crumpled in the corner, blood staining his clothes. His eyes stared sightlessly toward the ceiling.

A note of distress rose from her throat, and Jake moved into her field of vision to block her view.

"Don't look, Chels." He drew her into his arms, pressing her head to his chest and holding her body against his as she trembled. Or was he the one shaking? The tremors seemed to envelop and move through her at the same time.

"He's dead?"

"Yeah. It's over, babe. You're safe. It's all over," he whispered as he held her.

Chelsea let her muscles go limp, collapsing fully against Jake, soaking in the reassuring strength of his body cradling hers.

Behind Jake, policemen and court officials surrounded Brady's body, handheld radios crackling and tension thick in the cacophony of voices.

"Jake, I—"

He pressed a finger to her lips. "Wait. Let's go somewhere more private. I have something I need to say."

She nodded, and when she tried to stand, he swept her off her feet to carry her.

She shot him a shaky grin. "My shoulder's sore, but my feet still work. Let me walk."

He frowned his disagreement as she wiggled out of his arms. When her feet touched the floor, her post-adrenaline knees buckled like wet cardboard. Jake scooped her back up before she could fall and growled, "Humor me."

He carried her back up the stairs and into the courtroom where EMTs had arrived and were tending to the fallen bailiff and other injured spectators.

Jodi Israel spotted Chelsea as Jake brought her in, and rushed over. "Oh, my God, Miss Harris, are you all right?"

She offered a weak smile and nodded. "I am. Thanks to Jake."

"Bring her over here." ADA Israel led them to a less-busy corner of the courtroom where she righted a chair that had been knocked over in the melee. "Can I get you anything? Do you need a doctor?"

"I'll see that she gets to the E.R.," Jake said. He eased her down on the chair and crouched beside her. Sending the ADA a backward glance, he added, "Can we have some privacy for a minute?"

"Oh." ADA Israel backed away. "Sure."

Chelsea held her arm to her chest, keeping her injured shoulder immobile, and drew slow restorative breaths. "Wow. When I lost that twenty-four pounds for my health, who knew it would literally save my life?"

Jake blinked and tucked a wisp of hair behind her ear. "What?"

"I barely held on as it was. If I'd had those extra pounds dragging me down, I don't think I'd have been able to."

He shook his head and grinned. "You lost twenty-four pounds?"

She cocked her head in dismay. "You really didn't notice?"

"I… No."

She heaved a disappointed sigh.

"I mean, I noticed you looked beautiful, but you were beautiful to me before."

"Right." She rolled her eyes. "My *smile*," she said in a mocking tone.

Jake caught her chin between his fingers and angled her face toward his. "Yeah, your smile." His expression was stern, but his eyes were warm and a little damp.

Chelsea's pulse stumbled.

"Your smile is beautiful, because it's a reflection of the loving, smart, funny woman inside. But for the record, I find the rest of you damn fine-looking, as well. I happen to like curves on my woman, and the woman I met in January had one of the lushest, sexiest bodies I've ever seen."

Chelsea stared into his bright blue eyes. He was *serious.* She opened her mouth but was speechless.

"Now if you're happier having lost the weight, great. I'm happy for you and proud of the hard work that I'm sure it took to lose the pounds. But I don't love you because you have a hot body and a beautiful face or a smile like sunshine—"

Chelsea jolted, stiffened. He *loved* her?

"I love you because of who you are, because of the compassionate, courageous, sarcastic woman I got to know nine months ago. That will never change, Chels. It's yours uncondition—"

She covered his mouth with her hand to shush him. "Back up a minute. You love me? As in *love* love?"

He laced his fingers with hers and brought her palm to his mouth for a kiss. "Hell, yes. I love you, Chelsea Harris, with all that I am."

She blinked at him, unable to breathe. She tried to process his profession while a hundred doubts and questions assailed her. "But your job—"

His mouth tugged up on one side. "Yeah, I need a new one. Know anyone that's hiring?"

"And your promise to your mom?"

"I figure I've fulfilled it. I think she'd be happy with my choice. And I know she'd have loved you."

A pure, sweet joy flowed through her, warming her from the inside out. "I—I don't know what to say…"

He chuckled. "That's a first. Try 'I love you, too.'"

Tears spilled from her eyes as she nodded and threw her good arm around his neck. "I do, Jake. I love you, too."

Epilogue

A chill December wind nipped Chelsea's cheeks as she hurried into the posh New Orleans country club where Daniel LeCroix and his bride, Nicole White, were having their wedding reception. As one of the groomsmen, Jake had stayed behind at the church for a few pictures and was to meet Chelsea at the party. Chelsea had ridden from the church with Erin Kincaid, Alec's wife, and their toddler son, Joey.

"I didn't think New Orleans got cold," she said to Erin, holding the country club door for the young mother as she bustled in carrying Joey.

"This isn't cold. You should try Colorado in January." Erin set her son on the floor, and he immediately toddled off toward a Christmas tree lit with hundreds of white lights.

"I'm not complaining. Really. I swore after last January when I nearly died of exposure that I'd never complain about being cold again." Chelsea shivered at the memory.

"That's right." Erin's face lit with a warm smile. "Jake told us how you two met. You were really lucky Jake came along to rescue you when he did."

Chelsea grinned, unable to contain the happiness she'd found these past few months getting to know Jake better and helping him take care of his father's ranch. "I'm lucky Jake came along for a lot of reasons."

"Indeed." They handed their coats to an attendant to check, then Erin's smile slipped as she glanced at her son by the tree. "Oh, no! Joey, don't pull!"

Erin hurried off to prevent a Christmas-tree disaster, and Chelsea called to her, "I'll find our table."

In the ballroom, no expense had been spared in decorating. White candles, pink and red poinsettias, sparkling glass ornaments and organza drapes created a winter wonderland. A jazz band was already playing soft music, and the rich aroma of Cajun cuisine spiced the air. Chelsea headed to the head table, found her place card next to Jake's and settled in. Erin joined her a few minutes later...without her son.

Chelsea arched and eyebrow. "Where's Joey?"

"Nicole thought of everything for this wedding. There's a nursery down the hall staffed by no fewer than six of her teenaged cousins.

"Awesome. So Mommy's free to dance and party with Daddy tonight...."

She gave Erin a wink, and Alec's wife leaned close and pitched her voice to a conspiratorial whisper. "I wonder if they'd keep him long enough for Alec and me to slip back to the hotel for a...*private party?*"

Chelsea laughed. "I promise not to tell."

"Promise not to tell what?" Jake asked from behind her.

Chelsea spun around in her chair. "Jake! What about wedding party pictures?"

"All done. Told you I wouldn't be long."

Alec approached the table and kissed his wife before taking his assigned seat as best man, next to the groom. "Did you, uh…lose something, honey? Like our kid?"

While Erin explained about the nursery to Alec, Chelsea grabbed Jake by the lapels of his tuxedo and hauled him close for a kiss. "Have I told you how devastatingly handsome you are in that tux, Mr. Connelly?"

Jake cradled her cheek with his palm and returned her kiss with fervor. "You look rather delicious yourself in this sassy number." He ran a finger along the spaghetti strap of her clingy red-and-white candy-striped cocktail dress. He nuzzled her ear and murmured, "Are you supposed to look like a candy cane? Because all through the wedding, I kept looking at you and thinking how much I'd like to lick you." He gave her earlobe a playful nip, and Chelsea's cheeks warmed with a flush.

"Hold that thought, cowboy," she returned with a lopsided grin. "I know where we can buy peppermint body paint on the way back to the hotel."

Jake's eyebrows lifted, and his eyes darkened with desire and intrigue.

"Ladies and gentleman," the wedding director shouted from the door of the ballroom, "It is my pleasure to introduce to you for the first time…Mr. and Mrs. Daniel LeCroix!"

Chelsea, Jake, Erin and Alec all rose to their feet to applaud the happy couple. Jake loosed a piercing whistle, and Alec shouted, "About time, Lafitte!"

The band started playing Andrew Lloyd-Webber's

"All I Ask of You," and Daniel led Nicole onto the floor for their first dance. Chelsea watched the newlyweds sway and stare into each other's eyes with such unabashed and undeniable love that her own eyes misted.

As other couples joined the bride and groom, Jake took Chelsea's hand. "Dance with me."

She followed him onto the dance floor and drifted into his arms, feeling like the luckiest girl in the room to be on Jake's arm. As she pressed close to him and wrapped her arms around his neck, a lump under his tuxedo coat dug into her chest.

Chelsea levered back and patted the bump with a wrinkle in her brow. "What's this?"

"Well, it was supposed to be a surprise," Jake said with a wry grin, "but because you've found it, I'll do this now."

"Do what?" she asked as he stepped back from her.

Jake reached in the breast pocket of his tuxedo as he dropped to one knee.

All the air whooshed from Chelsea's lungs when she spotted the velvet jewelry box in his hand. Her knees started shaking, and the music faded to a drone as she gaped at him. "Jake?"

A wickedly handsome grin tugged his lips. "Chelsea Harris, you once told me not to deny myself the chance to love and be loved when I found the right woman for me. Well, you are the right one for me, and I can't imagine spending the rest of my life without you in it."

"Oh, Texas!" she gasped, fanning her face as tears of joy prickled her eyes. "I can't believe this!"

Around them, other couples on the dance floor realized what was happening and turned to watch, murmuring in delight.

Jake's smile widened. "Would you do me the honor of becoming my wife?"

Tears flowed from Chelsea's eyes, and her throat was so tight she could only squeak, "Yes."

A cheer went up in the room along with a round of applause. Jake slid the huge oval diamond solitaire ring on her shaking finger, then rose to his feet to pull her into his embrace.

Laughing and crying at the same time, Chelsea kissed Jake and repeated, "Yes. Yes. Yes. I love you, Jake. So, so much."

He brushed the hair back from her face and kissed her again. "You're the world to me, Chels. Don't ever doubt that."

"I don't. You've made me a believer." She stroked his jaw, remembering when he rescued her from Ethyl's trunk, the first time she saw his handsome face. "Turns out Brady did me a favor the day he kidnapped me."

Jake's smile grew pensive. "Yeah. Despite all the terrible things he did, some good came out of his evil."

Chelsea nestled closer. Held his gaze. Made sure he was paying attention. "Jake, good *won*."

She felt his muscles tense beneath her hands. Then he blinked. Exhaled. Smiled. "You're right. This time good won."

* * * * *

A sneaky peek at next month...

INTRIGUE...

BREATHTAKING ROMANTIC SUSPENSE

My wish list for next month's titles...

In stores from 17th May 2013:

❏ Special Forces Rendezvous — Elle Kennedy

& Secure Location — Beverly Long

❏ The Princess Predicament

& Royal Rescue — Lisa Childs

❏ A Billionaire's Redemption — Cindy Dees

& Star Witness — Mallory Kane

❏ Copper Lake Confidential — Marilyn Pappano

Available at WHSmith, Tesco, Asda, Eason, Amazon and Apple

Just can't wait?

Visit us Online

You can buy our books online a month before they hit the shops! **www.millsandboon.co.uk**

0513/46

Special Offers

Every month we put together collections and longer reads written by your favourite authors.

Here are some of next month's highlights— and don't miss our fabulous discount online!

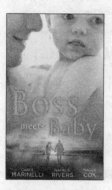

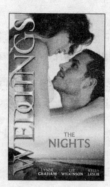

On sale 17th May

On sale 7th June

On sale 7th June

Save 20%
on all Special Releases

Find out more at
www.millsandboon.co.uk/specialreleases

*Visit us
Online*

0613/ST/MB418

Join the Mills & Boon Book Club

Subscribe to **Intrigue** today for 3, 6 or 12 months and you could **save over £40!**

We'll also treat you to these fabulous extras:

- **FREE L'Occitane gift set worth £10**
- **FREE home delivery**
- **Rewards scheme, exclusive offers…and much more!**

Subscribe now and save over £40
www.millsandboon.co.uk/subscribeme

SUBS/OFFER/I1

The World of Mills & Boon®

There's a Mills & Boon® series that's perfect for you. We publish ten series and, with new titles every month, you never have to wait long for your favourite to come along.

Blaze®

Scorching hot, sexy reads
4 new stories every month

By Request

Relive the romance with the best of the best
9 new stories every month

Cherish™

Romance to melt the heart every time
12 new stories every month

Desire™

Passionate and dramatic love stories
8 new stories every month

Visit us Online

Try something new with our Book Club offer
www.millsandboon.co.uk/freebookoffer

M&B/WORLD2

What will you treat yourself to next?

*Ignite your imagination,
step into the past...*
6 new stories every month

INTRIGUE...

Breathtaking romantic suspense
Up to 8 new stories every month

*Captivating medical drama –
with heart*
6 new stories every month

MODERN™

*International affairs,
seduction & passion guaranteed*
9 new stories every month

n o c t u r n e™

*Deliciously wicked
paranormal romance*
Up to 4 new stories every month

RIVΛ™

*Live life to the full –
give in to temptation*
3 new stories every month available
exclusively via our Book Club

You can also buy Mills & Boon eBooks at
www.millsandboon.co.uk

*Visit us
Online*

M&B/WORLD2

Mills & Boon® Online

Discover more romance at
www.millsandboon.co.uk

- 🌹 **FREE** online reads
- 🌹 **Books** up to one month before shops
- 🌹 **Browse our books** before you buy

...and much more!

For exclusive competitions and instant updates:

 Like us on **facebook.com/millsandboon**

 Follow us on **twitter.com/millsandboon**

 Join us on **community.millsandboon.co.uk**

Visit us Online | Sign up for our FREE eNewsletter at **www.millsandboon.co.uk**

WEB/M&B/RTL5